Without Fear

A Martha Beale Novel

Cordelia Frances Biddle

ISBN: 1-4392-6915-7
ISBN-13: 9781439269152

dedication: MY NUMEROUS THANKS to Marcia Rogers for the wondrous research materials she bestowed upon me: John F. Watson's seminal work *Annals of Philadelphia*, first published in 1857, and *A Memorial History of Philadelphia* edited by John Russell Young—1840s Philadelphia seeps from their pages.

And ever and always, my abiding gratitude to my husband, Steve. You give me hope and joy.

introduction: THE TITLE *WITHOUT FEAR* is taken from a prayer attributed to St. Clare. "Live without fear; your creator has made you holy, has always protected you, and loves you as a mother...." The message has a special resonance with me; I hope it does with my many loyal readers. I feel that Martha Beale, whom I continue to channel, would be especially moved and inspired by the first three words.

If you're familiar with my previous novels in the series, *Deception's Daughter* and *The Conjurer,* you're aware that the world of mid-nineteenth century Philadelphia had horrors aplenty despite its elegant, cosmopolitan ambiance. The grisly—and true—discovery of a headless corpse on the outskirts of the ice-encrusted city was one of them. To my knowledge, though, Joseph Bonaparte's palatial country estate, *Point Breeze,* never served as a backdrop for such a heinous crime. His years of residence there is just one facet of the city's fascinating history. A collection of Napoleon artifacts can be found at The Athenaeum of Philadelphia.

Labor conditions in Philadelphia's numerous textile mills were as grim as I have depicted them: children, women, and men working for inhuman wages under brutal conditions. As ever, I feel driven to address issues of social injustice. The interconnection between Philadelphia's textile industry and the slave trade was very real;

mercantile accounts register the amount of yard goods traded for human flesh. Although "polite" society was obsessed with regulations regarding appropriate etiquette and attire, it had its share of shameful secrets.

The Library Company of Philadelphia and The Athenaeum of Philadelphia continue to provide me with researcher's havens; their collections inspire me to burrow into the past.

I look forward to responding to questions or comments about *Without Fear.* Please contact me via my web site www.CordeliaFrancesBiddle.com. I promise a speedy reply.

.

Chapter I

Agnes

AGNES MUNDER WALKS AWAY from Quaker City Mill, walks away without a backward glance or a single misgiving about jeopardizing her employment, or that of her husband who so doggedly toils there. In fact, she gives him no more heed than she does the place itself, for she knows she's meant for finer things than the noisome floors of a textile manufactory. Cloaks of damask rather than cheap cottonade should be at her daily disposal, and silk slippers, and bonnets trimmed with aigret, or fur, or flowers fashioned from genuine French *peau de soie*.

Oh, yes, she's aware of what the other laborers will say when they discover that she's quit her loom again. They'll accuse her of imagining herself "above her station;" they'll mutter that she's "fanciful" and "capricious" and "prettier than she should be." Many will even accuse her of being "not right in the head"—which words they'll pretend to whisper, sending sidelong glances toward her poor, patient Oscar—although some will take pleasure in denouncing her husband for "sanctioning her wistful, hedonistic ways." And a few will add sneering queries regarding the childless state of a wife who's twenty-two and has been wed for five long years.

But what does any of that malicious cant matter? Agnes has inured herself to the combination of mistrust and envy. The other weavers, spoolers, throstle-spinners, carders, and cord-room hands can carp and cavil all they wish; and her masters can threaten and then dock her wages—as they've done repeatedly. And will do so again, she has no doubt.

She shakes her head in queenly forbearance of these triviali-ties, then pulls a red ribbon from her mantle pocket, ties it round her neck, and lifts her long skirt and smiles. Given her diet and station in life, her teeth are incongruously white; their only flaw a curious overlapping of the front two. Although, the effect makes her appear more winsome and naïve as if she were still half-child, half-adult and her years had been spent in pampered luxury.

"Ah," she sighs aloud; her smile grows, beaming upon those around her. Casting herself as a lady of stature and means, she be-comes one. So the true Agnes Munder is transformed, just as the streetscape improves, and the weather—the raw March day that threatens snow and worse—grows, in her invention, benign. Gone is the reeking, pulsing industrial heart of the city; gone is Fishtown and Otis Street where William Cramp and Sons build their vast iron ships, gone the Dyott Glass Furnace on Bank Street, the Vau-clain Boiler Works that spread viscous, yellow puddles on Palmer, the stink-enclosed calico printing factory on Beach, the tanneries whose choking stench affects all but the hardiest of stomachs, the smelting works and the sugar refinery on Church Alley that belch out so much noxious waste it's a wonder there's any wholesome air left to breathe.

Gone also are the snowflakes that now have begun spiraling through the waning daylight, increasing in number and density while shrinking in size—an unwelcome change that often presages a blizzard.

Agnes trips along, oblivious to the truth. She holds her skirt just so—between her forefinger and thumb in the same dainty manner as the wives of the mill's managers—while she drifts away from the docks that carry Quaker City Mill's finished products to

America's southern states or the great world beyond. For a moment, she considers how it would feel to be a bolt of cottonade or calico and wonders what marvels she'd behold if she were to be stored in the belly of a ship and then off-loaded onto foreign soil. How would those fantastical places smell? Would the sunlight blind the eye? Would there be music instead of grinding gears and catcalls and oaths? Would there be food aplenty—and not just food, but morsels of indescribable sweetness and delicacy?

As she wanders, her black hair comes loose, spilling down from the single braid coiled at the back of her neck until the locks make a frame for her face. She knows this haphazard appearance isn't seemly, because it garners curious and sometimes acquisitive looks from the men she passes. Agnes returns the hungry stares with a beneficent tilt of her head; to some men she even nods. Those who receive her attentions gape and then look away, frowning in recognition and confusion.

By now the snow is pelting down; it's like fire ash spewing from a dirty chimney, although, of course, it's white and frigid. The laborers employed along the wharfs or in the factories that comprise the city's commercial center glance upward in dread. For them, a continuation of the icy days of February is like doom. Pennies saved for food will have to be spent on additional fuel; sickly babies won't have the blessing of an early spring. Those men and women—and the child laborers among them—hunch their shoulders against the precipitation, lowering their heads as though waiting for God to strike them. Agnes remains unaffected.

Vanished wholly from her mind and heart is the filthy common privy built in a vault below the building she and her husband share with the other mill workers. Gone is the quarter of a day's wages withheld for tardiness, or the full day's earnings forfeited for poor work, or the salary paid but once a month when the rent

must be delivered fortnightly. Vanished are the children chained to
the looms' frames, whimpering while their hands and bodies keep
time with the steam turbines' jittering roar. Forgotten also is the
"spinners' phthisis," an affliction of the lungs that always leads to
death. Instead, she sings to herself.

A carriage stops. It's a very fine rig, a handsome brougham
painted glossy black, and the gelding pulling it is the same lustrous
color. The owner raps upon the door; the coachman reins in the
horse, and Agnes is hailed through the carriage's now half-open
window.

When she approaches, the owner's greeting is a discomfited
"My apologies, miss. I mistook you for an acquaintance."

Agnes is accustomed to this type of statement. Strange gentlemen in handsome rigs have summoned her before. How else
could she have afforded the silk ribbon at her neck, the lengths of
fabric for the cloak she's fashioned?

"It's no trouble, sir," she says. Her smile grows brighter, and
she tosses her hair, which elicits a sharp intake of breath from the
master and a quieter sigh from the servant who remains aloft, his
attention seemingly on the wet and steaming beast in the carriage
traces.

"Are you employed hereabouts?" she's asked, but her response
is a cagey shake of her dark curls. Agnes never supplies her name or
the name of the mill. "Or perhaps you work on your own?"

"Perhaps I do, sir."

"And perhaps you'd care for a ride in my equipage?"

"That I would, sir. Indeed, I would, especially with the snow
starting to make my path so treacherous. And me with such a sorry
excuse for shoes."

With that the coach door opens, and Agnes climbs up the
steps into an interior that smells of new leather, polished brass,

and *eau de cologne*. It's a heady, rich scent and far superior to the oily odor of smoked and curing river eels that has given Fishtown its name. She inhales the pleasant aroma as if by swelling her lungs with it she could grow as wealthy and self-satisfied as the gentleman seated in that handsome space.

The brougham's curtains are drawn shut; the owner taps his cane's silver handle upon the wall leading to the coachman's box, and the carriage moves away toward a less congested thoroughfare while Agnes smiles her glowing smile at her unknown admirer. "The hem of my dress is drenched," she says at length. "And my little feet quite frozen. I should have better footwear than I do."

Chapter 2
A Troubling Letter

NO MORE THAN A MILE distant from this transaction—although the setting might as well be one of those exotic climes for which Agnes longs—Martha Beale is seated in comfort. The surprise snowstorm that rattles the shutters and casements of her home on Chestnut Street and the night through which the blizzard rages are of no more consequence to her than the reality of the physical world is to Agnes.

Surrounded as she is by every manifestation of her wealth and her elevated position in society—the glossy suite of walnut furniture, the Turkey carpets with their lustrous crimson and indigo hues, the several layers of under and over draperies that cover the windows, the pier glasses, the landscape paintings in their gilded frames, and the myriad *objets d'art* that adorn all fashionable households—she should be experiencing the highest degree of peace and tranquility. In fact, the opposite is true. Martha stares into a fire that's been carefully banked and attended by her servants and sees woes instead of solace, hears the muffled sounds of domesticity—her adoptive children attending to their lessons in the day nursery on the floor above, the creak of polished wood planking as the *majordomo* crosses the foyer below—and knows only loneliness and heartache. Even the aromas of hot-house flowers and pomander and *eau de lavande* that fill her private sitting room seem stifling rather than soothing, and her clothes chafe and pinch and feel frigid against her skin instead of providing warmth.

She releases a sigh; her corset stays sigh with her; her feet in their embroidered slippers kick aside the tapestry footstool; and the letter resting in her lap—and which she's reread so often she has it memorized—slides to the floor. She watches the pages fall, then reaches an enervated hand to pick them up. Her eyes stare at the letters curled upon the paper until the lines blur and the words collide.

My dearest,
It is with heavy heart that I write you. I could not bear to call upon you in person in order to reveal my intentions, as I knew my resolve would weaken, and my plans come to naught. So I have chosen the coward's way and now steal off aboard a merchant ship that calls herself Red Cloud *before you can persuade me otherwise—before I can persuade myself. The vessel is a stout one; the captain seasoned and knowledgeable. . .*

She rises, carrying Thomas Kelman's missive to her *escritoire* where she flattens it on the polished surface as she's done numerous times since its arrival a fortnight prior. Her palm bears down hard upon the creases as if she were attempting to eradicate a stain.

Other letters also rest there—supposedly casual messages from gentlemen acquaintances whom she suspects of more inti-mate designs. She's an eligible heiress and, at the advanced age of twenty-seven, too old to put off marriage much longer. Those notes and invitations she bundles up, intending to consign them to a cubbyhole reserved for future correspondence. Instead, following some as yet unexamined motive, she grips the sheets of paper—thick, watermarked, many even scented with *eau de cologne*—and throws them into the fire, watching the flames flicker around the edges while her eyes pinch and her wide mouth sets itself into a merciless line.

The defiant act brings only momentary respite, however. The hurt, perplexity—and, yes, anger—that she feels cannot be absolved by attacking a surrogate. She returns to Kelman's letter.

I am fully cognizant of the fact that in leaving the city, the (mistaken) results of the Crowther investigation will be blamed upon my inaction or dereliction—or both—and that my failure to explain the circumstances surrounding the case will make me appear to have relinquished the field without having given consideration to the repercussions. In short, I will be vilified, and my decision to seek my future and my fortunes elsewhere will be deemed the act of a dishonest man.

It's not the missteps of the past that influence me, however, but you, Martha. The tragic conclusion to the Crowther affair—although deeply troubling still—has nothing to do with my resolution to quit Philadelphia.

In the eyes of the world, I am not your equal, nor will I ever be. You are a high-born lady. My parentage is base. You are in possession of a great fortune; I live by my wits. Forgive my bluntness in these matters, but I fear you would be ridiculed by your peers—and perhaps even ostracized—if they were to guess that you had given your heart to a person like me—and that mine had been pledged to you. As to matrimony, you and I both know custom is firmly against us. No matter how much we may wish otherwise, no matter how often we may have imagined otherwise, the fact is that the many levels of society that comprise the city would never countenance such a union.

I will write to you when I have determined where I will settle, so that your thoughts may be at rest, but as that will be some months hence, I urge you not to wait for my message. . .

Martha spins away from the desk. Her stomach churns; her gray eyes spark like hot coals. *Am I not allowed to participate in this debate?* she argues. *Thomas determines how both of us should behave, and I must keep my counsel? Reside quietly at home, my countenance serene, a vapid smile fixed upon my face as though my greatest worries were the visits we ladies are supposed to pay one another, or how often and how grandly I should entertain those of my acquaintance? Shouldn't I be permitted to choose whom I should wed and when? Couldn't Thomas at least have conferred with me before taking this drastic step— or given me a hint of warning about this* Red Cloud *and his plans? Am I to be treated no differently by him than I was by my father?*

The questions, though, are met with a litany of dull and practical evidence. As much as she wants to believe herself above public scrutiny, she understands that what Thomas writes is true. A city founded on the tenet of religious freedom may sanction marriages between peoples of one faith and another: Gentiles may happily wed Jews; Catholics may form loving bonds with Protestants; those originally hailing from New England may ally themselves with Southern, slave-owning families. But class lines are never crossed. The rich keep to themselves. As do the poor.

At length, her wrath begins to ebb, leaving her spent and weary. There's no Thomas to chide for adhering to custom, no dear, dear friend to touch her hand or lift her face up toward his own. There are no arms to encircle her, no scent of shaving soap and starched linen and maleness to breathe. The room is empty. It's as if he'd never walked through the door. Having grown accustomed to his presence during the past year, her sense of isolation feels more acute than it did during the years before they met.

She sighs anew; this time the sound is a groan. *Why must he journey on a merchant ship? And why to South America? Why not the western territories if he's so insistent on becoming a man of means? There's ample opportunity there—without the danger. With winter lingering, the Atlantic Ocean must be hazardous to traverse.* In her heart, she knows the answers to these objections. Didn't her father, the lauded financier Lemuel Beale, instigate trade in specie with the newest nations of the Americas? And doesn't she, as his sole heir, continue the practice? Why shouldn't Thomas also avail himself of those profits? Isn't risk part of life?

"Oh...oh...oh!" The words fly out with all the vindictiveness of oaths. If she were her friend, Becky Grey Taitt, the invective might be genuine, but Martha doesn't permit herself such hedonistic displays.

She studies her room, dim now and swathed in shadow, a pewterish color touching the silver toilette suite arranged upon her dressing table: the brushes and frizettes, the mirror and fingernail buffs, the jars containing pomade and rose water and bandoline. Here should be a realm so peaceable that no malign thoughts can enter. Instead, the ordinary seems fraught with ill intentions, and the unlit corners of the chamber lurk with demons.

AND SO THE DAY passes into evening and thence into night while the claustrophobic fall of snow upon snow encompasses the city. The stout walls and tall windows of Martha's stately mansion are cut off from her neighbors'; the street fronting her house is isolated from the lanes beyond; well-tended parks become no more than a dot or two of sulfur-colored light where the gas lamps glow; back alleys devolve into their own icy worlds.

At length, she sleeps, but her dreaming mind provides no respite from her waking thoughts. She envisions mountainous ocean waves: white-streaked, white-flecked, roiling green walls that blot out half the sky. The sound they produce is a bellowing growl that obliterates all other noise.

The waves crest and fall, spitting out yellow spume and shards of black seaweed; everything below is crushed. Barques, schooners, gaffe-rigged fishing boats, men of war, paddle-wheel steamers: all succumb to the mammoth swells until the splintered masts and spars, the shattered keels, and the broken bodies of the dead voyagers are tossed upon a distant shore. Thomas is among them, but unlike the blanched corpses surrounding him, his is covered in gore as crimson as the brightest sunrise. Martha screams out in the strangled voice of slumber, but is powerless to help.

Chapter 3
On Callowhill Street

THE TEMPEST CONTINUES unabated for eighteen hours longer, whipping snow across the city as though the stuff were so much fondant icing. When the winds gust—and they do mightily—the icing billows up to half-obscure ground-floor shop windows, carriage doors, the entries to iron-works and tanneries, and the broad marble stairs leading to the mansions facing Washington Square. The shrubberies in each park and esplanade disappear; the subterranean entrances to the town's ubiquitous oyster houses vanish; even the fire gangs that tear through the city are forced to keep indoors with their horses and wagons stabled. It's fortunate no kitchen blaze erupts for many blocks would be consumed before the conflagration could be subdued.

Throughout it all, Agnes remains ensconced with her new gentleman friend. His house on Callowhill Street is new and pleasant and delightfully warm. Coal cobbles glow in every grate, so she can wander, half-clothed, from upper room to upper room as though the ice spattering the window panes were of no more concern than an unpleasant dream. She washes herself by squatting in a copper hip-bath in steaming water provided by a dour (and, Agnes suspects, disapproving) female servant who never utters more than a grunt or two as she clatters the large urns upstairs and down until Agnes deems the temperature to her liking.

Refreshed, she dresses in one or another of the expensive peignoirs her anonymous admirer has provided, sips port wine until her head grows dizzy and her words issue forth in plumy giggles every time she speaks, then stretches out upon his bed and sleeps—or tries to. He's a most amorous person, for all of his refined manners and speech.

Several times she experiences pangs over quitting her Oscar in such an abrupt and unfeeling manner, but these she quickly squelches by promising herself she'll return to him some day.

Or perhaps she won't. Well, she'll certainly send word advising him not to worry. Then again, maybe she won't, because that act would be certain to produce jealousy or even a hunt to find her.

Or the gentleman might tire of her earlier than she'd like—like the last one, who only wanted her company for a day and half a night—and then she can creep home pretending to have been lost in the storm and rescued by a widow lady who spoke not one word of English.

Or she could have fallen into the hold of a ship bound for Wilmington or Baltimore and not found ready passage home. Certainly Oscar would forgive her misfortune if something as terrible as that were to occur! Even a week or longer would be excused if she were floating away on a creaky boat. And doesn't Oscar always pardon her forgetful, little absences? Nor ask how sometimes she returns attired in finer garb than when she vanished? Her husband has always been the kindliest of people.

These strategies build in Agnes's brain and evaporate just as rapidly while she hums to herself or nibbles at the preserved French plums the gentleman keeps in a handsome box or the colored sweetmeats layered so prettily among them.

The falling snow, she decides, is as beautiful as an imaginary elfin world. She hopes the blizzard never ends. Not until the very end of time.

Then she prays that her lover doesn't tire of their escapades too soon, and that when the sun again shines, he'll dress her in a fur-lined cloak and take her out for another ride in his snug and comfortable carriage. She'll insist he reveal his name, too; and she'll call him *Mr. So-and-so*, as if she were to the manner born. And he'll call her *Mrs. Munder*. Or maybe even *Miss*.

Chapter 4
An Elegant Rig

"MISS BEALE, I SUGGEST you postpone your examination of the premises until the streets have been fully cleared." This is Martha's chief clerk speaking, the only one of her father's former employees she trusted—and liked—enough to retain. The others either had the unhappy propensity of speaking down to her, as if a woman couldn't understand the financial affairs of men, or else they gazed at her in quiet disbelief. For a mere female to preside over a banking and brokerage concern...Well, no more need be said.

"No, Mr. Newgeon, I'll go. I need activity, not indecision. And besides, the factory can't be closed down due to the snowfall we received two days ago. If the circumstances are adverse, it will give me the opportunity to judge how well—or poorly—the trade is plied." Although Martha is seated in her formal first-floor with-drawing room as she delivers this speech, her body shows itself to be far from rest. A traveling bonnet is already upon her head; leather gloves encase her fingers; a fur-lined mantle is within easy reach. What the clerk can't guess is the true motivation for her insistence on proceeding with the journey. Worries about Thomas Kelman, about her future and her marital prospects influence ev-erything she thinks and does; and she simply cannot allow her-self to remain confined at home for another day, or even another minute. "If an unexpected blizzard can hinder production, then perhaps the business lacks stability." Having delivered this opinion, she stands, her spine rigid, her expression fixed. Her eyes shine brightly but not from hope or pleasure.

Newgeon regards her. Intemperance and stubbornness are part of the Beale character, as he well knows. In the father, those traits were always in evidence; in the daughter, they're habitually disguised as either quiet resolve or youthful zeal. Today, however, Martha seems a replica of her intractable parent. Pondering this transformation, the clerk shifts his feet in the heavy boots he donned for his walk from the Beale Brokerage House near the Mercantile Exchange on Third Street. "Quaker City Mill is one of the best in Philadelphia. When their looms cease producing, it's only to repair and clean the machinery—and that solely an hour before sunset on Saturdays. The mill's goods, according to all reports, are in high demand."

"Then let us not delay our visit."

"It's only your comfort that concerns me, miss."

An argument rises in her throat. Newgeon wouldn't have questioned her father's ability to travel on icy streets; there's no need to doubt hers. The words remain unexpressed; instead, she observes a pragmatic "I question why the owners are anxious to sell the company."

Newgeon permits himself the briefest of smiles. Although of middling years, he's of slight stature, hardly bigger or broader than a lanky boy, and with a head out of proportion to his torso as if all the numbers and facts he'd memorized on behalf of his former employer and that man's daughter were stuffed inside. His features, too, resemble lines drawn in accounting books: eyes, nose, ears, and mouth formed like so many divisors, parentheses, and percentage marks.

"Very astute, miss." There's not an ounce of condescension in the tone; rather, it's one of pride.

Martha studies him; her stern countenance momentarily softens. In the fourteen months since her father's death, she's learned a good deal about business transactions: why the Spanish currencies of the South American countries are stable and those of the United States are not; what commerce will prove a secure investment; what sections of the nation are burgeoning—despite the ongoing financial depression; which local districts will experience growth because of proximity to the anthracite depot; or where, like the industries in Northern Liberties and Fishtown, it would be wise to stake a claim. As the country's preeminent manufacturing and banking center, Philadelphia is attracting international interest; local financiers must keep pace or risk forfeiting valuable assets.

"Why don't they apply for additional capital rather than sell the company outright, Mr. Newgeon? If my father were alive, I'm certain he would have considered making a loan. And you know he was fastidious with his investments—and charged accordingly."

The clerk thinks. He has a habit of tipping upward on his toes, although the activity still leaves him a good deal shorter than Martha. "Perhaps you could suggest such a scheme, Miss Beale."

"No, Mr. Newgeon. I'm determined to purchase a factory. If Quaker City is offering itself for sale, and if their books and all else are in order, then I shall buy it. If not, I'll look elsewhere."

She says no more, although both Martha and her clerk know the rest of the speech: that her decision to become the owner of a manufactory rather than simply an investor is motivated by a desire to rectify what she believes are unfair labor practices. She's resolved that under her governance men and women will earn a living wage in healthy conditions; that no child will be forced into drudgery; that housing will be adequate rather than cramped. According to the new Utopian ideal she's been studying, she's also decided to add a school to the premises. Now, of course, she's more adamant than ever before.

"You'll come with me, Mr. Newgeon?"

"If you wish it, miss."

"I do. Your eyes will see what mine overlook."

The clerk hesitates a moment before speaking again. His boots creak; his shoulders hitch themselves higher. "You're aware, Miss Beale, of the conditions under which the men and women— and children—labor."

"Yes." A flicker of self-doubt crosses Martha's face. "At least, as much as I can imagine from what I've read. Facts and figures aren't the most inspiring of tutors. I do know, however, that a weekly wage of fewer than three dollars for a shift comprising upward of thirteen hours is poor payment indeed."

Newgeon nods but doesn't comment on the customary compensation. "You may be met with unkind words. Even the managers and supervisors aren't always treated with respect. And this unexpected return to winter may cause those unhappy with their employment to behave in ill-advised ways."

"I understand, Mr. Newgeon, but I wouldn't want anyone punished for speaking the truth. And I do mean to discover the truth in all things."

"There are other facts you may wish to consider before your visit, miss" is the tentative reply to this declaration.

"I'm sure they'll become apparent during my investigation of the operation. Now, shall we go? My carriage is waiting."

DESPITE HER BOAST to the contrary, nothing has prepared Martha for the reality of a large textile mill in operation. First there's the noise: The metallic din of gears and wheels and throstles and spinning bobbins and the blacksmith's staccato repairs combine with the deafening roar of human voices trying to rise above the cacophony of man-made things. Words are screamed out, but the only attribute that identifies them as human is anxiety. Even the wood floors of the building vibrate and hum, and the wide beams quake under movement so continual it feels as though the property were a gigantic, living organism.

Entering the main building, she takes a reflexive step backward, and in the next second, her eyes and lungs are attacked by the myriad motes that fly through the air; cotton dust, sawdust, particles of steel and iron turn what little air there is a dense and murky gray. She retrieves a handkerchief, holding it to her nose while her eyes fill with burning tears. "You'll get used to it, Miss Beale," she hears the manager assigned to guide her shout, but she doubts she ever will.

"Thirty-inch wide pantaloon stuffs, the looms produce," she's further informed. "Three-million yards per annum...nearly the same as the great Silesia Mill in Manayunk...."

But whatever the fellow is proudly declaiming, Martha ignores because her attention is arrested by the sight of people working other machines in the distance: women and children bent nearly double in order to reach the spinning frames that lie a mere two feet above floor level. If they notice a well-dressed lady in their midst, they make no sign; and Martha wonders how those tortured bodies straighten themselves at the end of the day, and whether they can hear anything but the constant drone or see images other than cotton strands for "pantaloon stuffs" rolling endlessly forward. Several of the children appeared tied to the machinery.

"Who are——?" she begins to ask.

"Families...We permit children...work alongside mothers..." is the disjointed reply. "It's a kindness we do them." Despite the noise, Martha detects duplicity beneath the boastful claim.

The word "charity" is added before her guide marches her into another room and another, then up and down more staircases. "The blacksmith's shop..." she hears, although the statement is no more than a whisper when compared to the clamor.

"Four-hundred power looms," she's told, "seven-thousand, one-hundred seventy-six spindles...adult weavers...adult carders...skilled mule spinners to man the spinning jennies." Here the manager stops. They're now on the building's third story and entering a room so thick with whirling cotton chaff that visibility is severely reduced. A laborer is pointed out to Martha, but the man appears unaware of the attention. "Munder...one of our best mule spinners...keeps pace for others...knack with drafting twist that produces the best yarns for warp and weft...make him a supervisor one day, if I was you...knows his place...Munder, stand up and greet the lady who may become your new owner."

The manager must tap the laborer on the shoulder before the mule spinner reacts. He does as he's been ordered, pulling off his cap and regarding Martha not with hope or bitterness or apathy, but with an expression of such apparent grief that she feels the emotion herself. Then he replaces the chaff-covered cap and resumes his work, and the manager leads Martha back toward the offices where Newgeon has been examining the mill's accounts. Her blue cashmere gown and capotte look as though they've been used to dust the dirtiest of houses.

"WELL, MISS BEALE? I believe you'll find your clerk has discovered all is in order here. I trust you were satisfied with your examination of the premises." It's one of the owners who addresses her. He's the only one on the premises and has the good Quaker name of Fox, although Martha finds him more closely allied to the animal than to his human forebears. He watches her with crafty eyes and a nose as pinched and sniffing as a snout.

Martha takes a proffered chair, flicking away clots of gray-white stuff that clings to her clothes. She's glad she didn't heed her maid's advice to wear her sable-trimmed walking dress, as this costume is ill-suited enough and makes her appear less experienced than she would like. "I cannot say I was satisfied, Mr. Fox, but I did inspect each of your floors and workrooms." She purposely doesn't look at Newgeon. "Before I can decide how I wish to proceed, I have some questions to pose."

He seats himself then leans back in his chair. He's attired not in the sturdy cottonade his mill produces but in elegant Jacquard. His cravat is silk; his fitted jacket of a fashionable crimson hue, his trousers narrow and fawn-colored. "You wish to know why my partners and I have decided to sell."

"No. I wish to discuss what influence our city's Guardians of the Poor have in this place. The agency can't be in agreement with the employment of so many children, nor with the conditions under which they toil."

Fox smiles, and Martha has the impression this was precisely the issue he expected her to raise. "The Guardians of the Poor is a well-meaning group, Miss Beale; more than well-meaning, it's an assemblage of exemplary citizens. But a textile mill must be a competitive force in the marketplace. If Silesia Mill out in Manayunk makes a practice of employing young laborers, so must we."

It's obvious from the smooth and patronizing tone that Fox intends to end his lecture there; the mention of Silesia Mill's arrangements would give any other industrialist pause because it's the region's largest and most influential factory. But Martha has inherited more than a little of Lemuel Beale's skepticism.

"Why is that, sir?" Her manner has become deceptively accommodating, and the owner is beguiled into thinking he's found a willing student.

"Profit, of course, Miss Beale. Do you think children earn as much as women? Or women as much as men? I needn't explain to you the effects upon the city and nation of the financial panic of six years past—which consequences we're still enduring. Your father was an astute investor and weathered the disaster admirably, but many large and small businesses faltered. Laborers were summarily released from their contracts, causing the pool of skilled and unskilled laborers to grow. Silesia took advantage of that surplus; as a result, the owner was able to reduce wages for those continuing in his employ. Naturally, we followed suit."

"Naturally" is Martha's reply although the word sticks in her throat.

"And, as Silesia's owner so persuasively states: 'It is charity that we provide when permitting children to labor alongside their parents.' "

"Charity, I see..." She can sense Newgeon regarding her, but she doesn't turn in his direction. Instead, she feigns interest in the room as though she were envisioning it equipped with furniture of her choosing and clerks of her hiring.

"If it weren't for our compassionate intervention, Miss Beale, they'd be forced to wander the streets while their mothers toiled. To say nothing of their little hands being more nimble and their bodies better able to accommodate our more compact frames—"

"I noticed small boys carrying heavy boxes up the stairs," Martha interrupts. Her delivery has become more pointed, but Fox is unaware of the change in attitude.

"Bobbin boxes," he tells her with satisfaction. "Some of our young fellows are good for nothing else but dragging equipment from floor to floor. Sixteen pounds isn't too much to ask; and the boys are glad of the work. It's a favor we do them. Else, as I said, they'd be left to beg upon the streets. Surely no one wishes that."

Martha nods; although encased in silk-lined gloves, her fingers clench with revulsion. "So the Silesia Mill determines how all other textile manufacturers conduct their business?"

"I wish that were not the case, Miss Beale, for I have no fondness for the owner. He's a boorish man—foreign, of course. But their cottonade is the industry model. With its popularity among the southern landowners, we'd be fools not to imitate his success."

"Ah, yes, the southern landowners," she echoes. Fox apprehends her confusion and permits himself another superior smile.

"Slave owners, naturally. The fabric is cheap and durable and, therefore, desirable. Our brokers in South Carolina and Georgia sell the stuff in bulk—"

"Slave owners?" is all Martha can manage to gasp out.

"Surely you understood the backbone of our business, Miss Beale?"

"That this is a textile mill, yes."

"The majority of whose looms produce an excellent quality of cottonade. It's for that very reason that Quaker City is in such an enviable position. Fashions may come and go, but the need for solid, well-priced—"

The explanation is interrupted as Martha rises. Beneath the several layers of her gown, her knees wobble in dismay. "I've taken enough of your time, Mr. Fox."

"But you haven't examined the mill's account books—"

"Mr. Newgeon did so for me." She looks at the clerk; astonishment and censure pass across her face. *You knew about this?* her expression demands, but the silent gaze he returns is impossible to decipher.

"Miss Beale, I must protest; there's a great deal more we need to discuss—"

"Not at the moment, sir. I fear I must bid you good day."

"I trust you're not ill, madam, or that I haven't offended in some fashion?"

What can Martha answer but the truth? "I must tell you, Mr. Fox, that I'm not happy to learn that you abet an activity as vile as the bondage practiced in the southern states."

He regards her in bewilderment. "People must be clothed, madam. You wouldn't have the poor creatures walk about naked, would you?"

"I choose not to profit from another's misfortune."

The owner's small eyes narrow further and his nose wrinkles as though scenting danger. "Madam, no one in business desires to be viewed in the despicable light you describe. My fellow owners and I are not ogres, nor are we the proverbial money lenders in the temple; we are simply men of affairs. The marketplace dictates our policies; it has always been thus—"

"Perhaps it's time human beings established the rules, rather than your 'marketplace.' "

"Madam, let us be rational. This is commerce, not a church aid society. Rather than castigate the men and women who produce the cloth, let us consider how fortunate the wretches are who receive it. Some folks sell shoddy goods to those lost African souls, but not Quaker City."

"Thank you, Mr. Fox—"

The mill owner isn't finished, however. "We take pride in our products, Miss Beale. And, yes, if you want my honest re-

sponse, I'm heartened to know the mill's goods protect bodies that
might otherwise go unclothed."

THE CARRIAGE THAT bears Martha and Newgeon back to
the Beale Brokerage House is wrapped in silence; even the coachman's verbal orders to the horse scarcely penetrate the space.

Her face averted, her body pressed against the door, Martha
watches the streetscape roll by. Snow mounds in front of shovel
shops and ironmongers; it nestles in the eaves of Reakirt's White-
lead and Window-glass manufactory and daubs the brick façade
of the neighboring coffin warehouse. The sun, now high in the sky
and very bright, glints down, producing a light that is painful to
the eye. Despite the sting, Martha continues to stare about her.
Slaves, her brain repeats, *yards and yards of cottonade sold to slave owners.*

"You knew about this, didn't you, Mr. Newgeon?" she demands at length.

"Yes, miss." He says no more for a moment or two. "But it
was my feeling that looms producing a coarse quality of fabric can
be altered to weave finer textiles instead."

"What you say may be true; although, I heartily wish Quaker
City were engaged in the creation of less tainted stuffs...worsteds
or carpeting, or even calico. I'll never be able to forget the product
that has built the mill's reputation—and its monetary value."

The clerk doesn't answer for several minutes. If Martha
looked at him, she would see his face reflecting the facts his brain
is reviewing, but she continues gazing out the window and so
doesn't recognize how troubled he's grown.

"Little that's manufactured is blameless, miss. Lives are often harmed during the producing of a commodity or the selling of
it. And that's because the mill owners and iron mongers, the factories that make whiting and lamp black, or tan the leather for your

gloves and your horses' harnesses must turn a profit or go under. So wages are kept to a minimum, and healthful working conditions are not what they should be. It seemed to me that Quaker City offered an ideal opportunity for improvement."

Her eyes still fixed upon the street, Martha considers the clerk's words. "My fine ideals must seem quite foolhardy to you, Mr. Newgeon."

"On the contrary, miss. I wouldn't have encouraged you to visit the mill if I didn't respect your motives."

Instead of a reply, she remains quiet; when she speaks again, her tone is flat. "Perhaps a calico-printing firm like the one we just passed would better suit my designs. It would be a smaller establishment with fewer laborers, and a good start, I think."

"Oh, miss, I don't believe a calico factory would fit your purposes at all."

With a rueful smile, she finally turns toward the clerk. "Don't tell me that it's also manufactured for 'southern landowners.'"

The clerk hesitates. His over-large head bobs in time to the carriage wheels' jouncing movement, his tall beaver hat bumping up and down until it nearly scrapes the carriage's padded ceiling. "Calico printed in Philadelphia is traded in Africa...along the River Niger...In exchange, ships transport human cargo to—"

Martha's ferocious words cut short the explanation. "Human cargo! But that vile business has been outlawed."

"A great many things are outlawed, miss. That doesn't mean they cease to exist."

"Oh" is all she can manage to gasp out. "If it's illegal, then how...?"

"The slaves are taken to Cuba, miss, and thence to Florida or Texas and so up into the southern states."

"And everyone is aware of this odious fact?"

"You were not, miss. And I venture to say many others are equally ignorant of the situation."

Martha releases an angry sigh and turns away. A new brougham is rounding the corner of Callowhill Street; for a moment, its appearance transfixes her for it's an elegant rig without a speck of dirt on its black body despite the cinder-laden roadway. Then the carriage disappears, and the mule spinner, Munder, enters her brain. There's obviously no connection between the laborer and the handsome coach, and so she pushes him and Quaker City Mill and each of the city's contemptible calico-printing factories as far from her thoughts as possible.

Chapter 5
What the Husband Knows

BY THE TIME OSCAR MUNDER quits the mill, daylight is only a memory. The stars—for the evening sky is now blessedly clear—glint down upon the ice-encrusted world, overlooking the brown-black pools of coal soot and the refuse and sweepings even the roaming pigs have left untouched while at the same time alighting on snowdrifts that are still gleaming white, making them shine as if they were freshly formed. When the moon rises, a full moon now, every blemish on brick or mortar or wood shingle, and every human stain as well, will be obliterated in a luminous bath. Then those still traversing the streets will appear cloaked in godliness; the tenements will look solid and sturdy, the narrow lanes welcoming; life will seem beneficent.

Munder has it in mind to take his Agnes out for a stroll after their meal, for she has always had a childlike delight in the magic a quixotic season like this can produce, and he imagines her *oohing* and *aahing* over the surprising effects of the scene. Then he reminds himself that she may or may not have wandered home while he was at his labors and that the fourth day of her absence is now drawing to a close.

Thinking of his errant wife, his face resumes its expression of loss, and his footsteps flag. He understands that her wages will be docked, just as they've been docked in the past; and it will require his urgent pleas to her supervisor to prevent her from being dismissed altogether. But he's also aware that that type of favoritism is certain to increase her unpopularity and make her—and him—the brunt of more ribald and cutting remarks. Although he knows he's stronger than his mate and can bear up under the harshest of circumstances. The harshest of conditions, as well.

By now his progress has halted altogether. *My little Agnes!* he thinks while his eyes, sunk within their sockets, survey a world which is growing less appealing by the moment. Indeed, the shops and factory alleys around him are starting to look no more genuine than the painted canvases that advertise a quack's bogus elixir. Munder has seen enough of those hucksters with their ramshackle wagons, the sides festooned with depictions of wholesome families quaffing nostrums guaranteed to cure all ailments. In each portrait the babies are rosy, the wives buxom, and the men smug—and rich beyond Munder's most fantastical dreams.

Considering those illusory pictures, the mule spinner glares until his eyes all but disappear. *Why must she be forced to toil at such an unhealthy trade? Why can't I, as her husband, earn enough for our upkeep or provide her with the little gewgaws she craves? Or with appetizing meals? Or a better home than a single room in a cramped and noxious-smelling tenement? Why am I a failure at twenty-three years of age when I should be in my prime?*

Munder's spine curves under the weight of all this self-rebuke. If he were a skeleton on display in one of the city's new anatomical classes, the students would worry that the thing were about to break apart and spill bones all over the table top. His head droops; his black hair, which is abundant and glossy despite the mill chaff blown into it daily, falls into his eyes and across his now-bitter cheeks.

He moves on. Starlight continues to spread a brilliant sheen across the landscape, and his hopes—despite his better judgment—begin to rise again. *Won't Agnes be excited when she learns the mill was visited by a fine lady? Won't she demand an account of every article of clothing Mistress Beale wore? And won't she clap her hands in delight when I tell her I've been singled out as an excellent worker? Won't she hug me and kiss me and ask to sit upon my lap? And then start planning where—and how—we'll reside if my lot improves?*

Buoyed by these fantasies, Oscar Munder increases his pace toward home. He pauses once when a fit of coughing overwhelms him, then discharges a stream of tarry, black stuff into the street and immediately kicks snow over the spittle as if he were afraid Agnes would discover it. With another fistful of the hard-packed flakes he wipes his mouth and bearded chin then tosses the dirty ball away. He's trying to recall precisely how Martha Beale looked, what she said, how she moved. Agnes, he knows, will demand the minutest of details.

He enters the long, narrow building where they dwell; the stench of excrement from the cellar privy, of the pisspots kept on every landing, of rancid soup bones and rotted cabbage assails him, causing him to cough again and hurriedly retrace his steps to the courtyard where he gags and then spits more black clots into the corner. *How is it that the place can stink thus?* he wonders. *The mill housing is a mere five years old, but even the stones of its construction reek as if they were formed not of schist and limestone but of human waste and the ammonia-like stink of rats.*

He climbs the stairs to the third floor, first intending to pose this scientific question to his wife, then deciding against it. He must be careful in his dealings with Agnes after she's taken it into her head to wander about; besides, he has a far more appealing subject in Mistress Beale.

Lifting the latch of his door, he's startled at first to find the room dark, although the neighbor who has peeked out to watch his approach is not.

"Scarpered on you again, did she?" the man demands. The voice is neither kind, nor unkind; and Munder turns to regard him. He doesn't answer, although his brain is finally reconciling itself to the truth. Agnes has not yet decided to return home.

"I'd cast her off if I was you, Mr. Munder. A wife should be a wife, not a—"

The mule spinner's throat makes a sound that's half-choking, half-growling; he strides inside and slams the door with such force that its frame rattles and its iron hinges clang.

"Suit yourself," he hears through the wood panel that bars the sight of the hall but never its sounds nor smells. "But you take my advice. Once they taste that way of life, there's no saving them. Wives or daughters both. And I should know, shouldn't I?"

Munder makes no reply; instead, he retreats as far into his one-room home as he can. A single window is set into the undressed stone wall and this he focuses upon, gazing at the four glass panes; although their surface immediately clouds with his breath, so his vision is not of other windows set in other buildings or even of the night sky, but of himself.

Thus mirrored, he sees what Agnes daily sees: the slack cheeks, the grayish skin, the unkempt beard in which all manner of lighter colored particles are stuck, the clothing that's winter-stained and rank. He watches this ghoul who's himself; the ghoul gazes contemptuously back.

At that moment, Oscar Munder finally understands that this time his wife has no intention of returning and that not one drop of hope, not one prayer or dream will ever transport her back into his arms.

Chapter 6
Home and Hearth

AND WHERE IS AGNES now, while her poor husband spends another fitful night in her absence and those who claim cordiality and fellowship mutter calumnies behind his back?

Hidden on the top floor of the house on Callowhill Street where no neighbors' preying eyes can spot her, removed from all association with the people with whom she's shared her labors and her life, do Agnes's aspirations persevere? Does the gentleman remain kindly and pleasant? Is the idyll everything she desires it to be, and is she still warm and well attended by the silent servant who prepares her food and heats the water for her bath?

Or has Agnes's lack of freedom begun to gall, and does she now regret her decision to leave her Oscar? Has she considered returning home—despite the disreputable passage of time and the thin shoes in which she originally braved the elements?

Or, perhaps, the situation is worse, and the gentleman has grown bored of his easy conquest and therefore callous, deciding to lock the stairway door during absences that have become increasingly lengthy. Maybe he's turned more than callous; maybe Agnes's passivity and childlike faith have aroused a latent cruelty, and he's chosen to deny her sustenance, clothing, light, and heat. Or maybe his impulses have escalated to more violent forms of physical abuse—as any madam of any bawdy house in the city can attest is a distinct possibility when gentlemen are dealing with hired companions. There are professional establishments catering to those types of clients, although their owners all know that retaining women willing to undergo that type of punishment isn't easy. Munder's wife, for all her foibles, would never be chosen to labor in one of those houses. Nor would she have wanted to.

So what of Agnes? If she is being kept against her will, and if her companion's behavior has cast off all pretense at nicety and grown vicious instead, then who will help her when the only other person aware of her existence in the house is a deaf mute?

"NO WORD, I TAKE IT?" The question is delivered by Becky Grey—now Mrs. William Taitt—to her lady's maid. The tone and accent are clipped, British still and also full of the former actress's much-vaunted vibrato.

"From the mister, madam?" the girl asks. With the exception of her baby's nursemaid (and that because William pays the woman handsomely), Becky can't keep servants. The result of the continual domestic turmoil is a persistent unease on the part of those in the Taitts' service—as well their mistress's inability to recall even one of their names.

"Of course, from your master. Who else would I be inquiring about at this ungodly hour of the night?" In her peignoir, with the maid carefully unpinning her elaborate coiffure, Becky glares at their dual reflections in the looking glass.

The girl knows better than to respond. When her mistress is in a mood like this, she's capable of anything: hurling silver brushes or combs, sweeping porcelain bric-a-brac from the mantel, rending a gown, and then blaming the destruction on those who wait upon her.

Unanswered, Becky's frown turns cruel. "Leave me," she orders. She waves off the girl's attentions, which isn't difficult as the lady's maid is a good deal shorter than her commanding mistress.

"Oh, but madam, I'm not finished. And you cannot go to bed without—"

"Leave me, I said!"

The girl quits her ministrations but doesn't move away. She'll be censured for the madam's haphazard toilette, too, she knows. "I could send for a footman, madam, and he could go to the master's club and inquire—"

"Stop your prattling. If I'd wanted your advice, I would have asked for it."

The maid bobs a curtsey, and then a second for good measure. "Yes, madam."

"With such a household and so many useless females idling about, it's no wonder my husband would rather spend his time elsewhere."

"Yes, madam." The girl starts backing toward the door, adding what she hopes will be a soothing conclusion to the conversation. "Shall I tell Nurse to fetch Baby to wish goodnight to his mama?" This is a mistake, however. Becky may call her infant "Baby;" she may refer to him as that when visiting her friend Martha who may then employ the same intimate abbreviation, but no mere servant should have such temerity.

"The child has a name, for pity's sake. Use it when you refer to him, or you'll be seeking another position."

The maid bobs up and down again; panic makes her eyes goggle. "Shall I tell Nurse to fetch young Master Taitt?"

Becky has grown tired of the exchange, however. "No. I wish no intrusions. Besides, it's too late to disturb the child. Now go."

Sidling out of the room, the maid is at pains to latch the door behind her with the softest of metallic rasps, but Becky watches the wood swing to, hears the scrape of iron and brass, and experiences not power over the cowed female in her hire but

38   Cordelia Frances Biddle

the opposite, for it seems that she and her servant are one and the same: two people wholly dependent upon the fickle goodwill of others. Recognizing the similarity, Becky feels hatred toward the girl, although the emotion has an equal amount of self-loathing.

Where is William that he deserts me for days at a time? her thoughts rail. *Why does he value me so little? What have I done to deserve this fate? Aren't I beautiful enough, cultured enough? Haven't I always been his willing accomplice in the marriage bed, and didn't I bear him a son? A young Taitt to rear in this hideous house with all the other dead and dreary Taitts sneering down at me from their haughty portraits.* Tears of wrath and helplessness fill her eyes; she lets them cascade down her cheeks, mindless of the powder still daubed on her skin, mindless of how mottled and ugly her complexion will become, or how inflamed and swollen her eyes. She has wept many times since she took up permanent residence in Philadelphia. She has no doubt she will weep many more.

And do I complain about that horrid plantation house of his in the Carolinas, or the slaves he keeps? I told him I wouldn't accompany him again when he journeyed there, but what of that? It's not a fit place for me. . .and wouldn't he rather keep me at a distance so he can enjoy his sordid dalliances with those unhappy women he owns?

Given her theatrical training, Becky should be able to sustain a high level of indignant ire and even a dramatic and self-serving sorrow, but true emotions aren't as conveniently manipulated as false ones, and she's soon spent and defeated. Her shoulders slump; her graceful posture sags. She looks nothing like the gilded London lady who once had princes and dukes vying for her attentions. *Why doesn't William come home? Why doesn't he love me? I'm not unsophisticated; I understand men's predilections; surely he knows that I would overlook a small romantic escapade here and there. Isn't that the mode I knew at home, and wouldn't I forgive it here? So why does he abuse me thus by vanishing for days at a time? Couldn't he at least create a satisfactory lie—if only for appearances' sake?* Catching sight of herself in the looking glass, she recognizes the answer. Who could love anyone as ugly as she? Who could feel empathy for such a pitifully formed creature? Why feign a cheery hearth and home when there is none?

She quits the glass and drifts toward the door, thinking to walk downstairs and see if her husband has returned while she was railing against her fate. Instead, she stands and listens, too overwhelmed by inertia to move further. In her mind's eye, she pictures the stairway, the paintings, the outmoded wall sconces and chandeliers, the mausoleum quality of a place owned by too many generations of the same family. Baby is now howling lustily in the distance, but the sound is so muffled by sealed doors and additional stairwells leading onto other landings that the noise might as well emanate from a neighboring house or the street. Knowing the nurse will attend to her child, will, in fact, be of greater comfort to him than his own mother, she ignores the wails and retreats further into her chambers. Her breathing and heartbeats have grown so slow that Becky wonders if she is dying.

Chapter 7

A Request

OF COURSE, BECKY doesn't succumb to heartache and despair, but she awakens the next morning with the bitter taste of regret in her mouth, her eyes swollen and painful and her brain still afire. Examining her reflection in the glass, a self-protective indignation takes hold; she determines to cast aside her morose behavior and seek out her friend Martha Beale and request her counsel regarding Taitt's waywardness. An heiress who can afford to dispense with polite society's nagging demands is the very person to aid her.

THE *TETE-A-TETE* and its resultant sense of well-being and resolve isn't as easily accomplished as Becky envisioned, however. Arriving at an inconveniently early hour at Martha's home, not only does she find her friend preoccupied and withdrawn, but also the very setting seems to conspire against her need for friendship and intimacy. The house, which she knows so well, seems suddenly the epitome of cold Philadelphia authority; there's no room for ambivalence or diffidence, no place for the awkwardness of marital confidences. Unable to achieve the desired personal tone or fully engage Martha, the former actress's attempts at a sociable demeanor serve to further alienate her—which, in turn, makes her efforts grow more fervent. Matching her escalating distress, her voice rises until it seems as though she were addressing an entire theatre full of people rather than one quiet woman in her private parlor.

"How do you tolerate this dreadful American snow?" she demands after one of her previous sallies fails to elicit anything more than a desultory response. "England is never subjected to anything like it. At least, not London. It's a pretty sight but only when viewed from the warmth of a comfortable chamber. In truth, I'd rather have all those white drifts painted on a scenery back-drop—then the setting could be exchanged for one of a more temperate clime. Wouldn't that be lovely! We alter our surroundings to match our moods!"

Martha watches the performance. At other times, she would be amused. Today, she finds Becky and her theatrics tiresome. Besides, the hour is an unusual one, far too premature for social calls. "And how is Baby?" she asks at length. Tea and the requisite cakes, biscuits, sweetmeats, and sugared fruits have been delivered by a footman, but the tray and its delicacies go untouched by both hostess and guest: Martha, through indifference; Becky, because she can't sit still long enough to eat.

"Oh, happy. Robust. No different than other three-month-old infants. At any rate, the nursemaid tells me so." Two sharp lines crease Becky's forehead while she speaks, then vanish just as rapidly.

"And William?"

This blandest of queries is avoided as Becky pirouettes on one foot and reaches out an arm to toy with the fur-lined pelisse and fur-edged bonnet she's tossed over the back of a chair. "Let us not discuss dull domesticity, my dear! Let us plan some exciting excursion instead. Take a sledge and visit your country house—"

"Which is shuttered until the warm weather arrives."

"Somewhere else then. I am simply dying for entertainment. William is quite well, by the by. Quite well."

"I'm happy to hear it."

"Yes. Quite well. All of us: fit as fiddles." Again, a frown knifes across Becky's face; again, it's banished. She throws herself into a settee near Martha's desk. "Don't tell me you've been working on those tedious banking figures again. Why not let a clerk attend to such an odious task? You have too much filthy lucre to waste your time on accruing more."

When her friend doesn't answer, Becky's words rush forward. "If you're determined to enter into the business of men— which I know you are—what goal can you have other than profit? At least it's superior to all this romanticized palaver about the sanctity of home and hearth." She laughs, but the sound is brittle. "You're a wealthy woman. You should be reveling in your autonomy rather than heaping additional burdens upon your shoulders. When you're married you'll have ample opportunity for care." She falls silent for a moment, plucking at a silk rose on her dress then fingering the lace of her sleeves. "Taitt told me that Thomas Kelman left the city several weeks ago," she observes at length. "I was surprised you didn't tell me yourself. My husband isn't ordinarily the bearer of romantic tidings."

"Yes" is Martha's sole reply, to which she adds a more genial "Yes, he's journeying to South America."

"The land of milk and honey. That's all Taitt talks about: how fortunes can be made there. He should have accompanied your Kelman. Two adventurous souls." A pause is followed by another scowl; if Martha weren't experiencing her own sense of loss, she would recognize Becky's distress. "It does seem unfair that a single unresolved crime should force the man to quit his home. It's not as though he was the culprit."

"No."

"An abduction gone awry. He shouldn't have born the brunt of the public's outcry when the girl was found dead."

"No," Martha repeats, and then changes the subject by describing the previous day's visit to Quaker City Mill as well as her discoveries regarding the institution's business practices.

"William keeps slaves at his southern estate," Becky states when Martha has finished. "I've promised myself that I will never visit there again. Not even if he takes Baby with him." With that, she again leaps to her feet, hurrying to the windows and throwing wide the draperies. "Forget your holy ideals; Emerson and Alcott and all those desiccated transcendentalists may trust in equality of life and labor. As for me, I believe that the day is beautiful and the sun is smiling. Let us go to the theatre. Let us have our fortunes cast by gypsies. You and I need to be out and about, not cooped up inside contemplating the errors of our ways."

Finally, Martha notices how her friend's cheeks blaze as she speaks and how her eyes burn. "Are you certain your health is what it should be, Becky? Three months after childbirth isn't a long recovery—"

"Of course, I'm healthy. Why shouldn't I be? My every desire attended to. My child so cosseted by servants I might as well be superfluous. Three months, I might add, is a very long time. I'm fully recovered, as you see. And dressed as I once was, although I must confess, my stays were never quite so uncomfortable before."

The answer, however, doesn't alleviate Martha's growing unease. She studies Becky who attempts to avoid the examination by moving away toward another corner of the room. "And William?" she probes.

"He's proud to be a parent, of course. As am I. Just as we're grateful to be wed. If he chooses to disappear from home on occasion, what of it? Men don't always wish to abide in a nursery atmosphere."

"But doesn't he wish to be with his son—?"

"An infant is an infant. They change little day to day. Nurse tells me fathers prefer their offspring when they can talk and display reason."

These words are no sooner uttered than a footman raps upon the door, announcing that another unexpected visitor has called: A Mr. Dumont now waits downstairs.

"Ah, a prospective suitor," Becky sings out. "Let me not prevent you from entertaining your gentlemen friends—unless it's the unfortunate Cornelius rather than his handsome brother Charles who has come to call." She makes a grab for her discarded mantle and matching muff, bundling them together as if she intended to rush outside with them still in her arms. "I should never have ventured out at such an untimely hour. The nurse will be wondering what has become of me." Her reticule drops, she swoops down to pick it up, then perches the purse atop the precarious pile. "It must be Charles, because, as everyone knows, Cornelius has a wife who—ah, enough gossip for one day."

"Becky. Stop. You came to visit me. What is it you wished to say?"

"Why, nothing at all. I decided to walk to your house out of friendship—and because I couldn't bear to be cooped up another second. Now, let me be on my way before I'm missed at home. Besides, I don't wish to intrude upon your *amours*—"

"Which this is not, I assure you. I hardly know Mr.—"

"Still waters run deep, Mistress Beale. You and I are both aware how sought after you've become since your year of formal mourning has passed." She laughs, the sound as false as before. "No wonder you seemed *distrait*. You were expecting another guest. And your Mr. Kelman only recently departed from the field! Martha, you are a wonder. Or should I say, 'Fie on you, madam—' "

"But I hardly know the Dumont brothers—"

"So you profess. However, I'll counter that the hour is an unconventional one. If I'm ill at ease paying a call this early in the day, then the gentleman downstairs must have been awarded special privileges. Now, let me go before Nurse and Baby realize I'm gone."

"Stay, Becky. We'll greet and dispense with this surprise caller together. Then you can explain the purpose of your—"

"Oh no, I'm not fit to be viewed by a physical specimen as perfect as Charles Dumont. I had a restless night, you see, and was prey to all sorts of nonsensical ruminations."

Martha regards her friend. "Something very great is troubling you, I think. I wish you would tell me what—"

But Becky has already fled from the room.

WALKING DOWNSTAIRS to the withdrawing room shortly thereafter, Martha can't dispel her worries over Becky. As she crosses the foyer, her fears escalate, and as she enters the room, she promises herself that she'll cut short the interview. Acting as hostess to a gentleman about town is the last thing she desires.

But there stands Charles Dumont. A fresh fire is now sizzling in the grate, and he has placed himself before the hearth in order to take advantage of the heat. Behind him, the light builds and flickers, making his long tawny-colored hair appear to glow. In fact, his entire figure seems to gleam as though his natural ease and confidence were a visible manifestation of inner grace. He bows, but his eyes—which are smiling—remain fixed on Martha's face.

"Miss Beale. It's so good of you to see me. I apologize for the oddness of the hour. I'm an impetuous person. At least, my brother is always telling me so. Warning me, I should say."

Martha wills herself to hold his gaze, although his appraisal feels uncomfortably intimate. "May I offer you tea, Mr. Dumont? And cake? Or ratafias and macaroons?"

"Nothing, Miss Beale. Your company is all I require." He sits the moment after his hostess has taken her chair, crossing one leg over another. Despite the cinder-laden streets, his boots are clean, his dove-gray trousers spotless. They're the clothes of a man who has never known want.

"May I ask the purpose of your visit? Or is this purely a social call—in which case, I extend my thanks." Again, Martha must force herself not to look away. Becky was correct. Charles Dumont is a well-favored person; if he were not, it would be easier for her to converse with him. Reflecting upon that anomaly, her discomfort increases. *Why should appearance affect me in this perverse fashion?* she asks herself. *Why do I feel tranquil among the ungainly and ordinary, and nervous among the elegant and refined? I possess a great fortune; don't I govern my own life?*

"Must there be a purpose other than amity, Miss Beale?" His smile grows until the expression wreathes his face; Martha must move her gaze to another part of the room. "Or has the lady who aspires to become a maven of industry already grown too methodical to enjoy casual visits from her acquaintances?"

"Where did you hear that bit of news?" Surprise makes the tone more breathy than she wishes.

"Why, from Fox, one of the owners of Quaker City Mill. He's not mistaken, is he?"

"Ah...Is that the meaning of your visit, then? To serve as Mr. Fox's emissary?"

Dumont laughs. It's a buoyant, cheerful sound, and Martha can't help but compare it to Thomas Kelman's sometimes pained introspection—which disloyal thought she hastens to dismiss.

"You're becoming as shrewd an opponent as your father was, Miss Beale."

"I didn't intend to become adversarial, sir, but I presumed my initial dealings with the mill owners were confidential."

Dumont shakes his head in mock disbelief. "This is Philadelphia, madam. Surely you're aware that nothing is private when every well-born family is intertwined. To newcomers we must resemble a giant coven. Perhaps not a wise analogy, but I was never one for wisdom—as Cornelius will also confirm. I admit I do have an ulterior motive for my visit."

Martha sits back in her chair, now prepared to hear paeans directed toward Quaker City Mill: how fine an investment it is and how amenable its laborers will be to change. Or, perhaps, as Becky suggested, a declaration that her guest wishes to enter the ranks of eligible men and seek her hand in matrimony. What she doesn't expect is what he says next.

"I'm aware of your reputation for aiding people in distress, that you brought two waifs into your home, and that your ministrations were a boon to a certain beleaguered family during their recent time of trial." He pauses; his tone turns softer and less assured. "Let me be blunt. I'm here on a mission for my brother. As I'm sure you're aware, he and I were born mere moments apart and resemble each other to a degree that most observers can't distinguish us. However, Cornelius is a very different person, diffident where I am garrulous, reserved rather than gregarious." Dumont hesitates again. He looks at the floor as though measuring how much to reveal. "He wasn't always so, but his wife is the focus of many callous rumors—which doubtless you've heard. She has a propensity toward fevers of the brain and so forth, and has spent considerable time under the care of physicians both within the confines of her home and at the Asylum for Relief of Persons Deprived of Their Use of Reason."

Martha is acquainted with the Asylum and its reputation for nurturing those suffering from melancholia and dementia as well as more nefarious afflictions, although she doesn't indicate as much. She inclines her head, urging her guest to continue, which he does, leaning forward until it seems as though he's about to kneel at her feet.

"At present, she's experiencing one of her more lucid periods, which my brother hopes is a sign of permanent improvement. I remain skeptical, but I'm a loyal sibling. Her return to full health would be my greatest wish...And this is what I now request of you, Miss Beale. Can you see it in your heart to befriend the lady? I fear others in your position might view her as a curiosity..." Dumont raises his hands in supplication. "Before you answer, let me further assert that my scheme—if I can call it that—requires no more time than a single day's congenial outing. If Cornelius's wife responds well to the activity, then I may approach you for further assistance. Or you may bid me *adieu* at once, and thank me never to call again. But I beg of you, please consider my request."

Martha doesn't speak for a minute. She realizes that the speech was rehearsed, although the fact doesn't displease her; she'd do the same if she had an awkward proposal to make. "I have no training in the medical arts—"

"I understand that, Miss Beale. I'm here to apply to your kindness of heart and to your natural empathy. With my hat in hand, I should add." He regards his empty fingers. "That is, if I hadn't given it to one of your excellent servants."

Martha smiles at this effort toward levity; he beams in gratitude. "I apologize for my ignorance, but how is your brother's wife called?"

"Called?" Dumont seems startled by the question. "Oh, I understand...Althea. However, Cornelius is fond of referring to her as Thea."

"Not an easy name."

"No. It's a trifle outmoded. But then, she is...reclusive."

Martha makes no further observation, although it's not the name's old-fashioned nature she finds curious but its reference to a mythological story from ancient Greece: a woman who murdered her son. "Has the couple been blessed with children?" The query is posed in a casual vein as though it had just occurred to her.

"No. Well, that is to say that there's no offspring living."

"Ah..." is the quiet reply, then she reminds herself that she's no learned professor plumbing the human psyche. "What are you proposing, Mr. Dumont?"

"A day-long carriage excursion north to *Point Breeze* with my brother, his wife, and with me. The sun and bracing air will prove beneficial to us all."

"*Point Breeze*? You mean the Bonaparte estate?"

"The very place. The vistas from the belvedere and parterre gardens are sublime, and as the house itself is no longer occupied, we won't be forced to encounter fellow travelers. Naturally, there are still servants on the premises, but we'll have the grounds to ourselves. It's very grand. I'm sure your father visited it. The billiard room alone is worth the trip."

"You're familiar with the house, then?"

"The Dumont name is of French origin, Miss Beale. We've been associated with the Bonaparte family for many years—long before the *Comte de Survilliers* arrived on these shores. In Paris, I would be called something that sounds like *Sharle Duemon*, and the country estate—which comprises some twelve miles of acreage— would be deemed a *chateau*." He applies an exaggerated accent, leaning as close to Martha as propriety permits. "Say you'll agree to my little scheme, Miss Beale. Please say you will. It would mean the world to Cornelius and to me."

"Mr. Dumont, you wear your heart on your sleeve."

"So Cornelius is constantly cautioning me. Please, Miss Beale. I know you have a reputation as the soul of kindness."

What can Martha say to this bit of flattery? That she wasn't always thus? That she's only recently felt comfortable enough to reveal her inmost feelings—and that solely because of her affection for Thomas Kelman? No, she must remain within the established order of polite conversation and murmur humble gratitude. Besides, Charles Dumont has no claim on her, nor will he. A pleasant young man—a very pleasant young man—but not someone with whom she will ally herself. "I'll agree to your request, sir, if I may also make one."

"Anything you wish. If you're willing to aid my dear brother, I'm at your command. Heart and mind and everything I possess."

"Be careful what you promise," Martha laughs then continues in a more serious vein. "A friend of mine is in need of the type of activity you describe. She's Mrs. William Taitt, who was known as Becky Grey—"

"I know the name well. Everyone does—"

"May we include her? Not her husband," Martha hastens to add. "Just Becky alone...I believe she'll be a compassionate presence to your sister-in-law, and the excursion would bring her so much joy."

"By all means, invite her."

Chapter 8

What the Party Discovers

WHEN THE MORNING of the excursion arrives, two days have been consumed in planning it—many of Martha's waking hours fraught with messages delivered from either Charles Dumont or Becky. Cornelius and his wife remain incommunicative throughout, but this is understandable given the nature of the charade the brothers are embarking upon and the fact that the women are to be introduced as last-minute additions to the party—acquaintances of Charles rather than of his twin. The stratagem is something Martha views with growing trepidation. Charles's missives querying what delicacies his guests would prefer for their picnic repast make it clear that he intends the journey to be a festivity of the highest order, but will his enthusiasm prove too taxing for his sister-in-law?

As to Becky, her worries seem to deal solely with her wardrobe. *Would a dress of Scotch plaid velvet trimmed with Honiton lace be more appealing than a new* gros de Tours *with a Grecian corsage?* she writes to Martha in a dashed-off note. That question answered she sends an additional message: *Coiffeur, would a Josephine comb be an attractive addition, or would the choice—named as it is for the emperor's wife—be viewed as an insult to his brother? On further consideration* (penned in another letter), *maybe the newest mode,* coiffée a la neige, *would be best.*

Martha shakes her head in wonderment. *What*, she asks herself, *would Becky do if she were preparing to encounter the real man—or the emperor—rather than a deserted residence?*

❧

"MISS BEALE, APOLOGIES for my tardy arrival. My brother's wife isn't yet prepared to set forth, so I called upon you first. If you permit a change of plan, the coachman will convey us to the Taitt residence and then return us to Cornelius's home." The speech is delivered all of one piece as Dumont escorts Martha down her front steps and into the waiting carriage. As might be anticipated, he's adept at handing the many layers of skirt and cloak in after her before also settling himself on the opposite leather seat. He raps his cane upon the coachman's box as an order to proceed, giving Martha time for only one query.

"Is your brother's wife well enough for the journey?"

"I assume she is. Cornelius didn't indicate otherwise." The brief verdict delivered, Dumont falls silent, although whether out of concern for Althea's fragile condition or the success of his party Martha can't determine. His face has taken on an unexpectedly grim cast, which she hopes will improve before the others join the party. Althea would certainly recognize herself as the cause of his discontent.

"I look forward to making Mrs. Dumont's acquaintance."

"Yes" is the equally hurried reply; then he seems to recover some of his former optimism. "Yes. And she you, as well. At least, I hope so...I'm most grateful, Miss Beale. Truly, I am."

"And I'm happy to visit a fabled house. So now we're equal in our debt to one another."

"No, Miss Beale, mine is by far the greater obligation." That said, he reverts to his uncommunicative state, and they journey to the Taitt home without further conversation.

There, however, they find that the lady hasn't finished her preparations, either. When she does appear—a full quarter of an hour later—Martha is amazed at her costume; a deeply winged bonnet all but conceals her face while the remainder of her body is so shrouded in fabric and fur as to be invisible. Not one of the season's newest fashions she seemed so eager to flaunt is in evidence. Becky apologizes for the delay, but her voice is thick as though from weeping. "I had a tumble upon the stairs," she adds, "which resulted in making me later than I wished."

"I trust it was nothing serious, Mrs. Taitt" is Dumont's solicitous reply.

"Not serious, no. I'm quite prepared to tramp the gardens and parkland, but I fear I did sustain some unsightly marks upon my face." She laughs, although the sound is far from joyous. "I expect my features will grow more hideous as the day progresses. My maid suggested a poultice of extract of lead, which I declined. It's one thing to be maimed, another to be encased in gauze and medicinal flannels. I would have resembled nothing so much as a cadaver on its way to a potter's field."

"I've been fortunate to see you perform when you first arrived in Philadelphia, madam, and I'll carry those lovely images with me forever. If you were capable of turning yourself into an ogre after a mere slip on a stairway, I'd deem it a testament to your craft."

Again Becky laughs, the tone as obligatory as before.

"We needn't go today," Martha offers. "We can postpone our adventure."

"No. An adventure is the very thing I require. Let us be off at once."

"But considering your fall, won't William worry——?"

"He's delighted to have me gone from the house and enjoying myself, Martha. His affairs have kept him away from home too often and me overly confined; I know he's pleased that I'm venturing forth at long last. Now, Mr. Dumont, tell me all about the wonders we have in store."

Which Dumont commences to do until the carriage halts at his brother's house. Cornelius stands alone upon the steps, without cape, hat, cane—or wife.

"Althea declines" is all he says, and Martha feels her heart lurch at the pain in his voice and the agony etched on his features. What Charles declared is true; in form and feature, the siblings are all but identical, but where the unwed brother's eyes light with a natural smile, Cornelius's expression appears too woebegone ever to have experienced mirth. When he ceases speaking, his lips clamp shut as if further speech will betray him.

"Then you'll come without her, brother," his twin advises from the open carriage door.

"No, I dare not. You understand that I'm the only one who can attend to her when these demons attack. She won't permit another person in the room, not even her maid; if I desert her, I fear she may do herself some damage."

"A few short hours' separation, surely—"

"No, Charles. I must remain at home." The voice is sharper than warranted, but Martha reminds herself that this is a man in an agony of worry.

"Mr. Dumont, is there any service I can render?" she asks.

"Thank you, no. My wife will tolerate only my company when she's thus afflicted. And sometimes, not even me." With that, Cornelius prepares to reenter his home while Charles leaps from the carriage, running up the steps until the two men stand talking together in quiet but obvious vexation. Charles gestures impatiently; Cornelius bows his head, and when he glances up again, his eyes are fierce. He shakes off the beseeching hand his twin lays upon his arm; Charles withdraws the gesture in an equal show of temper.

We needn't go, Martha yearns to call out, but the battle between the two men prevents her.

Moments later, the quarrel is past. Cornelius disappears inside; his brother enters the carriage and orders the coachman to drive on. "A pity," he announces, "however, there's no point in spoiling our day because of invented monsters. I assume you agree with my assessment, Mrs. Taitt?"

"Monsters, whether illusory or genuine, are dangerous companions" is her enigmatic reply.

"Ah, the craft of acting must enable you to conjure demons at will, Mrs. Taitt. And to banish them just as readily, I'll warrant."

When Becky doesn't answer, Dumont continues with a congenial: "My brother's wife could learn much from your experiences."

To this Becky makes no response.

THE THREESOME travels on, passing beyond the residential and industrial areas of the city as well as the shipyards and wharfs that have begun to stretch farther northward along the Delaware's banks. It's only when they find themselves in open countryside that anything approximating relaxed and agreeable conversation commences. Perhaps it's the homely sight of farm lanes and fields lying beneath layers of snow, or the wispy lines of wood smoke rising from the scattered cottages, or the peaceable cattle and sheep moving across the frozen terrain; whatever the cause, both Dumont and Becky begin talking at once.

"It's a veritable scandal that these outlying boroughs aren't yet—" he opines while Becky makes her own opening gambit.

"What's to become of the *Comte de Survilliers's* house now that he—?"

"I beg your pardon, madam. Please proceed and permit me to keep silent."

"No, you, sir. I didn't intend to interrupt."

Both begin again, only to repeat the tangle of words until Dumont concludes his prior remarks with an adamant: "Until a law is enacted consolidating Philadelphia's townships, every criminal wishing to escape justice need only flee into remote areas like these. Pretty though it is, if I resided here, I'd question my safety. Now, Mrs. Taitt, my numerous apologies for my outburst; you were asking me about the *Comte's*—?"

"Oh, sir, let us have no talk of crime. You'll have me fearing we'll encounter highwaymen on the path."

Dumont laughs. The sound fills the carriage; it's obvious his good humor has returned. "I promise you'll come to no harm, madam. My remarks were ill-timed—as always. And over-zealous, as well. If it weren't for that foolish dispute with my brother, I wouldn't have—"

"Still, highwaymen—!"

"My dear Mrs. Taitt, let me assure you that I and my coachman and footman are equipped with the means to defend ourselves should the need arise, which it will not." He graces Becky's still-shrouded face with a smile. "Now, shall we turn to merrier subjects and discuss *Point Breeze*? Although, I'm afraid you'll find my description paltry when compared to the original. Bare in mind that most of its construction was funded by a cache of diamonds—"

"Diamonds!" Becky gasps in showy appreciation.

"Indeed, a veritable trove of gem stones. And may I say that it takes a great *artiste* like yourself, Mrs. Taitt, to appreciate the extravagance of such a gesture."

"You're too kind, sir."

"Truthful, rather, madam. What I speak is from the heart."

"An admirable trait, sir, to be so honest and free with emotion. The American gentlemen in my acquaintance keep their feelings under lock and key."

"I believe your friend made a similar assessment of my character."

"Well, Martha is a wise woman."

Throughout this exchange, Martha has kept silent. She's aware of a shift in manner between her friend and their host. Within her obscuring garments, Becky seems to vibrate with renewed energy; Dumont does the same. By the time the winding carriage drives of Bonaparte's property are reached, the pair might as well be oblivious to the third person in the carriage. Relegated to the role of mute witness, Martha gazes out the carriage window, examining the lake with its artfully-sculpted islands, the Crosswicks Creek and its rustic bridges, secluded lovers' benches and marble statuary, the copses of tulip trees and honey locusts, and the swans and peacocks dotting the scene. Tranquility is the desired effect, but she experiences growing unease. *It's fortunate Taitt didn't join us*, she thinks, *his irascible nature would never tolerate this inappropriate display. What may be acceptable on the Continent will never find favor in Philadelphia.*

"I see we've arrived," she offers in a warning tone. "Perhaps we ladies should retire before luncheon. You did say the house was equipped to welcome us, did you not, Mr. Dumont?"

"Nonsense, Martha!" Becky chides. "Let us see and do everything. How can you be weary when all we've done is to sit in this agreeable coach? Of course, if you're tired I won't stop you from taking your ease. As to me, I give myself over wholly to Mr. Dumont."

"Then I suggest that we drive to the belvedere overlooking the river, madam," Dumont tells her. "The view is sublime. If the air doesn't strike you as too chill, we can enjoy part of our repast *en plein air* before examining the secret passages built below. It was atop the belvedere that the king staged suppers and open-air concerts—"

"Secret passages?" is Becky's excited reply.

"The *Comte* maintained that the subterranean rooms were constructed for the storage of ice, but I ask you, wouldn't a man who'd been forced to flee for his life maintain a ready escape route at any house in which he dwelt?"

▬▬

LUNCHEON, THEN. Luncheon, during which Martha's part is further diminished. Instead, Becky and Dumont take center stage. Hampers containing rugs and pillows to cover the belvedere's stone benches are unpacked—as are numerous other containers of food and drink. The footman dispenses handsome china and crystal goblets, while the former actress, her bonnet now tossed aside, gushes compliment after compliment over the galantine of veal, the oyster patties and sausage rolls, the pigeon pies and cabinet puddings—as well as upon the claret which makes her clearly bruised face glow pink. In vain, does Martha try to dampen her friend's giddy ardor or persuade Dumont to conduct himself more sensibly.

When she can tolerate no more of this unseemly flirtation, she rids herself of her plate and rises, turning her back upon the pair as if to better contemplate the view while Dumont, suddenly recalling that he has two guests instead of one, also stands.

"A handsome sight, isn't it, Miss Beale? The king chose this bluff because the Delaware shows itself to particular advantage here...Ah, and look: If I'm not mistaken, the snow is beginning to thaw. Our March sun is finally asserting itself. Aren't those green shoots appearing at the base of the wall?"

Just then a peacock screeches, the sound shrill and human, and Martha can't help but jump. The noise is like a person screaming in pain.

"Beautiful creatures," Dumont observes, "but their cries require acclimatization. I apologize if you were startled, Miss Beale."

Martha has no time to answer, because Becky has already claimed attention. "I was accustomed to hear the birds numerous times in my former situation, Mr. Dumont. The cries are a joy to me. If you had arranged to produce the sound just to make me happy, you couldn't have chosen better."

Again, Martha's presence recedes while Dumont announces that the tour will commence with a visit to the underground rooms before proceeding to the main house itself.

❦

DOWN, DOWN THEY DESCEND into a rank and low-ceilinged interior space whose wooden beams and stone vaults force them to walk in a crabbed and uncomfortable stoop. Dumont and the footman bear lanterns that fizzle in the wet, subterranean atmosphere.

"Phew...How noxious," Becky says as a foul odor attacks their nostrils.

"It's merely the result of the river overflowing its banks," Dumont tells her, but Becky isn't assuaged. She lifts her skirts to avoid a black-green puddle.

"Let us retrace our steps, for this is certainly unpleasant."

The party turns, only to discover that none of the varying tributaries in the brick-lined passageway appear to be their original point of entry.

"Are we lost, Mr. Dumont?" Trepidation causes Becky's voice to quiver.

"Inconvenienced, I would say, Mrs. Taitt. We can always raise up the household's servants to come to our aid."

"But how, when we're beneath the earth and surrounded by these stout walls?"

Dumont doesn't answer; instead, he orders the footman to move at a faster pace, hurrying the party along one corridor after another, the breadth of each expanding or contracting until the four are constrained to walk singly with their heads bowed and shoulders hunched and the women's skirts held close lest they scrape the slimy walls.

At length, the footman's lantern illuminates a double door, its massive iron hinges mossy, its several bolts pulled fast. "We must have reached the entry to the house," Dumont states while he and the footman strain to slide open the bars. The scene that greets them when the creaking wood has been pried open isn't a cellar stairway, however, but a hilltop overlooking the river. The stench the party previously encountered has become a fetid reek.

Becky coughs and runs toward the opening with her hand cupped over her mouth. When she reaches the supposed safety of the exterior, she tumbles forward, her figure disappearing as she slides down the ice-crusted hillside. Her voice trails behind her, thin with panic. "A body! A woman's body. A woman without a head."

Chapter 9

A Crimson Ribbon

THERE'S NO IMMEDIATE RETURN to Philadelphia, of course. The local constabulary must be called in (for *Point Breeze* is not only beyond jurisdiction of the city, but across the state border in New Jersey); the party of three and the coachman and footman must be queried, the *chateau's* servants interviewed, and an undertaker's cart sent for. The ladies are alternatively ensconced in the Bonaparte house, requested to retrace their steps through the labyrinth of subterranean passages, or escorted back to the hillside where the corpse remains swaddled in the same cloak of coarse fabric in which it was found. The sole difference to the grisly scene that Becky Grey Taitt first encountered and the one currently on view is the number of footprints clogging the snow: wide boots, narrow boots, heavy steps, uncertain ones; they circle the body's perimeter like the paw prints of wild animals sniffing at game.

When, at length, the undertaker's men—although not their master—arrive from Bordentown in order to retrieve the dead woman, daylight has begun to transform itself into evening, and the dripping boughs and newly exposed tufts of grass have started to refreeze, giving the sun's slanting rays additional hard surfaces upon which to glitter. For the space of twenty minutes, the confined universe that is *Point Breeze* turns copper-pink; the far-off statuary, the river's rocky beach, the bluff upon which the group has gathered, even the anxious faces of those in attendance all glow as if blessed with the divine. As the light fades, however, it robs everything it touched of life, and the scene looks more ominous than before.

The grim business continues, and the headless figure is finally shifted from the sloping terrain. Moving the body causes a crimson ribbon to tumble out from within the mantle's folds; the color, although spattered with the brown-black residue of death, gleams. Spotting this frippery, Becky's hands fly out; before anyone can prevent her, she swoops down and grabs up the thing.

"Oh, the poor woman! If this was her sole ornament, she was poor indeed." Becky gazes at the besmeared silk and all at once commences to sob until Martha comes to her aid, circling an arm around her friend's shivering shoulders while removing the ribbon and passing it to the constable in charge.

The constable and his men as well as Dumont and the undertaker's assistants stand motionless while Becky's tears roll on; and Martha can't help but yearn for Thomas's prudent presence. Whoever the dead woman was, she deserves a more meticulous investigation than these countrified guardians of the peace will accord her. If the behavior of a living—and innocent—person can confound them, what will happen when the culprit is discovered?

"My mates and I will need to make a fuller examination of the situation in the morning," the constable declares as he stuffs the ribbon into a jacket pocket. "Can't see nothin' now with the sun sinkin'. And we'll want to make a full inspection of the remaining property, too. Whoever she was, she had to come from somewhere. And it's certain she weren't done here, or we'd be seeing a good deal more blood." The tone rings with self-importance, although there's a hint of worry, too.

Dumont grimaces at the vulgarity of this speech. "Must the ladies be forced to endure further queries, sir? Not only is the evening growing chill, but they have endured a great deal of men-

tal distress." His manner is civil but just barely; disapproval of
the investigative process is written in every muscle of his jaw. He
regards the telltale ribbon, still partially visible within the constable's pocket. "I don't mind staying behind to assist you, but surely
you can release my two guests and permit them to journey back to
Philadelphia in my coach."

Whether the constable dislikes the condescending tone or
the lordly phrase "my coach," his response is a brisk: "Ladies, in
my opinion, make better witnesses than us gents. They notice
more, you see, and are apt to remember what they've spied. Why, if
it weren't for Mrs. Taitt here, that scrap of silk or what-have-you
might have been disregarded or even trampled underfoot—especially with the light getting so fluky. Not that I expect a length of
colored cloth will provide us with the lady's name, but there you
have it, sir. The distaff side, as my good wife likes to say, is smarter
than we give 'em credit for."

"But where is her...her head?" Becky manages to ask, although her voice retains the hiccoughing skip of heavy tears.

"Likely some fox or other creature carted it off, madam. If
the thing were ever hereabouts. Which we can't be certain, given
that so little of the lady's life fluid is evident. Severing all that flesh
and bone in a neck the size of a human being's is messy work. I'm
thinking we should be seeing signs of the effort instead of this neat
bundle you chanced upon. A master butcher couldn't have done a
tidier job."

The tremulous moan that greets this response does nothing
to curb the constable's graphic description. Rather, he seems to feel
he's dispensing a benevolent form of wisdom. "Don't you worry,
though, madam. We'll find the appendage. Though it might be the
worse for wear."

"Sir! I beg of you…My guests should not be subjected to these odious—" Dumont's protest is cut short as the constable orders his men to conclude their work. Then the undertaker's assistants heft the anonymous woman into the cart where her body briefly rattles the springs, although it's too light to cause a reaction from the horse. The beast turns his head only when his driver clambers back into the trap.

BY THE TIME the trio regains the house, Becky's audible sorrow has abated. In its aftermath, she's lethargic and quiet, agreeing with few if any words to whatever suggestions are made regarding the night's arrangements.

"Does *Madame* wish to view the available chambers before deciding on which would better suit her?"; "Does *Madame* care for hot water delivered upstairs in order to bathe?"; "Would a cold collation be preferable to a full dinner, and does *Madame* wish to take her meal in her chambers or downstairs?" Becky looks to Martha before replying then replicates each of her friend's answers. The ladies will retire to refresh themselves as best they can and reconvene for dinner with *Monsieur* Dumont. A servant will also be dispatched from the estate, advising those waiting in Philadelphia that the party will not return that evening. Then the woeful task of concluding the day resumes.

A SCREAM awakens Martha. It's a choking, mangled sound, and she finds herself on her feet and wrapping a shawl around her shoulders before the noise abates. It doesn't occur to her to worry for her safety as she hurries into the corridor fronting the numerous bedrooms.

There, she pauses, startled by her unfamiliar surroundings. Although her father insisted that his homes be opulent, that
paintings and statuary and other artwork abound, the two Beale
houses seem mediocre and provincial when compared to this palatial space: the portraits reaching from floor to ceiling, their regal
figures draped in ermine and satin; gold leaf decorating each piece
of furniture; gold coronets adorning every valance; even the marble
statues of semi-clothed females glow as if gilded. In the light created by a pair of vapor lamps that have been left to burn, Martha wonders if Bonaparte's estate isn't even more impressive when
shadows embellish its treasures.

She proceeds toward Becky's room, believing the sound that
awakened her may have disturbed her friend. She purposely doesn't
seek out Dumont as she's still in a quandary over his intentions
toward Becky, as well as hers toward him. Taitt may or may not
be the finest of husbands, but the unwelcome role of chaperone
weighs heavily on Martha's shoulders.

She raps upon Becky's door. When a groan is the only reply,
Martha depresses the latch and hurries inside to find her friend in
the midst of a nightmare.

"Becky. Wake up, my dear." Martha walks to the bed, push-
ing aside the heavy draperies that conceal the four posters and
frame. "Becky. Wake up. Your dreaming mind has been inventing
villains where none exist."

"Who's there?" The fright in the former actress's voice is
evident, a catch in the throat, an irresolute breath.

"It is I, Martha."

"Martha? Beale?" Confusion dulls the words. "But William…" Becky raises herself from her recumbent position. Even
in the darkened room, the bruises caused by her accidental fall are
evident. "Where am I?"

"At the Bonaparte estate, *Point Breeze*. You and I and Charles Dumont journeyed here yesterday."

"Oh, yes…yes…I remember now." This last is delivered in a moan. "The headless woman on the hillside."

"Yes." Martha pauses. "I expect you were dreaming about her."

"Dreaming?"

"I heard an odd noise. It frightened me, but I discovered you were its source. I expect the shock of chancing upon that body disconcerted you considerably."

Instead of speech, Becky sits upright, drawing her knees to her chest and wrapping her arms around them until her firm-boned figure contracts into a huddled bundle. "Who could do such a barbaric thing? What if we hadn't visited when we did? That woman would have been exposed to…to the wild beasts—" The notion is too horrible to pursue.

"The servants would have found her tomorrow, I'm sure."

"Are you? In my experience, servants like to remain as comfortable as possible when no one's overseeing their endeavors—or lack thereof. In that case, she would have been preyed upon by—"

"Becky, your lively imagination will upset us more than we already are. Let us turn our thoughts to—"

"I can't! Oh, Martha, who could have hated her so much to have not only taken her life but robbed her of her identity? A 'butcher's thorough job,' the constable said."

Martha sits on the mattress, the horsehair releasing a recognizable, brittle rasp, the feather bed lying upon it settling with a customary sigh. Nothing, save those two sounds, are familiar; the smells of the room are also foreign: a musky perfume rather than the cleansing tang of paste polish, a tapestry carpet still redolent of the Russian leather with which it must have been transported from France. "Perhaps the clothing will supply a clue," she answers although she doubts the truth of her own suggestion: a poor woman; who could possibly trace from whence her clothes had come? Or the cobbler who stitched her shoes? There was nothing notable about her attire except the colored ribbon, and that is an easily purchased commodity.

"Mr. Dumont said the king kept a mistress nearby," Becky announces in a nervous rush. "She bore him two children in secret; and the Bonaparte grandson now responsible for the estate views her and her offspring as interlopers—"

"When did he tell you that?" Martha interrupts.

"When we were picnicking. You seemed so preoccupied that I didn't draw you into the conversation."

"Ah, yes. Yes, I was." Martha recalls the scene and the steady bubble of chatter that filled her with unease.

"Do you think the woman could be she?" Becky's tone remains excitable and anxious.

"No. For one thing, she was too meanly dressed. And for another, I don't believe the grandson of a king would do anything so despicable."

"Oh, Martha, you're American to your core." A sardonic laugh accompanies the statement. "Who else has a motive for killing another person than someone whose succession is endangered?" Then the caustic mood evaporates. "To cut off a person's head! And then leave her. . .leave her for the—"

"My dear friend, don't create monsters for yourself—"

"What kind of a person would do this thing? Kill a poor woman and sever her head from her body. And why? Why?"

In reply, Martha offers a gentle: "I don't know. Now, do you think you can sleep again? Or shall we try to find you some warm milk or cambric tea?"

"Hate is a terrible thing, isn't it?"

"Yes, it is. Now, let us see about getting you—"

"How does your Mr. Kelman manage these grotesque situations?"

This time it's Martha's shoulders that slump. "I don't know."

"How can anyone be surrounded daily by the most depraved behavior and remain inured?" Without warning, Becky commences crying again, burying her face in her arms.

"Please...My dear...You'll harm yourself. We can do nothing to restore the woman to life. Nor can we discover her killer tonight. Now, let us get you something warm to soothe your spirits. Wrap yourself in your shawl. We'll make an exploration of this palace in the woods. Come. Dry your eyes. We'll aid no one by being morose."

"Taitt will be very angry that I left" is what Becky mutters in reply.

"But you said he was happy to have you go."

Becky doesn't answer, and Martha regards her with growing consternation. Questions spring to her mind, but she chooses a less judgmental approach. "I'm certain he'll be delighted to have you home and that whatever pique he may have experienced in your absence will quickly abate."

"Are you." The words are delivered as statement rather than question.

"Of course! He loves you, after all." Martha takes Becky's hand, pulling her to her feet. "Forgive my candor, but I wonder if your heightened sense of drama makes it difficult for you to value the ordinary emotions of us mere mortals. Now, let us find ourselves something warm and nourishing."

AS THEY WEND THEIR WAY down the staircase and are about to pass the library, the thudding fall of a heavy object arrests them; they press their bodies into the wall, regarding the room's closed doors with alarm.

A muffled sound of human movement follows the crash. Martha clasps Becky's fingers as they press themselves against the paneling, silently conferring whether to creep back upstairs or hurry past the chamber and seek out the servants in their distant wing. A loud noise within a shuttered room in the dead of night isn't a reassuring one under the best of circumstances, and these are not they.

Martha has learned a good deal about bravery and fortitude during her year as an autonomous person, however, and she decides she is not to be deterred. She lifts her head, sets her jaw, and proceeds down the final two steps while Becky trails behind, whispering:

"Let us seek out Mr. Dumont. We should have a gentleman with us—"

"No," Martha interrupts, although she's beginning to wonder whether she should put aside her misgivings for the moment.

"It's no time for stubbornness, Martha. It may be the murderer within."

The two women stop and stare at the shut portal, which opens unexpectedly and reveals Dumont who jerks backward in surprise. "I heard a suspicious sound emanating from this space—"

"So did we," Becky interjects, but Martha says nothing.

"My chamber lies directly above this one, and as the events of the day left me restless, I soon became aware that all was not as it should be. I found the library in disarray and was about to alert the servants when you ladies came upon me."

Becky's eyes grow wide as she looks at the door Dumont has now closed behind him. "In disarray?"

"The bookcases are singularly constructed: some of the shelving is genuine, containing true folios and other printed works; some is false and affixed with the spines of nonexistent volumes. A casual perusal wouldn't detect the difference because the Moroccan leather is kept oiled and the layer of gilded pages regularly dusted, but I was privileged to have this ingenious system explained to me. Behind the *faux* tomes are compartments where the Bonaparte valuables are stored. A number of those drawers now lie open."

Shock blanches Becky's face. "Are the valuables still in place?"

"Not that I was able to discern...Of course, the *Comte de Survilliers* could have taken the contents with him when he departed for France."

"Of course" is Becky's reply, although she sounds far from convinced. "But that doesn't explain the noises we heard, nor the fact that the room has been disturbed. Does it, Martha?"

"No." Martha's aware of how skeptical and challenging her tone is. She also recognizes that Dumont has registered the response for what it is: mistrust.

"I was on my way to apprise the servants," he repeats as he turns to Martha. "I'm heartily sorry you ladies were disturbed, Miss Beale, but I do wish you and Mrs. Taitt hadn't ventured forth. Your chambers are a far safer refuge than this hallway."

"Oh!" Becky begins while Martha takes the situation in hand.

"Let us go together then, Mr. Dumont. It would hardly do for us to separate now."

The suggestion is no sooner made than the *Comte's chef des domestiques* appears. With him are two burly men whom Martha assumes are employed in the stable and carriage house; not only do they smell of horse, but their postures have the obstinate heft of people accustomed to dealing with large, recalcitrant animals.

"*Mesdames. Monsieur.*" Like his absent master, the *majordomo* is a regal specimen. Gallic disdain at finding himself confronting ill-clad strangers in the middle of the night etches runnels down his cheeks.

"Someone has been prowling through the *Comte's* library," Dumont announces, to which the *majordomo* makes no other response but to open the door and process into the space. A paraffin lamp is burning, but whether it was lit by Dumont or the unseen trespasser else is unclear.

The *majordomo* moves from compartment to compartment, examining the bookcases; his two henchmen remain behind, arms folded across their chests, stances wide, guarding the exit as if they expected a stampede.

"*Bien,*" the chief of *Point Breeze's* servants at length concludes.

"Nothing has been removed, then?" Dumont asks.

"Nothing could have been removed, *monsieur*, for there is nothing here."

"The *Comte* took his possessions with him when he departed for France?"

"Those were not my words, *monsieur*." With that, the *majordomo* ceases speaking. Instead, he devotes his attention to the task of returning the room to its former orderliness.

"Someone did this damage," Dumont protests, "Shouldn't we be searching for the culprit?"

"I will inform the authorities in the morning, *monsieur*. I'm sure your testimony will be invaluable."

"But the person must still be in the house—"

"Perhaps, *monsieur*. Perhaps not. The sounds you—and the ladies—heard could have been produced by another source. Snow falling from the roof, perhaps—"

"It was not snow. Of that, I'm certain."

"Or who is to say that the *Comte's* unexpected guests weren't disporting themselves by exploring the place?"

"Me, do you mean? For you certainly couldn't be referring to the ladies in my company."

There's no reply to this irate query. Instead, the *majordomo* closes the final compartment and runs his hands across the false leather spines as if reassuring himself that all is well. In doing so, the right sleeve of his nightshirt (previously hidden beneath a broadcloth coat) catches one of the genuine books aligned on the shelf below, toppling the volume onto the floor. The noise produced is significant, but what occurs as a result of the accident is even more startling.

A hidden door swings backward revealing a chamber decorated—or so Martha surmises—almost exclusively with mirrors. In the midst of it is a bed embossed with the Bonaparte crest. Another mirror is affixed to the ceiling above; and the lamplight sheering in from the library multiplies itself upon the reflective surfaces.

"Oh," she can't help but gasp, although it's not the clandestine room that has transfixed her, but the bed's condition. Here is no pristine testament to an absent owner; rather, the welter of quilts and pillows reveal that someone has recently arisen, and from a tempestuous repose.

Then the *majordomo* slams the door shut, and the room disappears from view.

Chapter 10
"I'm Not Who You Think."

WHILE MARTHA retires to her *Point Breeze* guest chamber for the second time in the same night and then immediately drifts into exhausted slumber, the man she sorely misses stands sleepless on deck aboard the southerly bound *Red Cloud*. The moonlight peeking through the icicle-daubed window overlooking the Delaware River is the same that washes the merchant ship's graying wood planks, although here the clouds embellishing the night sky scud along with the brilliant luster of day while the breeze eddying around the masts is dulcet and tender, a warm wind never found in a northern clime. Thomas Kelman leans against the rail, breathing in salt air and salt mist. Below him waves rush against the hull; breaking apart, they are as white as the clouds, as pure and foamy as snow.

"Journeying to Havana is my guess," a fellow traveler tells him. He has a long, square head that looks as though it had been grown inside a rectangular box; and he goes by the name of "Joule, Egbert," which he announces in a single gush of sound as if laying claim to two disparate selves. Ostensibly an American (although his accent is hard to place), he booked passage in Charleston; where he plans to eventually disembark, he hasn't revealed. It could be Havana; it could be Key West—where the ship is now heading. It could be some other port; Joule, Egbert keeps his cards close to the vest.

"Yes." Kelman answers. He says no more, not from hostil-
ity or mistrust, but because he wishes to concentrate on the ocean
spilling around him. *What would Martha make of this vast expanse?* he
thinks, although he knows the answer. She'd be as awestruck as
he. In the entire world, there appears nothing else save one vessel
upon a body of water so supreme it seems as if every speck of land
has been engulfed. Halyards, stanchions, and spars jangle with the
ship's motion; the sole response to the noise is the repeated rush
of waves and spray flying upward like wraiths conjured from the
deep.

"Been there before, have you?" Joule, Egbert has struck up
his pipe; the smoke blows off with the wind making it difficult to
keep the tobacco lighted.

"No."

"Ah, well. I would have guessed otherwise. You have a rather
wild look about you—which I intend as a compliment. A man of
many travels. As am I."

Kelman maintains his silence but doesn't move away, and
Joule misinterprets the lack of speech for permission to continue.
"An interesting place, if your blood runs to that type of thing.
And busy, too. The port does a fair trade. More than fair. Fellows
laboring night and day, and not just the common sort, but men
like you and I. Never seen anything like it." He rattles on, puffing
intermittently at his uncooperative pipe. Kelman gazes seaward;
Martha is still very much in his mind and heart. The miles sepa-
rating them may increase by the hour, but it seems that his need for
her grows rather than diminishes. *What am I doing?* he asks himself. *I
insist it's for her own good that I quit Philadelphia, but is that true? If I examine
my deepest feelings, do I find altruism or something base? Or do I find fear?*

"Say what you will about us Americans and our commerce;
nothing compares to the Spaniards in Santiago. You bring in a

live cargo, they don't waste a minute getting it settled and watered and whatnot. No matter the time of day a vessel arrives—dawn, midnight, whatever you like—the cargo's dispatched the moment the ship heaves to. Gunpowder's the same. But then, no one wants combustible stuff like that sitting amidst a welter of other vessels, waiting for any rowdy to do mischief, do they? No, sir. As you can imagine, Santiago's a haven for those nefarious types; the *señor Alcade* and his minions have a devil of a time coping with them. Prison or no—which I can tell you isn't a choice accommodation. Not much above the *barracoons*, in fact—"

"The *barracoons?*" Kelman finally asks. Concentrating on his own self-examination, he has only heard a smattering of the man's words.

"The slave depot. Where the live cargo is kept. That's why you're traveling, isn't it? You have the look of a purchasing agent. And originally hailing from Galveston or Houston, I'm guessing. I know those are big markets out there and the profits equally—"

"The slave—?" Kelman interrupts.

Mistaking the question for one of amplification rather than surprise, Joule, Egbert continues in a tutorial vein. "*Barracoons*. It's the Spanish lingo. If you don't speak it now, you'll learn soon enough. That's where the live African cargo is confined until auction days—which it must be, of course. You can't risk having the damn creatures run away. Nor do you want them stolen— not at three-hundred dollars a head in Santiago and thrice that price on American shores. That is your trade, sir, isn't it? You are a purchasing agent, are you not? And, of course, you must speak the lingo—" The man's loquacious speech abruptly ceases. He frowns; in the moonlight, the creases in his face intensify the expression, making it pinched and crafty. He squints at Kelman who

gazes back, his black eyes mirroring the brilliant sea while revealing nothing of his thoughts.

"Is that why you're aboard *Red Cloud*, Mr. Joule? Are you also
a purchasing agent?"

A smile reveals doglike, yellow teeth. "Not me, sir. Goodness, no. Not me. And I see I was mistaken about you, too. After all, the game's illegal, isn't it? Peddling imported flesh. That's
not me, sir. Not Joule, Egbert. And I'm relieved to know it's not
your business either. Greatly relieved, I might add. One can't be
too careful about whom one chooses as comrades, can one?" He
studies Kelman further, noting the silvery scar slashing diagonally
across his left cheek. The wound makes the man look like a character no reasonable person would dare to cross. "A military man,
are you? Not that I wish to pry, mind you; a man's affairs are his
own. Or *former* military, maybe."

Kelman says nothing. The word "former" echoes through
his brain: a man who once worked at the behest of the mayor of
Philadelphia, a man who fell in love with Martha Beale, a man
whose hopes have ended.

"Me, I'm an engineer. Joule, Egbert at your service. I've been
enlisted to help manage the coalmines in Havana that the Spaniards can't seem to tame, help educate the locals on how to dig
holes without the tunnels collapsing on their sorry heads." He
wraps his hammy hands around the ship's rail as if the calloused
flesh were proof of his employment. "I may know a thing or two
about the *barracoons*, but we all do down there. You can't help what
you learn, can you? A port like that, and the trade so central to
everyone's livelihood. Not that I'm in agreement with it, mind you.
Not by a long shot. But you can't dictate what your ears take in,
can you? I'm an honest man." The unsmiling canine grin opens to
reveal more teeth, but Kelman gazes calmly back. He also places

long fingers on the wood rail, which gesture Joule construes as threatening.

"I see I'm mistaken, sir. You're obviously a gentleman. Born and bred. Those hands gave you away. You can't play the piano nor waltz at cotillions with mitts like mine." The tone grows more plumy and ingratiating. "I see my error now. You've been dispatched to assist the American consul, who I've heard is in trouble again. If that be the case, let me utter a word of caution, one voyager to another: the consul's good lady is the granddaughter of our former president, Jefferson, and both of them—"

"I'm not who you think," Kelman interrupts. He pushes away from the rail, away from his erstwhile companion, striding toward the bow and then disappearing onto the vessel's leeward side.

Joule, Egbert watches the tall man vanish from view. He detects a state of inner turmoil and wonders if the fellow's in full possession of his faculties, if perhaps he'd sought out this solitary spot with the notion of throwing himself overboard. He makes no move to follow, however. Whoever the gent is, he has the stamp of officialdom upon him; those types are better left alone.

Chapter II
"Let This Be a Warning."

DURING THE DAYS following Martha's return from *Point Breeze*, the city becomes increasingly consumed by the grisly details concerning the body discovered there. Given other circumstances, the remains of a female corpse found in rural New Jersey might not stir the interest of those dwelling within the sophisticated metropolis of Philadelphia, but the fact that every newspaper, broadsheet, and penny press trumpets the Bonaparte name, the former king's history (as well as his brother's more famous one), and the decidedly un-American sumptuousness of the residence makes the story impossible to escape. Even the staid *Philadelphia Gazette and Commercial Intelligencer* devotes fully half its front page to the tale until the flimsy pages seem to swell as though engorged on hyperbole.

Martha, Becky Grey Taitt, and Charles Dumont's presence at the exposure of such a hideous crime is equally elaborated, so much so that their inclusion in the reports becomes, if not sinister, at least dubious. *Why was the trio partaking in a bucolic jaunt during an inclement season? Why was William Taitt not present on the outing? Was his wife acting as chaperone for Martha Beale and a would-be suitor? But if that were the case, shouldn't the pair have secured the services of someone more acceptable to polite society than a former actress? And what of the* Compte de Survilliers' *avaricious nephew? Or the American-born mistress and her love children who have been so meticulously kept out of sight?* The scribes writing for the popular press tumble over one another in their attempts to cast aspersions on everyone present when the body was found, or upon those peculiarly absent. Royalty brought low is always a lucrative theme.

Naturally, it's only a matter of time before Oscar Munder is affected by the tale. Cycling throughout Quaker City Mill, the names Bonaparte and Beale become nearly synonymous, creating a whirlwind of intrigue that passes from picker house to carding room to mule spinners, boiler menders, and carpenters like yarn debris blown into an all-encompassing cloud. The excitement at having glimpsed Lemuel Beale's heir as she toured the manufactory permits even the lowliest of employees a sense of participation in the affair. Every moment of her visit is recalled; every facet of her clothing, posture, and speech is scrutinized and argued over—as are those whom she singled out with a glance or word of conversation, which, of course, includes Munder.

"Maybe it's your runaway lady the picnicking party found," one of his so-called mates announces. The tone isn't friendly, although it's hard to recognize either words or implication above the roar of machinery. "The reports say the body had a pretty red ribbon concealed upon her person."

Oscar Munder doesn't speak; instead, his fingers navigate their way around the spinning jenny. For such fleshy and muscular hands (and they are preternaturally large), they're surprisingly gentle as they coax the long fibers called "rovings" into place, moving in unconscious rhythm with the intermittent suck and pull of the apparatus.

The boy dogging his heels, recently hired as "scavenger" and "creel tender" whose job is to make certain that none of the precious fibers are wasted on the shop floor, springs forward, hurrying as though the machine were an omnibus he needed to catch. "Like this, mister?" he yells in order to make himself heard, but his new master doesn't answer him either.

Rather, it's Munder's cynical mate who does; he cuffs the lad across the back of his head then raises both hands, placing his forefingers on either side of his head in order to mimic the boy's outsized ears. Winking at the other scavengers, creel tenders, and "piecers," he encourages them to join in the joke while Oscar Munder's eyes remain fixed on the winding yarn.

"It's a wonder Fox and his minions don't give you the sack—now that you've grown all dreamy-like. Women are women. Limp rag dolls are no use to them." The statement is accompanied by a lewd gesture that causes the other adult workers as well as the young hirelings to snort and snicker, producing their own obscene gesticulations amidst the pulsing whir of steel and wood and spinning thread.

Only the newest scavenger remains stalwart in support of his master. Instead of speech, he bares his teeth, making his ears all the more conspicuous. "Fangs, too!" a bass voice shouts. "Mind you don't bite no one, Master Bat."

The taunts of the other children join the jest. "Bat. Bat. Master Bat bit a rat and ate him for his supper."

Munder, however, continues insensate, which provokes his fellow laborers to greater heights of cruelty. "I seem to remember she was fond of that type of gewgaw," the initial tormenter resumes. "When she could find someone to pay for it. Your chaste little Agnes."

At the name, Munder's head finally jerks up. "Agnes?" Confusion etches ruts in his dusty brow.

"That's right. Your vanished missus. With her fancy tastes for pretty things."

The scowl on the mule spinner's face has no sooner turned into guarded comprehension than he lunges across the narrow floor space between the machinery, grabbing his foe by the throat

and flinging him to the ground—which action immediately produces the overseer.

"You! Munder!" he shouts, gesturing to the other spinners
to haul the two men apart. "That's docked wages for you. Mr. Fox
don't tolerate fighting on the premises. Nor do I. You know that.
You should. You're one of my best."

Pinned to the wall by his erstwhile friends, Munder can
only pant out a wordless, impotent rage while the overseer regards
this formerly exemplary laborer with a combination of ire and distress.

"I'll have an apology to this here gentleman, or you won't
work again this week. Tell him you're sorry for what you done and
shake hands. We all have our problems. It's best you recall that
lesson."

Still Munder doesn't speak. His companions release him,
but he remains with his back pressed against the stone and his
arms fixed by his sides.

"Apologize, man. I'm ordering, not asking."

When no words are uttered, the overseer's frustration boils
over. "Present yourself to Mr. Fox at once. And take that boy of
yours with you—"

"He's not my—"

"He's working at your behest, so he's yours. Now, take your-
selves out of my sight before I send the both of you packing. I'll
not have subversive actions in a room under my control. You may
be a good hand, but I'll thank you to remember that you're easily
replaced. And I'll let Fox know the same."

HATS IN HAND, the pair are led into Fox's presence where man
and boy stare at the fine and burnished space: the handsome woodwork, the large secretary desk, the lamplight rather than tallows,

and the maroon and indigo carpet that stretches across a shining floor. Having no cognizance of woodland creatures, Munder decides Fox resembles a rat. A rat with its snout pointed toward a bit of garbage.

"I'll not tolerate fighting at these works," he says, to which the mule spinner nods in his quiet fashion.

"Speak, man. Your silence is as offensive as your brawling."

"Yes, sir."

"Yes, sir, what, mule spinner?"

"Yes, sir, Mr. Fox, sir."

Fox glares. "You have a wife——" he finally intones.

"I do, Mr. Fox, sir."

"Who I'm told has left your home."

Munder swallows and nods again; his eyes are fixed on the floor.

"I won't have my men brutalizing one another, nor their wives or children."

"Oh, sir, I would never do that. I love my Agnes, sir."

"Wives don't quit their husbands without reason, mule spinner. Practicality keeps women homebound unless they fear for their lives, and sometimes even then they remain. A few minutes ago and without provocation, you attacked a fellow laborer. I assume you've shown similar ill-temper to your wife——"

"No——"

"I'm not finished, Munder! Now, what you do or do not during your free time is not the purview of Quaker City Mill. More's the pity, in my estimation. However, I will not have any hand of mine acting in a scurrilous fashion. Your wife may be addled in the brain; she may be inconstant or slatternly or a drunkard; she may have any number of unfortunate attributes, but if I hear that she's returned only to escape again, then I will intercede—no matter the mill's policy. You've been a respected laborer until now, but all men are capable of change. And most of them for the worse… Let this instance serve as a warning. If you so much as jostle one of your fellows in passing, or make even the smallest and most oblique of threats, or in any other fashion act in a belligerent manner, you'll be promptly released from service, is that clear? I will not tolerate brutishness amongst those in my employ. Now go. And take your boy with you—"

"He's not my—"

"Take him, I tell you! You lose a week's wages commencing today."

"MR. MUNDER. Mr. Munder."

It's night at last, and the new boy hustles along, scampering to catch up with a master who seems intent on putting as much distance between himself and his place of employment as possible. As they pass the docks abutting Quaker City Mill, the twin shadows of man and child grow together or leap apart.

"Sir. A word, if you please."

Munder finally ceases his determined progression and turns, startled to spot this scrawny lad chasing after him. His eyes take in clothes that are either too small or too large as well as a frayed cravat that looks like something retrieved from a rubbish heap. "What is it?"

"Don't you know me?" The boy doffs his cap although the action is hesitant as though he wished his unfortunate ears weren't his only memorable feature.

"No."

"I'm your new scavenger, sir. Scavenger and creel tender rolled into one, that's me. Findal Stokes."

"Ah." The mule spinner begins to turn away. Findal, in his desperation, hops in front of him, then scuttles out of reach lest those big fists swing through the air and attempt to slap him away.

"Yes, sir. Stokes. That's me. I'm known as a bit of a finder in my own fashion. That's on account of me keeping my ears to the ground." The boy grimaces at this familiar if distressing usage then forges ahead with the initial part of his plea. "If what the other fellows is saying is true, and your missus—"

"You'll not speak of her." Menace reverberates within the words.

Findal dances backward several additional steps. "No, sir, I won't. If that's how you wish it." For good measure, he holds his hat to his chest as if making a pledge.

"How I wish it." The threatening tone has gone; in its place is a sound that's echoing and faraway like pebbles dropped in a well. "How I wish it." Munder lifts his head, gazing past the boy at the street, its snow heaps now bemired with horse and pig dung, the entrances to alleyways angling off into inhospitable darkness. Visible at the end of the lane, the masts of the harbor stretch black lines against a less black sky. When the river's tidal motion stirs the vessels, the masts quiver, producing an inky blur as well as a cacophony of sound: metal bracings, stays, halyards, and spar grommets colliding with one another. It's a bellicose noise.

"You frequent one of these taverns, do you, sir?"

"Frequent...?"

"Or perhaps you have family hereabouts?" Anxiety to please makes Findal's words bounce.

"I have no family but my wife."

At that moment, a pair of bawdy women stalk out from an unlit alley, laughing as though the world and the night were made for their exclusive entertainment. Spotting them, Munder steps back while Findal's eyes slide around to observe what seems a likely confrontation.

"I see this gent's already taken," one of the women cackles. "And by a boy no better attired than a beggar. Ah well, what some customers *fancy* is more than my brain can fathom."

Her companion guffaws then commences hiccoughing uncontrollably. It's clear both are drunk and don't mind who notices. "You wouldn't want to take silver from such as him, my dear. Your wares are for the discerning customer."

"Or a gentleman *discerning* enough to equip me with a prettier costume than I'm currently sporting."

"Ah, the *change* a few coins can produce."

Their inebriated mirth builds until their hiccoughs and hoots permeate the otherwise quiet street. Linking arms, they nearly force Munder and Findal from their path.

"Ladies. Excuse me, ladies."

"Oh, *ladies*, is it now? I expect the gent has determined that dirty little lads are not to his liking."

"Or he wants us two for two," the other drawls, and the supposed sally sets them chortling again. They weave together, nearly doubling over in their hilarity.

"Have you noticed a woman named Agnes hereabouts?" Munder persists. "A pretty woman with black hair. Long, curling black hair."

"If it's raven-colored tresses you hunger for, I could alter my locks in a moment's time—"

"No, it's Agnes I want."

"And I can become *Agnes*, too. But the revisions to my person will cost extra."

"I don't want you" is the ill-considered response. "I want my wife."

At this pronouncement, the two women straighten, their good humor gone and with it any evidence of beery revelry. "Then you'd best not truck with us." The tone is frigid but also wounded.

"No, you'd better not," her friend agrees in an equally icy vein. "If it's a loving mate you're hunting for, you won't find her among such as we."

They lock arms again, preparing to leave Munder in their wake. In the dim light, their young faces display a progression of emotion: hurt, valor, regret, vindication. "Worn out brood mares is not what we aspire to be. Or didn't you imagine we've had our share of legitimate suitors? And better dressed than you—and healthy, too."

"No, you misunderstood me" is Munder's earnest reply. "I'm searching for my wife because she wandered off—"

"*Wandered* off, is it?" one of the pair sneers. "Most likely she left you a-purpose, mister. Because you're a dull-witted clod who wastes the time of professional ladies—"

"I didn't intend to insult...I only asked if you've seen my—"

"Maybe you should reflect on your own failings and ask yourself whether this fine wife of yours had reason to run off." With that, the women parade away, although this time without a word.

IN SILENCE, MUNDER continues his journey; equally mum, Findal trudges at his side. Several times, the boy begins to speak, for he has an important question to pose, but on each occasion, his courage deserts him, leaving in its stead a grimace of self-reproach.

Munder seems as unaware of the child's unease as he does of his presence.

Thus preoccupied, the mule spinner roves the alleys and lanes of the waterfront, pausing in front of the taverns to listen to the voices within but never venturing inside. If Agnes were in one of those establishments, it's clear he wouldn't reveal himself but would lurk in the shadows until she quit the place. Intuiting the motive, Findal's chest throbs with pity as if he were transformed into a man and Munder a child.

When the beer halls and rum parlors are finally exhausted, the mule spinner turns toward home then pauses again, staring in astonishment at the boy who has stuck by him all this time. "What is it you want?"

"Nothing, sir. Just to be sociable is all."

"Sociable past midnight sounds like a lie to me, boy."

"It's Stokes, sir, Findal Stokes."

Despite the yearning tone, Munder doesn't repeat the name. "Tell me what you want or be gone." He raises a hand in a dismissive gesture. Findal skips away; it would take one inconsequential blow from that wide fist to knock him flat.

"Sir, I'll be plain. I'm new to the mill and don't yet have wages I can count my own."

"Nor will have for a month. Surely you were told that when you hired on."

"I was, sir. Yes, indeed. Not for a month the gentleman said." Findal hesitates, gazing up at Munder until a glint of recognition shimmers in the man's eyes.

"You have no place to sleep."

"No, sir, I don't."

"And you want me to set you up?"

"I intend to pay—"

"Not without wages, you won't." Munder frowns. "How do I know you're not a thief?"

"You don't, sir" is the honest answer, for, indeed, Findal once earned his livelihood as a pickpocket and cut-purse. "I swear I'll be true, though, sir. I'm only asking a space on your floor. Just a warm place to lay my body till the weather turns. And I can do chores, too. I may look small, but I'm strong. And older than I appear, for I believe I'm thirteen—"

"And agile," the mule spinner interjects.

Findal recognizes suspicion in these words. Nimble children are the preferred accomplices of felonious masters.

"I won't steal from you, sir."

Munder considers this statement. The gleam of understanding in his eyes has now dulled, and his expression returned to the opaqueness of sorrow. "No, you won't, boy. Because I'd thrash the life out of you if you did."

Findal nods, then glances again at the man's hands. "I won't give you cause to beat me, sir."

"See that you keep your promise. And you don't look thirteen years to me."

Chapter 12
We Reap What We Sow

AS FINDAL MAKES a nest on the Munders' floor and Agnes's husband sinks into his lonely cot nearby, the hallowed enclave known as Society Hill bears witness to quite a different scene. Founded as it was by Penn's Society of Free Traders, the area has long since cast off its egalitarian beginnings, and the tall brick edifices with their curving marble entry stairs and elegant fanlights now serve as home to the city's ancestral elite. Among revered names like Cadwalader and Shippen, Dallas and Biddle, reside the Taitts. It's here that a particular perfumed boudoir belonging to the lady of the house rings with rage. Against the chill night, the room blazes with light and heat, and the looking glasses and the crystal drops on the candelabra augment the sheen until even the air is tinged with gold. If young Stokes or his grudging protector were shown such a chamber they would never believe that evil could occur there. And yet, it will.

"A journey to *Point Breeze*! Whatever were you thinking?" William Taitt's *à la mode* high heels pound across the floor. Treading over the carpet, they create noise and vibration and cause the decorative furbelows filling the chamber to rattle and jounce. Aside from his suit of clothes and the familiar hereditary profile, he's a different man than he is in public. The patrician face may be as finely carved, his brow as high, his spine as straight, but the bonhomie that softens his features and figure when in company with his peers is in short supply when his sole witnesses are his spouse and servants.

As she has for the past half hour of this tirade, Becky remains seated, her eyes upon those angry shoes, her hands folded in her lap. This woman who was the toast of London is as meek as any as green kitchen maid and as silent as her husband is loud.

"And your name—*my* name—circulated far and wide amongst the most common of people! Cried out on street corners, scoffed at in oyster cellars and other insalubrious spots! This time you've gone too far. Indeed you have." A narrow smile curls the corners of his mouth as if he were tasting something either sour or cloyingly sweet, while his gaze retains the steeliest of lusters. "What am I to say to my friends and acquaintances? That my wife has taken leave of her senses? That some brain fever engendered in childbirth has rendered you incapable of reason? Certainly, your actions attest to a dangerous malady. And you do understand the fate of women thus afflicted, don't you? Look at Cornelius Dumont's wife if you want proof. Or those less fortunate wretches who are locked away in asylums for the remainder of their lives."

Becky waits, imagining herself far from this scene. For a moment, she recalls the lovely picnic Charles Dumont provided: the cold, tangy air, the handsome vistas, and his equally handsome visage. But the pretty picture devolves into horror. She shuts her eyes against the memory. Her husband views the reaction as rejecting his instructions.

"Don't feign ignorance, madam. Or close your eyes to the truth. That's always been your way, hasn't it? To provoke me in any manner you can. Surely you didn't believe I'd condone this little escapade of yours? Or feel you could shield yourself by hiding beneath the respectable cloak of Mistress Beale? And don't try to tell me Dumont is currying favor with your friend, for I won't believe it. She can, and will, attain a better partner than he."

Becky considers a reply. Indeed, she *could* invoke Martha's name because her husband, despite his slur, sets great store in wealth and heritage. But, no, she decides, that choice won't do; it feels disloyal and craven. Whether apprised of his judgments or not, Martha shouldn't be subjected to Taitt's sneers.

While she ponders, her husband's vexation increases. "Are you dull-witted, woman? I want answers, not sullen silence."

"I didn't believe you were finished speaking, William."

"And when has that stopped you from voicing whatever inconsequential thing was on your mind?"

Becky inclines her head but doesn't otherwise respond. She's glad that the house is now abed and that her husband hasn't been out imbibing with his friends, but then reflects that the harangue may last longer as a result of his sobriety.

"You have no idea the difficulties I've faced since marrying you! An actress and a foreigner, when I could have had my pick of any woman of quality I'd wished."

This argument is his customary refuge; Becky knows better than to challenge it. The rationale behind his decision to wed—ordinary lust, or a desire to thumb his nose at convention, or even a secret pride in becoming a man admired for his daring as well as the ripeness of his bride—is too complex a riddle to solve. Besides, Becky had her own reasons for accepting Taitt's proposal of marriage, and none of them involved love.

"I've tried to alter my ways," she offers at length. The tone is intended as placating, but a hint of rebellion surfaces, and this emotion her husband instantly hears.

"Oh, have you, my dear? By taking yourself off on a lunatic journey where you stumble upon a headless corpse? Is that your notion of assimilating yourself within polite society? It's a wonder you don't take a lover, as I know you were accustomed to do in your former existence. Or is Charles Dumont the lucky man? He's certainly pretty enough. And vapid, too. You'd make quite the pair—"

"Oh, William, how can you? Such a question is beneath you."

"Do you climb on your high horse, madam? Your hobby horse?"

Becky stifles the urge to march out of the room. She knows histrionics will only add fuel to her husband's wrath; nonetheless, her eyes flame in outrage. "I've never been unfaithful to you, William. And I never will be."

"Ah, but isn't that the fashion on the Continent? For women to have their little *amours?*"

"This is not the Continent, William, and I—"

"Regret that it is not."

"Those weren't my intended words" is her reply. "What I meant to say is that I'm grateful to be an American, a Philadelphian. And I'm thankful to be the mother of your son."

Taitt receives this statement as a challenge rather than as an allusion to family life, and so rounds on her again, leaning down until his face is inches from hers and the furious heat spilling from his body floods hers, as well. "Take care, Mistress Grey. Take care whom you warn about motherhood and parental custody. You know the law. My son isn't the product of some dalliance I'd like to forget; he's my heir, *my* child. *Mine.* Just as you, for good or ill, are also mine."

"Yes, I know my place." Her voice is level, but her damp fingers clench and unclench.

"And yet you persist in—"

"I was invited to join an excursion. An innocent excursion. It didn't occur to me that you would disapprove. Besides, you enjoy your own adventures and are oftentimes absent—"

"What I do is of no concern of yours."

"No? Aren't I your wife? What if Baby fell ill while you were off disporting yourself—?"

"Enough, woman!"

"I'm not a servant, William; nor am I a black-skinned slave girl waiting for your summons. I will not be dictated to in that manner."

Without warning, Taitt laughs, the sound fulsome and loud and mean. "You'll be dictated to in any fashion I wish, my dear, and under any circumstances. This is my house, and I'm its master. You would do well to remember the fact." He swoops down again, grabbing her face in claw-like hands and kissing her full on the lips. Becky tries to withdraw from this violent embrace, but he holds her fast, his tongue and teeth prying open her mouth while his fingers begin to tear at her skirts and pantalettes and stockings. "You do remember that, don't you, Mistress Grey?"

His stronger body forces hers to the floor, his hips thrusting back her hips, his knees pinning the half-torn-away skirts in place—and with them her now partially-clad body. She utters not a sound but arranges herself as best she can. She's aware of the wool of the carpet chafing her neck and bare shoulders, of her husband's long fingernails gouging her skin, of the sticky weight of him, the bones that grind into hers, and the jarring ache of hard floor below and harder body above. None of these details seem worth deliberation, however. He pants in her ear, rips away her bodice, wrenches her breasts from her corset, and crams her underskirts under her buttocks while her mind roves free.

There's a smell of tobacco leaves, a residue of the preservative in which the tapestry was rolled and stored during the summer months, and she wonders briefly about the conscientiousness of the upstairs maids. But that query is gone almost before it began, dissolving into memories of more fervid encounters in other rooms upon other carpets less clean—and a good deal less costly—than this one.

Becky sees a series of ceilings over her head: plaster cupids; smoke-blackened oak; a chandelier whose owner's jouncing motion made the thing sway and jitter until she was afraid it would come crashing down on them both. Strangest of all, she sees herself staring upward as though she weren't a woman lying on her back but a disembodied spirit hovering in the air. She has a sense of a pair of angelic hands reaching down to save her, but Taitt's final bursting groan obliterates the vision. Immediately, he rolls away, also gazing ceiling-ward while his face, as she knows from experience, blanches with self-disgust. She doesn't bother to look in his direction; in fact, her neck feels so bruised she's not certain she can twist it.

"Forgive me," he mutters at length. "I am base; I'm driven by the vilest of urges: fornication, impurity, drunkenness. I should not behave thus. It's unseemly and contemptible, and you are wrong to permit it. Very wrong to permit it." She can hear him grinding his teeth; she can hear his chest heave. Then, grasping the arm of a chaise, he pulls himself to his feet and turns away to re-button his trousers, which leaves Becky to struggle upward also and attempt to put her ruined costume in order.

"Jealousy, envy, lust: corruption of the flesh in all its venality...We reap what we sow, as the Bible warns us."

She knows better than to answer; instead, wrapping her ripped garments about her, she stands in the attitude of weary hostess hoping the last guest will depart. Tears well in her eyes; she forces them not to fall, but her sight blurs and the carpet design and colors swim together.

"You and I, madam, we reap what we sow. Cruelty, avarice, the death of the soul. If I falter, you're complicit. I bid you good night. Order a new gown if you must. That one never suited you."

Chapter 13
A Disconcerting Encounter

THE MORNING FOLLOWING, which is Sunday, finds Martha at worship services at St. Peter's Church located at Pine and Third Streets. The day is clear and bright, the sky the dense cobalt hue peculiar to winter in Pennsylvania, and the sun so strong that its rays, alighting on what remains of the snow or window glass—indeed, upon any shiny object—are painful to the eyes. Even within the concealing wings of her bonnet, Martha has been forced to squint or raise her hand to shield her sight as she traversed the city streets on her way down to Third Street. Becky Grey Taitt, who entered the tall south doors almost immediately after and then was seated in the same pew, copied these gestures just as she now clings to her friend's side.

Unusually silent (for Becky prefers gossip to hearing the Lectionary), she seems scarcely cognizant of her surroundings; and Martha's polite observation, "I trust William is not indisposed this morning. He's such a stalwart member of the Vestry that it seems odd not to see him here," is answered with a small and fleeting smile. Lesser acquaintances are accorded a brief nod as if Becky were anticipating a message from on high—or suffering a virulent toothache.

"Let me walk with you to your house, Martha," she begs after the recessional hymn concludes, and the two pass along the priest's receiving line and step into the harsh white light of the still-icy memorial garden.

"Oh, but that route is out of your way. And I know what store your husband sets on a prompt Sunday dinner." Martha pulls her fur-lined mantilla closer and smoothes her kidskin gloves. "I hope he wasn't too outraged at your deserting him five days ago. You should have told him, Becky. Gentlemen can be peculiar when it comes to their spouses exercising authority. At least, in my observation they can."

"Yes, you're correct as usual," Becky begins in a jaunty vein that then subsides to a whisper. "William does mind my name being connected to the crime."

"Mine is also. I trust he recognizes the fact."

"But you're a Beale. And I am——" Rather than conclude what she began to say, Becky turns mute. She trudges at Martha's side. Her preoccupied countenance and the grim set of her shoulders make her seem older and less handsome than she is, and it would take a careful observer to recognize the once-lauded performer lurking within the shadows cast by her bonnet. Her step, too, has none of its habitual verve, which adds to her transformation. Several gentlemen of their acquaintance tip their hats to Martha as they pass while regarding her mysterious companion with sympathy, as though she were a shy and countrified friend unaccustomed to city life.

Martha marks Becky's altered character but decides to say nothing. Taitt's behavior toward his wife is very much on her mind; however, she reminds herself that her judgment is far from impartial. Even before his marriage, she neither liked nor admired the man.

"We shouldn't have gone to that awful place, should we, Martha? Or at least without a larger party present."

"We did what we did. We cannot undo it. Besides, our presence may bring a criminal to justice. Repellant as the notion is, if you hadn't made your discovery, there's a likelihood the poor woman's body might have gone unnoticed until there was very little left of her."

"Still, I wish we hadn't gone."

"So, William has criticized you, has he?"

"He is irked, yes" is the faint reply. "His reputation is important to him."

"Perhaps he should also consider that his wife may help solve a murder, and then his good name will increase within the community."

"That's kind of you to say, Martha, but I don't believe my husband would agree."

"Well, if it hadn't been for our excursion, what does he imagine would have occurred? You said yourself that servants don't like to quit their cozy hearths during inclement weather. If Charles Dumont hadn't made his request, if we hadn't agreed, or taken our picnic where we did, or gotten lost in that labyrinth of tunnels, why the outcome would have been far different. It was good fortune that placed us there."

"I would not deem it 'good,' " Becky rejoins, "for the accident has brought me nothing but woe."

"Oh, Becky, cast off your misery. Your William will change his attitude—"

Whatever Martha intended to add is interrupted as her friend grabs her arm. "There's a man following us. A beggar, from the looks of him."

"I shouldn't wonder, dressed as we are. Let me give him something—"

"No! Don't turn in his direction. He might have wickedness in mind."

"Oh, come! On a Sunday morning? And in such a public arena? In fact, it's the ideal moment to aid a person in distress."

"Martha, no. There's something unnerving in his stance. He looks a dangerous character. Let's walk on as if we haven't noticed him until we can report the incident to a member of the day watch."

"Becky, my dear, I fear the experience at *Point Breeze* has—"

"Walk on with me. Please!"

Despite this ardent plea, Martha's curiosity gets the better of her and she turns. Noticing her gaze on him, the man stops, doffing his hat and then twisting it in his large and none-too-clean hands. Becky's correct; his posture could be termed ominous and he appears intent on approaching the two women. But he also looks vaguely familiar. Martha can't imagine why, unless it's simply that she's noticed him soliciting strangers before. A boy hovers at a distance, his own hat clamped firmly on his head and his face purposefully obscured, although the rigidity of his body betrays his concentration upon the scene.

"Miss...Beale..." The man's words are halting, the sound no more than a gurgle.

"Yes?" As she responds, Martha feels Becky's fingers tighten their grip on her arm.

"Do come away! He could be planning mischief and have treacherous accomplices. Besides, what will William say if further disasters befall me?"

"I mean no harm, miss. Indeed, I don't. And I have no companions. Good or ill."

"Isn't that urchin over there yours?" Becky demands.

"That—?" The man spins around in the direction indicated then shouts a perturbed "You, boy! Be gone. I won't have you traipsing after me like that."

The boy moves, apparently disappearing into the crowd, but Martha can still spot his wiry figure dodging here and there, trying to remain close at hand while not having his presence noticed. Again, she has a curious sense of familiarity.

"Miss Beale," the father repeats (for Martha assumes he's the child's parent). "Miss Beale, I will be plain."

"Oh, come away, Martha! You don't know what this type of person can do." There's genuine fear in Becky's voice, more so than Martha feels the situation, or her friend's normally courageous character, warrants. She pats Becky's hand, hoping to impart reassurance, but the former actress only shrinks further into herself. "How do you know my name?"

"The mill, miss...the mill...I'm Munder."

"Munder?" Martha is dimly cognizant of having heard the name before.

"Oscar Munder, mule spinner."

"Mule—?"

"The foreman made special notice of my work, miss, when you was touring Quaker City."

"Oh, yes, of course." Although she doesn't recall the event as fully as Munder obviously does, she answers as though she did.

"And you wish to ask me about employment, is that it?" Martha studies his nervous stance, the manner in which he keeps kneading his hat, and then realizes he must have followed her from the church, at least, if not from her home. The fact sends the first prickle of apprehension down her spine—which emotion she inadvertently transmits to Becky. "You've taken a good many pains to find me, Mr. Munder, but I must inform you, it's not certain I'll become your employer."

"I trailed after you from the church, miss. I heard tell that your father was a great, rich man. And he's buried there, isn't he?"

She makes no answer, although another stab of dread attacks her.

"So I reasoned I should find you there, miss, if you was the noble person you seemed."

Becky murmurs something inaudible, or else she simply whimpers while Martha considers Munder's two speeches; both seem forthright as well as disconcertingly peremptory. "I repeat that I'm in no position to help you in regards to your labors, Mr. Munder. Nor may ever be. Now, I must continue on my way—"

"Yes, you can help me, miss! You—"

"I'm not mistress of Quaker City Mill, Mr.—"

"I don't care a hang about the mill, miss! It's my Agnes I want." With these words, Munder lunges forward a step. Martha instinctively flinches back.

"I know of no one named Agnes. Now, I must ask you not to hinder my path—"

"My wife, miss, which was stolen from me."

"Oh, Martha, do come away. This man has evil in his eyes." Tall though Becky is, she cringes against her friend until Martha appears the more imposing of the two.

"Which was stolen away from me!" Munder repeats. "And now my mates are yammering on about some dead lass wearing a red neck ribbon like my Agnes's...And you was there, miss! You was there when she was found."

"Oh, my dear God," Becky gasps while Martha assesses the surprising information.

"You believe that lady was your wife?"

"I don't know, miss. In truth, I don't. But my Agnes, she went away. And she hasn't come home. And now the other mule spinners are giving me dark hints about a murdered lass found on a gentleman's estate. A king's mansion, they said, and you among the party that discovered her."

"Yes, I was there. . ."

"Martha, no good will come of this conversation. He means to implicate us, and then what will William—?"

"Yes, Mr. Munder, I was at the estate you mentioned," Martha states in a stronger tone. "But there was no identification on the woman's body. As far as I know, no determination has been made, so I think your companions—and you—are making unnecessary conclusions. Besides, the estate is a long way from here and I don't imagine you or your wife have ever traveled that far."

"But you did, miss."

"Yes, I did. In a large and well-equipped coach."

"Well, who's to say my girl didn't do the same?"

"Mr. Munder, I don't believe—"

"Mayn't I see the lass, Miss Beale? To discover if it's my Agnes?"

"That, I can't answer. You'd have to apply to the constable in charge." Even as she makes this proposal, Martha realizes how problematic it is. If the fellow leading the investigation hasn't changed his manner, he'll either dismiss Munder's plea out of hand or arrest him on suspicion of murder.

That troubling idea enters Martha and Becky's brains simultaneously, and both send worried glances down toward the mule spinner's wide and sinewy hands.

"I'm afraid I can't help you," Martha concludes in a sterner tone.

"Oh, but you must! You was there. You and another lady. And a gentleman. A lady and gentleman of quality. Like you yourself."

Although Oscar Munder hasn't identified her, Becky draws in a horrified breath. "Let us leave, Martha. Please...William won't tolerate—"

"Would the likes of them come to my aid, do you think, miss? If you won't?" Munder insists with increasing agitation. "If it's my dear Agnes dead, I must know."

At this point, Becky frees herself from her friend's side, stepping resolutely out of range as if she means to put as much distance between herself and this odious conversation as she can. Martha, however, stands her ground, and her expression turns from empathy to impatience.

"Mr. Munder, I'm an ordinary citizen like you, and a citizen of Pennsylvania, not of New Jersey where the crime was discovered. There's nothing I can do to help you find your wife. I'm sorry, but that's the fact of the matter. Now, be on your way, and do not follow me further. The day and night watches could deem your actions to have unlawful intent."

But the mule spinner is not to be dissuaded, and the intemperance he displayed at the mill again emerges. He flings down his hat and clenches his fists to his breast, beating the bone as if he wished to attack someone else. "I'll find them other two folk what was with you. Their names must be in the gazettes. Yes! I remember now. They told me one was an actress—"

"Be warned, Mr. Munder" is Martha's steely reply, "or I'll inform the constabulary of your intentions. Come along, Becky. You were correct. This fellow is a menace."

"Becky! Yes! That was it. Becky something," Munder shouts at which the former actress undergoes another metamorphosis.

Instead of dragging Martha from the scene, she reenters the fray although terror rather than bravado are etched upon her features.

"You could interpose with that constable at *Point Breeze*," she mutters while turning her back to Munder and averting her face. "With your name and reputation, he couldn't very well refuse you."

Martha stares at her friend. "You just insisted we hurry away from this person. Not champion his cause."

"I've changed my mind" is the *sotto voce* answer.

"But the man may be mentally unbalanced. In fact, it seems more than probable. We can't risk—"

"I thought you wanted to aid the downtrodden. Now is your opportunity."

"Oh, Becky. If William could hear you—" Those simple words, spoken in the most reasonable of tones have a terrible effect. Becky's face contorts then begins to quiver in helpless spasms.

"William must never learn about our encounter with this person! Promise me you won't mention today's conversation."

"But—"

"Promise me, Martha!"

Martha draws back, studying her friend. "Ahhh...I see..." is all she says before releasing a worried breath. "Oh, Becky, Becky... We must find help for you. If you're being ill-treated—"

"There's no help for me. None. Taitt is who he is. I am his wife. Now, what can be done to convey this Munder to Borden-town before he works his mischief in my home?"

"There's help for everything" is the gentle response.

"No, Martha."

Throughout the exchange, Munder has remained silent and watchful; a kind of craftiness has settled in his eyes, making him look guileful rather than innocent. When Martha again regards him, she recognizes the change; like his big hands and ready rage, it frightens her.

"I can arrange to have you escorted to the place in question," she states, "and send word to the constable in charge that you wish to view the dead woman's body. But if you behave as you just did, if you act in a threatening manner or raise your voice, or drag the names of innocent persons through the mud, I won't be held accountable for the judgment of the authorities, nor I will extend any further assistance. Do you understand?"

"Yes, miss." So quickly has his subservient behavior returned that Martha's not certain she witnessed another aspect of the man.

"Good," she says while Becky repairs to a safer distance. "And what about your son? You don't intend to take him with you, do you?"

"I don't know who you mean" is the gruff answer. "Agnes and I, we have no little ones."

"The boy accompanying you," Martha reiterates.

"I don't have a boy."

Chapter 14
Evidence in the Case

THE PLAN TO AID Oscar Munder as well as to identify the remains of the woman found at *Point Breeze* miscarries, however. The mule spinner is no sooner delivered to the undertaker's establishment in Bordentown, where the deceased's body has been stored in a bier shed used for those awaiting burial, than his emotional state betrays him.

Presented with the headless corpse, he wails when he recognizes the mantle and dress in which the body is wrapped, then collapses in a faint from which he's aroused after administrations of water and vinegar are splashed over his mouth and nose. The customary sal-volatile, or concoction of warm brandy and water are rejected as being a needless expense for a common laborer.

Revived, he's dragged to his feet.

Instead of regaining his composure, however, his grief increases, and he buries his head in the corpse's clothing, sobbing his wife's name repeatedly. When the undertaker's assistants and the constable in charge of the investigation try to wrench the dress from his hands, he leaps upon all three, felling them with manic ferocity. Alerted to the battle, a sergeant and another watchman rush into the shed and wrestle Munder onto the sawdust-strewn floor. Manacled, hand and feet, he bellows that he must view his "dear wife's face" and accuses everyone present of "brutalizing her lifeless body."

Arrested for "the murder of the Philadelphia mill hand, Agnes Munder," he finally recognizes his predicament and screams out that it's not his "wife lying on the table, but another lass."

Naturally, no one believes the contradictory statement.

Munder is remanded into custody. Being a quarter mile distant, the local jail is chosen, although the constable expresses his misgivings. No one in the small New Jersey community wants to have a murderer on their hands; besides, both victim and spouse were and are residents of Philadelphia.

All these details are contained in a report sent to Martha by special courier. Much rhetoric is expended in order to impress her. The constable describes Munder as "a brute with hands large enough to twist a woman's neck in twain," as "suffering from treacherous delusions of the brain," and "a beast not fit to walk abroad." Concluding that he's "confident the fiend will hang," he adds excessive gratitude for Martha's "activities on behalf of all law-abiding citizens of this great state of ours, of the Commonwealth of Pennsylvania, and of the nation."

Reading this last paragraph, Martha feels at once cold, then feverishly hot. *What have I done?* she rails inwardly. *I shouldn't have interfered. Oh, why isn't Thomas here to set this disaster aright? He would know what to do. What made me think I could enter the business of justice? I have no training in investigative practices, nor ever will.* Her face flushed and taut, she begins to stalk her chambers (she'd just risen for the day when the missive was delivered), her taffeta dressing gown crackling like desiccated leaves.

What if Munder is innocent, as he claims? Or what if the dead woman isn't his wife? Could he have mistaken the costume? Could his sorrow have convinced him that the deceased was his missing spouse and led him to confuse one ordinary dress and mantle with another?

The queries lead to others; she ponders the distance between *Point Breeze* and the city and the cost of transporting either a dead—or living—person. Surely if Oscar Munder wanted to dispense with his mate, there are closer and easier places. But then she recalls the man's propensity for violence and her recognition of his conniving nature. "How I wish Thomas were here to sort out this dilemma," she groans. Her hands ball themselves into fists; her jaw clenches until her flesh looks as though it might shatter.

At last, she remembers Munder's boy. "Now the child has lost both parents. What's to become of him? Oh, what have I done!"

At that moment she finds herself glaring down at the street; and a plan of action appears in her brain as though she saw it sketched upon the cobbles.

THE FIRST PART of this scheme meets little success, however. Locating Munder's dwelling and persuading the building's superintendent to unlock the mule spinner's door, Martha discovers no son, nor any vestige of a youthful presence.

When she expresses her surprise, she's informed that the couple was childless, and her reiteration that she saw the husband in the company of a boy is met with a blank and disinterested gaze. "Could be one of them mill urchins, I suppose," he finally allows before adding a censorious "Often times, they lurk 'round their masters, hoping for a handout. Best beware of their likes, miss. They're little felons, most of 'em, and ain't got the scruples of a swarm of bees."

If there's no trace of the mystery boy in Munder's room, there's ample evidence of his wife. The adornments she used to decorate the room are poignant in their meagerness: a row of colored paper cut in starry shapes and glued to the wall, a feather in a broken crockery cup set upon the window sill; around it, pieces of this and that are arranged in a spiral: river pebbles of varying colors, a shard of something shiny that looks like a scrap from a gilded picture frame, dried flowers turning to dust. On a nail, there's a dress of summery stuff as well as a straw hat—all that remains of Agnes's wardrobe. Martha has never come into intimate contact with poverty like this, and it creates a hole in her stomach that fills with sorrow and rage.

She gazes about, trying to see the scene as Thomas might if he were researching the crime, but the weight of Agnes's ghostly presence prevents her from rational observation. All she can think is *If this man murdered and then decapitated his wife, how can he live with her possessions still in evidence? Wouldn't her tortured spirit haunt him night and day?*

The ruminations are interrupted by a noise mounting from the street. The Penny Press has grabbed hold of the news, and the boys hawking the papers are shouting out the story: "Mule Spinner Murders Wife and Saws off Her Head!"

Fleeing, Martha makes her retreat down the several flights of stairs, where the voice of the building's overseer momentarily arrests her. "I had him as a tenant," he's declaring to the gawkers now gathering at the site. "He seemed quiet enough, but you never know, do you? And the wife? Well, she led him a dance. Many's the time I warned him she was up to no good. I knew it, you see, even if that Munder fellow didn't. I knew it all along."

It's then that Martha leaves for her next visit.

"I'M NOT CERTAIN I can help you, Miss Beale." This is the eminent Dr. Emil Rosenau speaking. He rises from behind a pristine desk as she's escorted down a double flight of stairs into his subterranean receiving room and gallery. Although the materials used to construct the room's display cases and bookstands are of polished walnut, the floor well carpeted, and the paraffin lamps neatly arranged, the effect is lugubrious. But then, so many skeletal remains would make even a silk-lined boudoir look grim.

Martha can't help but stare. Row after row of bleached and hollow-eyed crania gaze sightlessly back from the shelves while the full-sized or child-sized spines and legs and arms and hands and feet that once supported warm, human flesh appear to hover within their glass-sided cabinets as if waiting for life to be breathed into them once more.

"I'm not knowledgeable about murder, Miss Beale," Rosenau continues as if his surroundings were the most ordinary of places—which to him they are. "Unless you consider that a number of these specimens came from the gallows. Not the children, naturally...It may seem an unusual practice to acquire the corpses of the newly executed, but it's how we scientists often obtain the cadavers we require for our anatomical work."

He pauses in thought and presses the tips of his fingers together. He's excruciatingly thin, as if made of no fleshier stuff than the articulated skeletons surrounding him, and his voice scarcely carries in the quiet space. Martha must keep still and not permit her clothing to rustle if she is to hear him. "But with the furor in England over the despicable duo who killed in order to supply the surgical colleges—as well as rumors of body-snatching and 'resurrection men' and so forth—well, let us say that public scrutiny can be a deterrent for such repellant activities...However, let us also admit that chronicling the human figure and the diseases that attack it takes genuine flesh and bone, and further conclude that persons sentenced to hang are generally in the prime of life. For obvious reasons, the dissection of a youthful specimen is superior to an elderly one."

"Some of these remains belong to former murderers?" Martha manages to ask, at which point Rosenau turns aside to regard his eerie collection. There's a sense of sadness in his posture, as if his visitor had criticized a beloved dog.

"What you see displayed improves the physician's skills, Miss Beale. I posit that the criminals here have made a unique contribution to society. Unwittingly, perhaps, but that doesn't make their gifts less useful. Look at these vertebrae, for instance—" Which Martha does, although with reluctance as the example is terribly misshapen, and it makes her stomach churn in revulsion. "You'll note the gross deformity of the spine, how it twists upon itself as though weighted. In life, this man—yes, he was a notorious murderer—would have been an ugly creature both physically and mentally. He suffered from a bone disease we call '*Struma*;' I won't take your time in describing its characteristics. Someday, it's hoped that such diseases may be curable, perhaps even preventable."

"And the. . .and the crania? Did they also belong to murderers?"

"A few. Although the specimens here were assembled by a specialist who used them to measure cranial capacity, and thereby further his theory of racial attributes. I purchased the collection for my phrenological work."

Rosenau picks up a nearby skull, cradling it in his palm as though it were a melon he was considering purchasing. "This woman suffered from *Mania Furiosa*, which was caused by an injury to the frontal lobe. I shan't detail her crime, other than to say that it was vile." He sets down the skull and takes up another. "This example shows disease of the parietal lobe, resulting in *Melancholia*, which in this man's instance manifested itself in dangerous perversions and delusions. . .Have you read Samuel Morton's *Crania Americana*, Miss Beale?"

Martha shakes her head, her eyes fixed upon the vacant holes gaping back from the physician's hand. *Dangerous perversions,* she thinks and shudders.

"No...Naturally, you wouldn't have. The work isn't intended for the lay person...One of its theses is the questionable practice of molding the heads of newly born infants in order to inhibit evil instincts...But I digress. Your note indicated you wished to discuss the cadaver discovered at the Bonaparte estate."

"Yes." she tells him as he returns the skull to its shelf. In the light reflected by the glass cabinetry, Rosenau's skin looks as white as bone.

"A case of decapitation, I gather." With seeming reluctance, the physician turns his back on his collection and focuses on his guest. "So, alas, no use for the phrenologist's skills," he adds with the wryest of smiles.

"No," Martha begins to answer, then changes her mind. "Unless you'd be willing to examine the husband who's been arrested for the crime."

Rosenau thinks. "Let me consider the possibility. I regret to say I'm more comfortable with the deceased than the living. A dead man doesn't challenge a prognosis that his 'propensities' run to acquisitiveness, combativeness, and destructiveness. Nor does he insist he's not a pickpocket and thief as a result."

"You can tell all that by simply looking at a person's face?"

"It's more complicated than that, Miss Beale. But I assure you 'cranioscopy,' as the science is deemed, is no clever parlor trick...So what is it you wish from me as regards this case?"

This time it's Martha who pauses. "Oscar Munder has denied the crime—"

"But has been imprisoned as the sole suspect."

"Yes." She hesitates again. "But I'm beginning to wonder whether some deeper mystery is involved." Then she recounts the details of the constable's report, her abbreviated examination of Munder's dwelling, and concludes with the picnic at *Point Breeze*.

Rosenau listens. Unlike Thomas Kelman whose concentration requires the full use of his body as well as of his brain, the physician doesn't move; he almost appears not to breathe. "Is it possible, Miss Beale," he asks at length, "that you've been duped by this fellow? You view the wife's clothing and so forth and experience empathy—and therefore the onset of a dilemma. You can't imagine a husband living with those obvious reminders of his crime. Or going to such pains to rid himself of her. However, the skeletal remains of the people who surround you had no such scruples. The torturer who started experimenting with cats and dogs, of necessity graduated to human life. It's possible Munder took pleasure from viewing his wife's effects and knowing justice had been served. Especially, if she was as wayward as you inferred. As to why *Point Breeze*, the man could simply have a loathing for royalty."

"For a man devoted to science, sir. You seem surprisingly familiar with the vagaries of the soul."

Rosenau doesn't speak for a moment. "The 'vagaries of the soul' as you put it, Miss Beale, may not be a systematic study, but it's what impelled these people during their lifetimes. I'd have to be dull-witted indeed not to feel their presence or wonder at the thoughts that led them to commit the crimes they did. So, I repeat, it's possible this Munder may be a very wicked man."

"It's also possible the dead woman isn't his wife."

"Yes."

"Will you examine her, sir? In order to determine whether or not the corpse belongs to Agnes Munder?"

"I can examine the body, certainly, Miss Beale. I can also dissect it, although commencing that process produces great disturbance to the remains. But I have no identifying clues to hunt for.

"She was a mill hand. Her age and height and outward appearance are known—"

"Which only supplies me with the facts that her hands were probably outsized, the skin calloused, and that her spine may have been bowed from unhealthy working conditions—too little to differentiate her from countless other women. If her corpse were intact, perhaps...Well, no matter. It's not."

"The constable has hopes of recovering the severed head in the neighboring woods," Martha interjects.

"Which seems unlikely given the passage of time since your party was there." Rosenau moves away from his visitor and walks the length of his room. His footsteps make no noise, nor does his clothing chafe or creak. He might as well be gliding across the space. "Before I agree to your request, I'd like to meet with the husband. My reasons are several: If I determine that his physiognomy and behavior are those of an innocent man and that his claims regarding the deceased can be verified, then we will have discovered who the mystery woman is *not*. On the other hand, if my phrenological work reveals propensities associated with destructiveness and so forth, then Munder can be viewed as a *potential* murderer, and I will accordingly endeavor to learn his wife's physical attributes as clues when examining the body. A criminal is often more talkative than is wise. 'Love of approbation' is the term in scientific parlance. Either way, my efforts should bring clarity to the case."

"Thank you, Dr. Rosenau," Martha answers. "I'll arrange to have Munder transferred to the Moyamensing Prison in Philadelphia."

"Shouldn't this be official business rather than one of a private nature, Miss Beale?"

"Oh, it will be, sir. A word from Lemuel Beale's daughter has the benefit of bringing swift results—both in public and individual enterprises.

Chapter 15

Unanswered Questions

ON THE MORNING FOLLOWING Martha's meeting with Emil Rosenau, a card announcing a gentleman visitor is delivered to her second-floor sitting room. As this occurs immediately after she dispatched a letter recommending that Oscar Munder be transferred to the Moyamensing Prison in Philadelphia, but before she can depart for the Beale Brokerage concerns, she receives the news that Charles Dumont is downstairs and requesting to see her with an expression of impatience. She hasn't been contacted by either brother since the ill-fated excursion to *Point Breeze* and can't help but feel that those events have irrevocably damaged a friendly acquaintanceship. As to Dumont's behavior toward Becky Grey, and hers toward him, no more need be said.

As if discerning her altered opinion of him, his attitude as he's escorted upstairs and shown into the room is all apology and consternation. He takes the chair she indicates with obvious reluctance, and even then he perches on the edge as if he'd far rather stand. "I blame myself, Miss Beale," he repeats several times. "If I hadn't insisted on that journey…" The words trail away; his hostess replies with a brisk:

"It's better that the body was located in a timely fashion, Mr. Dumont. Horrific as the situation was, no one would have wished the poor woman to remain there any longer."

"No…No, of course not." He sighs; Martha can't help but notice how greatly his appearance has changed. Instead of carefree youth, he now resembles his downcast brother. His lower eyelids drag as though freighted with heavy thoughts; his skin has turned yellowish; and his expression of habitual amity has grown wary. He adds a dismal "At least Cornelius and Thea weren't present. God knows how my unfortunate sister-in-law would have reacted. Not well, of that I'm certain."

At this admission, Martha's heart softens. From her place on the settee, she turns to face him rather than maintain a frosty profile. "How do they fare, your brother and his wife?"

"Not well. Miss Beale, not well. I've begun to realize the situation will never improve. Never. My good and compassionate twin is wed to a woman whose psyche is too fragile for this world. She's a melancholic and will always be so."

"And has your brother sought additional help for her condition?" Martha asks as discreetly as she can.

"Do you mean from the physician at the asylum or some other private practitioner?" Dumont's eyes cloud. "Yes. Yes, he has. As he's done on numerous previous occasions. But Cornelius also informed me that he refuses to deliver her into anyone else's keeping again. Like me, he understands that his dear Althea is doomed by dementia. Or perhaps he's always known it; and I've been the fool clinging to useless hopes and impossible visions. Like a sojourn to a pretty estate on the river. What folly that was! And Mrs. Taitt! What misery she must be experiencing on account of her discovery."

"You're not at fault for what occurred, Mr. Dumont. Nor for your brother's marriage or his wife's mental state." Martha clasps her hands in her lap as the remaining embers in the fireplace grate fall to the hearth's stone floor. Realizing she must soon depart, she's loath to call in a servant to rekindle the flame. Besides, the cooling air proves a momentary distraction. "Before we journeyed to *Point Breeze*, you mentioned that it might be beneficial if I were to visit Althea. Know that I stand ready to do so. If it would aid her to see a new face or engage in a solely female conversation—"

"I'm afraid that's no longer possible," Dumont states. "Thea has become a danger not only to herself but to others. Even her maid has fled. Oh, Miss Beale, the world can be a sorry place." For a moment, Martha's afraid his emotions will overcome him, but he rallies, straightening his shoulders and gazing into her face. "I didn't come here to discuss private woes, however, but to sincerely and abjectly apologize for involving you in the hideous affair at *Point Breeze*. I'm aware that the journalists can't get enough of the story and that your name—as well as Mrs. Taitt's—unfailingly appears in each and every report."

"Happenstance doesn't always affect us for the good, Mr. Dumont. As your name is also needlessly bandied about, this affair can't be easier for you than for me—or Becky."

"No…All the same, I blame myself. We men are tougher than you ladies. I also fear I may have acquired an enemy in William Taitt. Luring his wife into an unsavory terrain—"

"There's nothing you can do to alter his opinion of the excursion or anyone else's. What's done is done. My friend, as you know, went willingly. And on my suggestion. So I'm the one who should be censured, not you." It's on the tip of Martha's tongue to tell Dumont about her visit to Emil Rosenau. Why she doesn't, she's not certain, but she keeps the information private.

"A fascinating place, *Point Breeze*," she continues, trying to lighten the conversation. "A clandestine chamber hidden behind a bookcase, there's more mystique and romance within those walls than we Americans are accustomed to. At least, this American. Were the servants able to discover who had left the library in such disarray?"

"If they did, I'm not aware of it" is all Dumont answers, then adds a doleful "I was more concerned with what had transpired earlier in the day."

Martha thinks back. Dumont's retelling of the event is not the scene she remembers. "Of course…Although I seem to recollect that you were certain that whoever had done the damage was still in the house."

"Yes," he answers after another gloomy pause. "Yes, I was worried on account of you ladies. My nerves were more jittery than they should have been. The *majordomo* didn't share my fears, as I recall."

"No…" Martha watches the man. A mixture of doubt and uncertainty prickles her mind, but it's too amorphous a sentiment to decipher. "Were there truly valuables stored in the room?"

Dumont looks at her; again, his shoulders pull back as if accepting the cloak of responsibility, and his personality undergoes another transformation. No longer the pleasure-loving scion of a wealthy family or a worried brother, he appears a man of affairs— and a full ten years older than before. "I believe I mentioned the Dumonts' historical connection to the Bonapartes. In fact, the relationship is more than casual. I'm currently engaged in assisting with legal matters concerning the *Comte's* grandson and a lady purported to be the great man's mistress."

"Ah, yes…the *Comte's* elusive lady. My friend Becky shared that information with me. Do you know she even suspected that the *purported* mistress might have been the murder victim?"

"But the dead woman has been identified as Agnes Munder. And her husband has confessed to the crime and is now in custody—thanks to your efforts, from what I've read. Mill hands, the both of them; and from your Quaker City."

"It's not my mill, Mr. Dumont" is Martha's quick retort to which she adds a gentler "I refer to Mrs. Taitt's and my private conversations during that difficult night we spent at *Point Breeze*. However, I assume that in your capacity as legal advisor to the *Comte's* grandson, you must know whether or not the mistress is alive and well?"

Dumont's response is to rise without answering the question. "I've wasted too much of your time lamenting the misadventure I forced upon you and your friend. Let me take my leave and ask you again to forgive me for the troubles I've caused."

"You didn't answer me, sir. The woman does live, doesn't she?"

"I've had written communication from her."

"Recently?"

"Miss Beale, the *Comte's* grandson is an honorable man as well as a friend of mine. Whatever his relations with the lady in question, he would never do anything untoward—or illegal." The statements made, Dumont still appears to wrestle with his thoughts. Standing, he looks as though he couldn't decide whether to go or stay. "Oh, Miss Beale, I'm afraid I've done a very foolish thing. It was your regard and favor I sought when I invited you to *Point Breeze*. My brother and his needs were secondary to my base motives. In fact, I lied. And now, I fear...no, now I'm certain that I've lost you."

"*Lost* me, sir? What do you mean?"

"You imagined I was directing my full attentions on your friend, but it was *you* I was attempting to impress. Now I recognize that I've abused Mrs. Taitt as well as yourself. What an idiot I've been. Cornelius is correct; I have no sense. None."

Astonishment floods Martha's face. She doesn't speak.

"I see I disgust you, Miss Beale. How I wish that were not so. But, alas, you're quite justified in reproaching me—"

"You misinterpret my reaction, Mr. Dumont—"

"You're kind, Miss Beale. You seek to absolve me from my numerous blunders, but I perceive the truth. Indeed, I deserve your condemnation. And I deserve the Taitts', too. Mrs. Taitt's, especially, for feigning an interest I didn't have. I hope you'll tell her how repentant I am—"

"Oh, sir," Martha begins. She hardly knows where her thoughts are leading, but her guest seems unaware that she has spoken.

"What miserable times these are! Just yesterday, I was apprised that a business venture of mine had failed. This morning, I come here to bare my soul and beseech you to consider me as a suitor and again fail—"

"Oh, sir—"

He's too full of self-loathing to hear anyone but himself. "'Ships sink,' Cornelius said, 'or pirates attack them and make off with the cargo. If you have goods to sell, place them locally,' that's what he told me, and yet I wouldn't listen—"

"Neither my father nor I ascribe to that notion, Mr. Dumont. The countries in South America are—"

"*Red Cloud!* What a hideous name! Why didn't I ask myself if there was an evil omen in it? That's the sailor's fabled warning, isn't it?"

Martha feels as though all the air had left her body. She parts her lips; her throat is parched. "I know a ship of that name—"

"Well, you know it no longer because I've been informed by a source I believe reliable that she disappeared. A storm off the Florida coast or some such misery...Oh, what does it matter what befell the vessel? Although if you also had a shipment aboard her,

then I'm heartily sorry to be the bearer of bad tidings." If Dumont
took time to notice Martha rather than bewail his fate, he'd recognize how pale she's become. "I take my leave of you, Miss Beale.
Some day, I hope to regain your goodwill, but I know it can't be
now."

Left alone, Martha doesn't stir in her chair or walk to a
window or rekindle the fire. If she draws breath or blinks her eyes
or moves her fingers or toes she's unaware of it.

The room grows cold; the day progresses; she hears her
adoptive children return from school for their midday meal; she
hears knocks on her door, youthful voices calling her name. Then
the same voices shushed by the new governess who quietly escorts
Ella and Cai from the hallway. In other parts of the house other
shoes tread other floorboards, but they also turn stealthy with curiosity and consternation.

Outside, the life of the street rolls by, but the noise becomes
a meaningless hum within the louder clang that rattles her brain.

It must be another ship, she tells herself over and over. *Another vessel
entirely. It's a common enough name, after all. Or Dumont could have misheard
it.* Red *something. . .or something* Cloud. . .*Yes, that must be the case. Dumont is
wrong. Or his supposedly reliable source is wrong. Didn't he confess how often he's
in error? Wasn't that the purpose of his visit? To atone for his mistakes?*

The arguments repeat themselves, circling around and
around and around, but they bring neither solace nor relief. *If
Thomas were drowned, wouldn't I know it? No matter how far away, wouldn't
I feel him dying? Wouldn't I?*

Chapter 16

Fingers Trained for Skilled and Nimble Work

DURING THE TWO DAYS that Oscar Munder has been confined to the prison in New Jersey, ill usage and anguish have taken their toll. A person who grows less human by the moment has replaced the mild-mannered man Agnes married and the conscientious mule spinner who was once the pride of his overseer.

Nor does Munder care. There's no pretty, little Agnes to fret when he coughs up welts of black-red phlegm; no Agnes to remind him to clean his beard or brush his hair; no sweet wife to gently chide him for the grime and filth that now cling to his clothes and hands and face; no one to reflect his better nature, or soothe the sobs that wrack his body, or answer the bellows that he aims at his jailers, or at the curious townsfolk clustered outside the small prison, or even at the carrion birds whose nests straddle the trees surrounding the place. Their caws, meant only for each other and having as little concern over the man chained to the stone wall as for a cake of soap, make him shiver with rage. In his ears, their cries to one another sound like human voices. Like mocking and deriding comments, like laughter, like jeers. Like all the futile endeavors of his twenty-three years.

"No!" he roars and shakes the bars until the wooden trestle that serves as both table and bed jolts on the dirt floor. "No!" But the word becomes no word, only a spilling out of sound that devolves into a choked weeping which the spinners' phthisis that's destroying his lungs finally turns into violent and spasmodic gasps for breath and air.

"You in there, shut your trap," he hears yelled by one of his keepers. Outside and venturing as close as they dare, neighborhood boys take up the chant while the crows rise in alarm and scream their noisy contempt.

It's in this defeated and semi-human state that Oscar Munder is bound, hands and feet, and thrust into a roomy cage for transfer to the Moyamensing Prison in order to be first examined by none other than Dr. Emil Rosenau—and then to stand trial for murder. The cage was formerly used for the transportation of a valuable and ill-tempered breed bull; the wagon is the same wagon that carried the precious animal and the driver—proud of reminding everyone of his prior service and the stoutness of the moveable prison's construction. "You could carry a pair of them mountain panthers in this," he boasts, "and come away with nary a nick. Unless you were fool enough to lean too close—which I advise against at present, seeing as how this fellow sawed off his wife's noggin."

The boys who watch as Munder is shoved inside shriek with terror and glee at the driver's warning and at the fearsome sight of the villainous mill hand.

SO BEGINS THE JOURNEY back into the city. The sky is overcast, the air cold; spring seems more distant than the sleety rains of November. Munder huddles within a space engineered for a creature ten times his weight and shivers, holding his arms to his side as best he can; although the manacles prevent him from wrapping them across his body, and so providing a little warmth.

Beneath his matted hair, he gazes at the same road Martha saw: the farms, the smoke rising finger-thin and ineffectual against the frigid sky. Where the snow remains, and there is still a good deal of it filling pastureland and woods alike, it has taken on a stamp of dirt and age; where the earth is uncovered, it looks gray and dead, its grasses broken.

The miles plod past, the driver jesting continuously to the keeper who's accompanying him on this jaunt into the metropolis. Their crude banter brushes past Munder's ears, as do the ever-ratcheting descriptions of the nefarious escapades the two intend to indulge in once they're "rid of the cargo." In a show of either humor or scorn, they toss the horse's blanket across the cage's roof, thereby screening themselves from their prisoner's dull gaze. The covering does nothing to diminish the loudness of their exchange; instead, the words "hang" and "gallows" and "gibbet" seems to increase in volume when trapped beneath the sweat-heavy felt.

What does Oscar Munder think of while the wagon jounces along? Does he ponder the lives and fates of the farmers whose stone buildings dot the solitary route? Does he consider the deer that shy through the woods or the cattle hunched over the unyielding ground? Does his mind play out scenes from his past and envision his Agnes alive and laughing?

"A red ribbon," he mutters through chattering teeth, which phrase the keeper unexpectedly hears above the more boisterous conversation.

"The fellow's in possession of human speech, after all," he sings out and then bangs upon the cage's top with his cudgel, shaking down oat chaff and pulverized hay upon Munder's head.

"Tell us how you done it, before you spill the beans to the judge," the driver joins in. "How you cut the lass's head off. And where you stashed the bloody appendage." He laughs, whips up the horse, and adds an oath for good measure.

"You'd be doing yourself a service," the other interjects. "Especially if the lady wasn't the darling maid you claimed her to be. Might be your sorry lot would garner a bit of pity among the members of the jury. There's not a fellow in the city who's unacquainted with women of easy virtue."

Munder glowers at the disembodied voices, then the scowl turns inward, and he begins to recollect the true nature of the history he and his wife shared: her deceptions both little and large, the new garments she tried to hide, the unaccustomed smells on her body, the breath that had consumed unfamiliar foods—and drink.

Examining these pictures, the mule spinner's heart sickens. "But I wouldn't have killed her because of what she did to me," he promises himself. "Not for all the world."

"But you did, didn't you?" the driver exclaims as he slaps the reins and takes up the whip again. "Ah, well, many's the time I would have liked to throttle my missus, too. Though she's not the piece of baggage you was saddled with. I don't know how a man can live with a trollop like that. I guess the answer is: you can't."

"You're right about that," the keeper guffaws. "Wed one of them wenches, and your trousers won't know a minute's peace."

"Oh, they'll know peace all right, my friend. But it'd be better if the *member* of the reconnoitering party could stand up and salute once in a while. A cease fire is a painful time."

"Especially if you've got plenty of shot to discharge."

During this lewd exchange, Munder's face contorts with rage and his hands ball themselves into fists. He raises them to his face, but whether to tear at the skin with his teeth or bash his face against the iron fetters, he doesn't know.

Instead, the fists hang in the air. The laughter above his head rollicks into a bawdy ditty while Munder regards the manacles, uncoiling his fingers as though suddenly remembering they were there. "I didn't kill my Agnes," he says in the barest of whispers. "But I will murder the man who did. And whichever fine lady's protecting him."

Then he turns his back to his unseen escorts and touches the door to his cage. Unlike the breed bull previously incarcerated there, he has hands—and fingers—trained for skilled and nimble work.

Chapter 17

A Desperate Plan

IT'S FINDAL WHO spots the fugitive gliding from shadow to shadow beneath the building where he and Agnes kept their dwelling. For a moment, the boy can't believe it's the mule spinner, so stealthy and wary are his movements. Nor does it seem possible that the man is a living human creature and not a phantom gliding through the moonless alley.

"Mr. Munder, sir." The words are on Findal's lips, but he swallows them back, shrinking into himself as he watches.

Young Stokes has stood sentinel in this spot ever since Sunday, when his one-time master accosted Martha Beale. While not simply waiting (although he's not sure why he does so), he's spent his waking hours prowling along the exteriors of the adjacent structures, hoping to garner news about Munder's fate. What he's heard thus far has made him shake with fright, for Findal believes every allegation and every gory detail concerning the jealous husband's vengeful crime. And there've been more than enough blandishments to the tale, and most related by supposedly reliable sources.

Why he hasn't turned tail and fled, he can't explain. It's not because he intends to sneak inside the mule spinner's room and pilfer whatever he finds of value (although he could have done so, and has in other homes on numerous occasions in the past); and it isn't that he plans to win a reward for pretending to have overheard the man relive the crime in his tortured sleep (though that's possible, too). No, instead, Findal has stuck to the place out of a kind of heart hunger. The scraps of food he has scrounged during his vigil have done nothing to feed the ache he feels inside. Although their acquaintance was brief, Munder was kindly, and so the boy has remained, wandering around and around the spot where once someone gave him a warm place to sleep and a bowlful of supper and the quiet ease of trust.

But what to do now with the bogey-man? The boy creeps after the mule spinner, dread making him feel queasier and queasier by the moment. He imagines the man's huge hands dripping with blood and flesh, imagines the knife that hacked away his victim's head (a butcher's slick saw is what Findal envisions), invents the death struggle and the horror-struck wife—whose form he conjures up from the clothes he saw hanging in the couple's room.

"Oooh..." he gasps and then stops in panic lest the monster hear him. In the night air that envelopes the city's streets, his eyes are huge and white. Picturing himself as he must appear, Findal squeezes his eyelids shut before Munder can turn and discover those bright orbs burning.

The murderer moves on, or rather drifts forward in his sinister fashion, and Findal is saved.

He follows. He feels his heart pounding although the cause is now both fright and grief. *Why did you do it, Mr. Munder?* he yearns to ask. *I thought you loved the lady. Why would you want to harm her? Wouldn't she have left off her bad ways if you'd asked her to? I would have, sir, when you took me in. And I'd be good as gold now; I would.*

This internal argument ceases the moment Oscar Munder begins muttering to himself. "Whoever the man is," he says, although at first the words are indistinct, "and that Beale woman who set me up to hang. Sending me out to Bordentown as if it were a favor she was doing!" He coughs, stifling the hoarse rasp as best he can and then hawking onto the already smeary cobbles. When he takes up his rant again, it's louder; although a sing-song quality makes it sound like a drunken ramble rather than coherent speech. "She knows who did this villainous thing, I'll warrant; that's why she agreed to my plea. Wasn't she there with my girl? Wasn't she there?"

At this, the boy finally finds the courage to escape. His footsteps gather speed the farther and farther he runs from Oscar Munder. But oh, how the choice pains the child, how the street's stones wound his feet and legs, and how the icy air turns his tears to stinging frost and the salt of his mouth to bile.

WHEN DAWN RISES, its lavender light finds Findal curled in a ball near the service entrance to Martha's house. Clad in a dark jacket and trousers and a man's black boots and covered in the grime of the street, as well as whatever cast-off straw and rags he's been able to accumulate, his huddled figure looks like a stray dog sleeping in a nest of its own manufacture. None of the early trades-people driving past with their sleepy beasts give the sight a second glance. When a thin ray of sun brushes the boy's sooty face and alights on his uncovered ears, their size and surprising pinkness startle a few of the drovers, but they turn their heads away, believing they've spotted new-born mongrel cubs nursing and hoping the mother won't decide to rise up in protective ire. A weary horse is easily spooked, especially by a cur leaping out of the shadows.

"Ugh!" The under housemaid whose job it is to clean both front and rear steps before the rest of the household arises looks in disgust at the grubby mound coiled at the foot of the brick wall. She also notices the rosy flesh but decides it's a nest of baby vermin hidden in a beggar's discarded coat. "Filthy creatures," she mutters and attacks the mess with her broom, whereupon an exhausted Findal leaps to his feet, shouting.

"Leave off hitting me, missus. Can't a person sleep without being struck on account of it?"

At this the girl screams, although she doesn't drop the broom. Watching infant rats spring up and take human shape leaves her mouth hanging open in unbelieving disgust.

"You never seen a boy before?" Findal demands. He notices her staring googly-eyed at his over-sized ears and clamps his hat back on his head.

"Get off with you, you dirty thing! You have no business hiding next to good folks' houses." Her young eyes narrow in self-righteousness, and the hands holding the broom clench as she raises it in a gesture that is both defensive and intimidating. "I'll wager you was planning mischief, you filthy little thief. The city's too much burdened of the likes of you, and that's a fact."

"I'm no thief." This isn't technically true, but no matter.

"Well, you're not a chimney sweep, that's for sure."

"I am," Findal insists, although this statement is also false.

"Well, the flues here are fine. And we don't need ugly boys like you scaling around inside them, nor creeping around the parlor when you're done." She brandishes the broom like a weapon. "Get along now, or I'll call for the watch."

"I want to see Miss Beale."

"Of all the nerve! Get off with you, you miserable urchin." Her eyes squint tighter, and her lips follow suit. "How did you know this was the lady's house?"

"I'm acquainted with Miss Beale. You can tell her it's Findal Stokes calling. And that it's most urgent."

"And I'm acquainted with the Queen of the Fairies," the girl scoffs. "Now you make tracks, Master Stokes, if that's your real name."

"It is." Findal senses he's losing ground, and so he plants his feet more firmly on the brick sidewalk. Here the snow has been fully cleared, but hoarfrost has made the surface slippery, causing him difficulties in standing firm.

"Well, *Master* Stokes, I'll lay some *strokes* on your head if you don't shove off—"

"It's danger, I'm talking about. Miss Beale is in—"

"You're the one in danger, lad. And don't you mention her name again. Go along, before I have you hauled off for loitering."

"But—"

"Shoo! Be gone!" With that, the girl begins swatting at the boy, walking down the marble stairs as though advancing into battle. "Get!" she shouts. "Shoo. I don't want to catch you here again." Having driven Findal across the street, she stops and glares, then rearranges her pinafore and dusts her skirts before parading back inside where the scullery maid is lighting the kitchen fire.

"You certainly took your time sweeping the rear entry. You'd best step lively if you want to clean the front before Miss Beale comes down," she observes without glancing at her fellow laborer whose cheeks still glow rosy-red from exertion and indignation.

"The back was particularly dirty, but I took care of the problem. Besides, last night weren't you muttering about the mistress taking ill sudden-like after that gentleman left her and that she's likely to rest abed today?"

"We don't tolerate gossip in this house" is the hiss that answers this brazen observation.

"I'm only repeating what you said. 'A handsome gent,' were your very words, 'fairer and better than the one who deserted her.' "

"You keep what I said close, do you hear?"

"Then don't you go reminding me of my duties."

NATURALLY, FINDAL doesn't hear this exchange; even if he did, he's not so easily defeated. A mission is a mission after all. He dodges out of sight but remains on the scene, scrutinizing every door and window of the house as if he expected its residents were capable of issuing forth like swallows on the wing.

After an hour or more (time stretches on forever in his mind), the new governess and her charges issue forth. Findal has spied upon the threesome on other occasions and so has memorized their practiced route to the school on Locust Street and back again. The lady (she's far prettier than the old nursery maid) will be talking partly in a curious language she calls "French" and partly in normal speech. He watches them leave, the little mulatto boy named either Cai or Casper now holding the governess's hand rather than his adoptive sister, Ella's. He seems happier than he once did, and fatter and stronger, too, but it's Ella who commands Findal's devoted attention. She's taller than she was when he first encountered her, nearly as tall as he is, though he believes her to be younger by a year or maybe even two. Her beautiful blond plaits bounce upon the shoulders of her velvet coat; her cheeks shine like polished apples; she's as fair and perfect as any living girl could be. He longs to follow in her footsteps but tells himself he must wait for Martha Beale.

More time passes; the governess returns (her name is *Mademoiselle* Hédé), but no fine personage issues from the house. In his mind's eye, Findal pictures Munder arriving on the doorstep, wielding a weapon, maybe, and forcing himself inside. What deterrent would the law be to a man in his demented state? You can't kill a person twice. Findal peers over his shoulder, gazing down the street and back up again. Invented villains come and go; the boy's eyes ache with watching.

Then *Mademoiselle* Hédé again embarks for school, and this time, Findal creeps after her. He will explain his fears to the girl Ella, and she will repeat them to her mother.

THE EXCHANGE doesn't take place until late afternoon, however. Recognizing Findal from an encounter the previous autumn, Ella understands the curious significance of his presence, but freedom isn't something children of her station possess. School must end; the trip home north along Eighth Street and thence west on Chestnut must be accomplished before she can slip away from *Mademoiselle* Hédé and sidle outside to meet him. By then dusk is encroaching and Findal's terror rising.

"A bad man is going to hurt your mam," he says without introduction. The two have sequestered themselves down the block, well out of view of Beale House. Findal trembles with cold and hunger, but he holds himself as still as he can, lest the shaking be misconstrued for weakness.

"You told me that once before, and it came to naught." Ella's tone is lordly—it was lordly then, too. But Findal doesn't challenge her; he knows precisely what happened on that earlier occasion because the man in question was his father. He also understands why the girl doubts him now, for she has no cognizance of how it happened that Martha Beale—and Ella—escaped the elder Stokes's clutches.

"A fellow with big hands. He killed his wife and cut off her head with a butcher's saw—"

Ella's nose wrinkles in disgust; she makes a spitting sound to match. She may be attired in a dress, coat and hat, and all the full mimicry of adult garb, she may be learning elegant manners and elocution and languages and music, but she's still a product of the squalid environment that spawned her. At eleven, or maybe eleven and a half or even twelve, and despite too intimate a knowledge of the streets, she's also a child. "Leave off your nonsensical inventions."

"It's no invention. Everyone's talking about it. He's a laborer at the Quaker City Mill—which is where I'm now employed."

Ella studies him. Her expression has turned sardonic and wise beyond her years. "No longer a thief, are you?"

"No." He yearns to say more, but can't, yearns to boast of the escapade that rescued this girl and her guardian, but won't. Ever. "You never found your true mam, did you?" he asks after a painful silence.

"No thanks to you, I didn't. You told me you'd keep your big ears to the ground. That's what you said."

Findal overlooks the insult to his physical appearance. Only Ella is permitted this liberty, although she doesn't appreciate how privileged she is. "Maybe you don't want to find her anymore. You're set up nice and comfortable—"

"How do you know what I want?" she demands. "I had a sister and a brother, too. How do you know I don't worry over what befell them when I was sold to that awful place!" Tears of hurt and indignation make her eyes gleam.

"There, there…don't take on so…"

"Going to offer me a handkerchief, are you, Master Stokes? Act like the honest gentleman you are?"

"There's no cause for meanness, Ella."

"Miss! I'm 'Miss' to the likes of you, a dirty urchin like yourself. You shimmied down our chimney once, and not because anyone hired you, either."

"To warn you, that was why. You and the small boy—"

"I think you were making that silly story up. Just like you're fashioning tall tales now—"

"No, Ella, I'm—"

"Miss!" At that, she starts to weep, snuffling and hiccoughing and snorting like the child she is, and Findal begins to fret that a passerby will hear the commotion and blame him for annoying this well-accoutered lass. He's also mortified to feel his own eyes puddling with tears. He blinks them away before Ella notices.

"Mother made Mr. Kelman go away. On a boat…on the ocean…and before he could find my family like he promised he would. Just the same as you! I think she did it on purpose, because she wants to keep me for herself and didn't want Mr. Kelman investigating. That's what he does—what he *did* till he left us. Now I'm Ella Beale, Mother told me, and will be until the day I marry. And even then I'll remain her dear daughter forever—"

"But Ella…Miss, you've got such a nice home. And good food, I'll wager, and plenty of it. And you're warm, and look how prettily—"

"You wish to live with us, I suppose. Which is where all this loony talk of wicked folk comes from—"

"No, miss. What would I do with a life like yours and the little boy's? School and all your fancy garb and being marched back and forth with never a moment to call your own? I like roving free—"

"Pigs roved free in most of the places I've lived, but I doubt they liked it" is the trenchant reply at which Findal ventures a crooked smile.

"Well, now miss, I've been compared to lots of things, but never no swine."

"Ella," she murmurs at length. "Call me Ella. I don't want to be 'miss' to you—ever. Besides, you're nothing like a pig. You don't have a snout, do you?" She also smiles. It's a sheepish expression but genuine in its contrition. Spoken apologies are for grown-up people or adults attempting to teach children manners. They are words mouthed and words accepted; youth recognizes what's true. Ella's smile is real and so is the touch of her hand on his sleeve.

"Who is this man? And what would you like me to do?"

So young Stokes explains everything he knows, beginning with his first day at the mill and culminating the previous night when he discovered the escaped prisoner near his one-time home. He also describes his clandestine presence when the mule spinner followed Martha Beale from St. Peter's Church.

"You must come inside and tell Mother," Ella declares after he's finished.

"That I cannot do, miss."

"Ella."

"Ella. You tell her."

"She's not a frightening person, Findal. She's good and kind. She'll give you food and new clothes and a place to sleep. We have a big house, you know, and many extra chambers. Come inside. This man may be dangerous to you, too. And you're shivering—"

"You tell her for me. I meant to do it myself, but now you have all the knowledge from me."

"I think Mother will believe you more than me, though. You were there, after all."

"See how you call her 'Mother,'" Findal offers after a moment and in the gentlest of tones. "That's the fourth time you've said it."

Ella doesn't respond to the observation; instead, she orders a decisive "Wait here while I bring hot food and better clothing. Don't you hear how your teeth chatter? You'll freeze if you're not careful."

"I'm not going inside with you, Ella. I can't live as you do—"

"I never claimed you could, did I? Now, stand in this very spot. No, better yet, come near to the rear entry so your supper will stay warm." Without waiting for an answer, she flies back up the street and into her home.

Findal can't do as he's commanded, of course, not because he wishes to hurt Ella's feelings, or because he's certain she'll bring Martha Beale, or that he fears his motives might be misconstrued when the night watch is summoned to probe the matter, or that he'll be detained in Moyamensing Prison for further inquiry, but because a life of strictures and niceties and rules isn't for him.

He leaves, but he'll never be far away.

Chapter 18
Red Cloud

WHAT OF THE VESSEL *Red Cloud*? Has it sunk as Charles Dumont indicated? Or is it proceeding on its expected course and drawing mile by nautical mile closer to Key West, from whence it will depart for Havana? And how does Kelman fare, if that's the case? Is he still intent upon completion of his journey? And what of the fellow passenger who calls himself Joule, Egbert?

Martha believes she would intuit Thomas's death if he drowned, but would she? Could she? After all, the "understanding" that exists between them is relatively new and unknown to anyone other than Becky Grey Taitt. The strictures of society and the differences in their backgrounds have made courtship impossible; and the amount of time the couple has spent alone in one another's company can be measured in hours, rather than days. So what of Martha's claim? Wouldn't it take years of intimacy to achieve the type of spiritual unity that enables the ghosts and disembodied voices of those dearest to us to fling themselves through the void and spread messages of departure and comfort? When Martha's nightmares conjure up sea disasters, are they visions invented by a terrified brain, or are they real?

WHO CAN TELL how the blaze began? An improperly trimmed oil lamp, a candle left burning in an unguarded location, or a storm that knocked the ship's hull in such a fashion that a simple flame leapt onto a piece of grease-coated wood?

Open fires are hazardous on any vessel, and ones laboring through heavy seas especially. All hands are required to battle the waves, to stow loose objects, to trim the sails, to batten down. A little spark that begins in a forgotten corner becomes several flickering sparks in jig time; they light others that quickly find new lengths of smeary timber to enkindle. Then the blaze roars through one cabin or cook room, through the hold where the cargo is stored, or into the crew's forward berths, or the captain's more spacious aft quarters until the single blaze grows to an inferno that soon engulfs the ship.

If the disaster occurs at night and in rough weather, what hope is there for personal salvation? The sky is black, the ocean blacker—and colder, and cruel with hungry fish. The only light is the burning vessel, and that must be left as far behind as possible, and as quickly, too, lest the flames rain down upon the longboats cut free from the mother ship and so consume them. If gunpowder was listed among the cargo, then escape on a smaller boat may be impossible.

When dawn streaks the sky after such a cataclysm, little, if anything, remains. Not the smell of charred human flesh or livestock, not half a smoldering hull, not the blackened mast burrowing among the waves, or rent sail canvas floating hither and yon. If there's been a storm—as there was in the case of *Red Cloud*—the seas at daybreak continue thunderous and strong; their green waves build and sink and push out in all directions like a vast and foamy blanket shaken by capricious, underwater gods. The sun may shine, the sky burn blue, the wind that buffeted the heavens may have begun to ease, but the damage can't be undone.

It's as if the ship never existed.

Chapter 19
Missing

THE CITY IS GRIPPED with frenzy as details of Oscar Munder's daring escape begin to circulate. Caged though he was, it's reported that he managed to bodily assault his captors, knock them senseless, and thence vanish without a trace. Naturally, the story is encouraged by the pair entrusted to deliver the mule spinner to Moyamensing Prison. What good would it serve if the citizens of Pennsylvania and New Jersey discovered the truth? Certainly the men's employment would be terminated and their reputations as trustworthy guardians of the criminal class would be destroyed. So Munder is transformed into a demon capable of changing shape and outwitting and outfighting anyone—or any number of men.

The day and night watches hired to protect the city turn jittery; rumors that the killer has been spotted in the north or south or east or west of the town abound. Citizens begin to fear for their safety even when engaged in the most mundane of tasks, and in broad daylight, too. The areas around Quaker City Mill fairly jump with anxiety; not one of his former mates or masters feels free from reprisal, nor do the young piecers and loom tenders for whom the mule spinner takes on all the aspects of a vengeful ogre.

That one man can cause such disruption to daily life isn't strange. Despite its expanding population and its new residential and commercial areas, Philadelphia has continued to exist within an antiquated form of policing (the watches were among the earliest mode of governance); and those civil servants are often hard pressed to keep order. Like the fire brigades, the watches are under the jurisdiction of no centralized authority; their turf is local, cooperation nil. During the previous year's riots in which Negro houses, businesses, and a church were burned to the ground or the Weavers' Rights riots that also set the city aflame, the militia had to be deployed in order to restore peace, which occurred only after a significant loss of property—as well as life.

Now there are complaints that the militia should be summoned again and marched, weapons at the ready, through the streets. The suggestion may seem absurd; Munder is only one person, after all, but given the fact that no one feels safe, the notion remains.

Martha, warned by Ella, should pay closer attention to the warnings circling around her, but she refuses to listen. Newgeon, her *majordomo*, and even her lady's maid issue entreaties that fall on deaf ears. Ella and Cai may be tutored at home by *Mademoiselle* Hédé for the time being, but Martha walks back and forth between her home and the Beale Brokerage offices with her concentration solely on Thomas Kelman and a ship that may or may not have sunk off the coast of Florida. Like Munder's fantastical and macabre strength, that too is rumor.

LEAVING THE HOUSE on the fourth morning following the mull spinner's escape, she encounters Emil Rosenau on his way to confer with her. Spring has finally arrived in full force. Where the streets are dirt-packed, they're mired in mud several inches deep; the thoroughfares paved with cobbles and Prussian block are only slightly more passable, and the earth in every park and garden plot squelches with moisture. What snow and ice linger leach rivulets into already sodden turf, producing a continuous sound of running water as if Philadelphia were built atop a series of creeks—which much of it is. The sun-streaked sky cares little for the slough bubbling beneath it, however; the air is dry and brisk, and the still-leafless tree branches alive with returning birds.

"Miss Beale," Rosenau calls as he picks his way across the road. "Happily met. I was on my way to call upon you."

Descending her front stairs, Martha turns at the sound of his voice; with her concentration of the vanished Thomas, the polite smile she affixes is an effort.

"Surely you're not venturing out alone?"

"It's my custom, Dr. Rosenau. The fresh air and changing streetscape invigorates my brain." Despite this avowal, she looks far from energized; quite the opposite, she appears wan and weary.

"But, madam, you must know the peril in which you place yourself. A madman on the loose, and one whose crime you had the misfortune to encounter. Reports of his abilities may be exaggerated, but in my professional estimation, men and women who've lost their use of reason often have superhuman physical prowess as well a lack of fear."

Rather than respond to this advice, Martha resumes her journey. "Will you walk with me, sir? If you intended to visit, then you must have news to impart."

"Alas, I have no information regarding Munder. I'm certain my services won't be required since the man is obviously of a depraved and choleric nature. However, because you applied to me in the manner you did, and because my curiosity has been piqued, I wonder whether I'm exercising my civic duty in keeping aloof from the case."

"A missing man cannot be examined, sir."

"No, naturally not. Not until he's caught and imprisoned again. And then what difference would it make if I declared he possessed a propensity for abhorrent acts? We know that to be true already. No, I refer to his deceased wife. You asked me if I would examine her remains. I stated that the work of dissecting a body, though scientific, is akin to butchery and that I had no specific physical clues to search for and identify. I will not burden you with the details of the dissection procedure, as they are not only unpleasant but unseemly for a lady's sensibilities. However, given that Munder's escape is an obvious form of confession, I feel it would be beneficial to a court of law to have a full description of the corpse rather than refer to it merely as a headless woman found at *Point Breeze*. The man must pay for his crime, but proper protocol should be observed. Not that the outcome will differ given my findings, but we are a civilized people and must provide our judges with all possible expertise."

"I understand," Martha tells him; her tone is vague though, and he recognizes how little attention she's giving the conversation.

"Are you quite well, Miss Beale? Naturally, I'm not privy to your habits, nor do I wish to pry, but you seem unnaturally fatigued. Perhaps an elixir would be beneficial."

"What I suffer from isn't a physical malady but a mental one, Dr. Rosenau. No elixir can cure me, I'm afraid."

"Ah, too many facts and figures when you would rather exert yourself over the 'vagaries of the soul' as you put it." If Rosenau took the time to notice her reaction to his comment, he'd see a face gone slack with sadness, but he's too intent upon his own circumstances and scarcely gives her a glance.

"What you propose sounds like an admirable plan, sir" is her eventual reply.

"Good. Now, should I apply to the authorities in Borden-town myself, or do you wish to retain your sphere of influence? Which I recall is quite impressive."

"I'm happy to help if you wish it. Although I can't imagine a scholar of your stature requires my aid."

It's decided, however, that Martha will write a letter recommending Rosenau's examination of the corpse and that he will carry it with him to New Jersey that very morning. The missive delivered into his hands, Martha bids him goodbye at the brokerage house her father built up, and then turns her jumbled thoughts to the business of banking.

AS THE HOURS grind forward toward midday and Martha tries to quell her anxieties with the dry practicality of facts and figures and Rosenau travels northward to Bordentown, Cornelius Dumont's house becomes the scene of shocked disbelief. Clustering in the hall outside the mistress's room, an upstairs maid, a downstairs maid, a scullery maid who has no business in this part of the residence all give voice to their dismay. Their master stands among them, equally distraught. Anger and grief and despair seethe just beneath the surface of every gesture and every word.

"But she was reasonably well last night, sir. I heard her moving about when I left the flagon of tea you ordered."

"And early this morning, too, sir," the downstairs maid hastens to add. "I paused right here, as I always do before going down to kindle the dining room fire. I don't like to think of her cold, you see…although I know we can't risk an open blaze in her chambers. Her footsteps were quiet but peaceful—"

"And I rasped an apple for her breakfast," the kitchen girl interjects.

The words are no sooner out of her mouth than Cornelius rounds on her. "The physician recommended no such thing. Nor did I order it."

She bobs a curtsy, then another for good measure. She's young, fifteen at the most, and new to the household's many strictures. "No, sir. I took it on myself. Well, the upstairs girl here, she knew, too. Surely there's no harm in an apple, sir—especially one soft enough for a baby's gums. And I believe the missus likes them, because the plate always comes back empty. My gran were the same. Even when folks don't recognize their own kin, they enjoy a bit of a treat." Her knees bend as she dips into another worried bow, and her cheeks flush crimson with apprehension.

"Your grandmother has nothing to do with my wife" is the ill-tempered reply—for which Dumont is immediately forgiven by those gathered around him. He's their employer, after all.

"No, sir."

"Nor should she be likened to an infant."

"No, sir." Disgraced, the scullery maid glances at her sister servers, but they avoid the silent appeal and turn their faces away.

"None of you saw my wife during your several sanctioned or unsanctioned visits, then?"

"No, sir! You said we mustn't peep in on her." This is the upstairs girl responding. Self-righteousness and a need to distance herself from the others makes her voice louder than necessary in the confined space. "That would only rattle the poor dear further. As to the rasped apple, sir, I certainly never—"

"Damn the apple!" Dumont rages. "What do I care about pieces of fruit or flagons of lukewarm tea? I want my wife, not idle cant."

His servants bite their lips and stare at the floor, shifting soundlessly on their feet as if ready to run from the scene—which all would like to do.

"I want my wife. My wife! My dear wife. Oh, why didn't I look in on her this morning when I awakened? Why did I let her silence lull me into thinking she was still asleep, that her dreams weren't troubling her, that she was at rest?" He hangs his head, and then reaches out his hand to caress the closed door. Inside, not a sound issues forth. The hired women say nothing; instead, they watch their master's hand stroking the painted wood. It looks to them as though he were saying farewell to the thing he loved most in this world. "Why was I so careless?"

"Sir," the downstairs girl finally ventures. "Shouldn't we notify—?"

"Notify? What do you mean, 'notify?' Notify whom, and about what?"

"The authorities, sir. Someone must be told, I think. That's how it was in my former employment. When the mistress's father died." The suggestion disappears into a breathless hush that neither of the other two servants dares break.

"Ah...I see," Dumont answers at length. "Yes, I see how it is...Yes, we must. Delaying the inevitable is useless. Someone in authority must be summoned." He shivers, and the three recognize the distress the proposal causes. Strange and unmannerly men walking through the house, peering at his wife's sequestered chambers, judging her hapless state. Those are the very lessons they were warned about as soon as their employment began: Don't enter the mistress's room under any circumstances—unless specifically ordered to; Don't speak to her through the door or answer if she calls out; Don't gossip about what you've heard. "Yes, you're correct," Dumont repeats. "Of course, it must be done."

"A genuine search party is what you need, sir," the scullery maid ventures. She doesn't look at the others as she speaks but lifts her chest like a child trying to seem taller. "Not just us in the household scaring about the neighborhood and hallooing the missus's name. Hired men in a proper team who will know how and where to look."

"Yes." The tone is flat. Dumont straightens his shoulders but remains staring sightlessly at the closed entry to his wife's room.

"Maybe she hasn't got far, sir. She knows the city, after all. She should do, being raised here from what I've heard. And she's not always as bad off as she might be. She could be hiding quite close by, too. Just to give us a bit of a scare, like."

"Ahh…"

The women look at one another; protective empathy makes them inch imperceptibly closer to their master. "You'll need to summon a member of the day watch, yourself, sir," the downstairs maid offers. "Or tell the *majordomo* to do it."

Dumont moves his hand on the paneling. For a moment, it appears as though he were going to depress the latch and step inside; instead, he withdraws, and the place is left in its shuttered state. "A search party. Yes."

"You must take heart, Mr. Dumont, sir. Someone will find her and bring her home. She's not a person of no account, after all."

☙❧

A PUBLIC STAGECOACH is drawing away from the city limits, journeying west and north toward the coal and lumber regions of central Pennsylvania. A sole woman sits inside the cramped conveyance, and her appearance among the fraternity of travelers is an oddity, for not only is she female but expensively attired. Her male companions are of lesser social stature and affluence: a dry goods merchant, a school master, a tannery owner, an itinerant preacher, an iron monger hoping to find better circumstances in one of the raw towns built along the Susquehanna or Lehigh Rivers.

True, the clothes she wears have a certain eccentricity; the colors are a bit garish and ill-matched as if she'd taken one shirt-waist and paired it with the skirt of a different gown, or a bonnet or mantle intended for another ensemble, but they bespeak money, nonetheless.

The men eye her, noting the fine leather of her shoes (shoes that look as though they'd never trod a city street), the fur-lined muff, the aigret-trimmed bonnet, and begin to make private con-jectures as to who she might be and why she's traveling alone—and in a common coach, among companions clearly not of her ilk. No fine lady would journey in such a fashion. Separately, each man decides she must be running away from her home. A cruel spouse, perhaps, or domineering parent, or perhaps she's an unwed lady who has found herself with child and the fear of scandal impels her.

Whether she's aware of their curious glances or not, the woman keeps her head pressed to the isinglass of the window, star-ing outside as if nothing in the world were as wondrous as the passing scenery: the trees now clustered into a forest, farmland and pastureland suddenly appearing within the rolling verdure, a homestead far off, a cottage close by, the snows of winter clinging to the higher elevations, and the blue and white-capped mountains that beckon in the distance.

Dusk advances, the coach rolls on, the horses are whipped up the long inclines, and the brakes squeal on the corresponding descents while the woman hums a silent song whose notes eventu-ally creep out peep by peep into the gloom.

Chapter 20
Fine Garments

NO SOONER HAVE two members of the day watch left the Dumont household with promises to summon others in the constabulary than Althea's anxious husband issues a call for additional able-bodied men to join the search. In less than an hour, the assemblage is gathered in front of the home; coins change hands; directions are given; Dumont even employs the city's most notorious fire brigades: the *Weccacoe Hose Company* and sinisterly named *Killers*. Because of the metropolis's lack of a centralized administration, the "fire boys" are a necessary evil; the blazes they combat are often superfluous to the wars they wage upon one another while houses burn to their foundations. When decently paid, however, the men prove loyal enough; Dumont's largesse will ensure their devotion, at least temporarily. Representatives of the Humane Society, a well-to-do group dedicated to rescuing would-be suicides from the rivers, join the motley, and sometimes rowdy, band that begins traversing the streets and alleys, calling Althea Dumont's name. Cornelius and Charles are among them, the former always in the lead.

Dusk appears; the light dims; the searchers continue to fill the byways: black-coated and black-hatted men looking like so many hungry starlings hopping over the ground. When they reach the Delaware, however, they stop dead in their tracks.

With the sudden advent of warmer days and the thaw that now drenches the city, the river roils with cresting waves. Banks have been breeched; vast tree trunks carried from inland forests hurtle past, plunging beneath the foaming waters one moment and exploding skyward the next. Some of the commercial quays are nearly buried under the rising tide, and the liquid road connecting William Penn's city to the greater world appears twice the size and five times as dangerous as it does during the summer months. Anyone slipping upon the rocks lining the shores would be swept away in a trice. No need to fill coat pockets with stones as suicides generally do, sinking would be easy; staying afloat and safe from those murderous logs well nigh impossible.

Staring at the treacherous scene, the silver waves now turning as dark as tarnished pewter, the group disbands: a few here and there slinking silently off, clusters of ten or more making brave comments about how quick the lady's end must have been. Drowning seems the probable conclusion to her life's story. Despite Dumont's demands that the search be resumed the following day, no one suggests exploring the city's western boundary, which is the Schuylkill River. If his wife ventured in that direction, she would have found another lethal body of water. Her end would have been the same.

Cornelius is the last to leave the Delaware's banks, and only then because his twin pulls him bodily away.

All this Martha hears in person from Charles Dumont. Like her conversation with Emil Rosenau that morning, the exchange takes place in the street outside her residence; the difference is that the hopeful light of day has been replaced by the melancholy gray of evening; the similarity is that Dumont feels equally compelled to chide her for her rash behavior.

"Oh, Miss Beale!" he exclaims the moment he has finished his heartrending report. "You mustn't walk abroad like this! Alone and with no guardian. Why, any ruffian could accost you. And when I consider that beast, Munder—"

"Gone from the house?" Martha interrupts; it's doubtful she even hears his remonstrations regarding her safety. "How can such a thing have occurred? Was your sister-in-law accustomed to that type of freedom?"

"No. At least not recently."

"But then?"

"Who can say, Miss Beale? A home isn't a fortress. Servants walk in and out. Milk and eggs are delivered—"

"Oh, your poor, poor brother. He must be beside himself."

"He is." Standing on the brick pavement, Dumont has a bedraggled appearance not in keeping with his habitual fastidiousness. Seeing Martha assess the change to his person, he adds a forlorn "The roads, as you know, are exceedingly muddy, and the flats near the Delaware worse."

Words fail him, nor does Martha speak. Instead they remain motionless, letting the sounds of day's end surround them: the market carts retiring from city; householders traveling homeward to a supper already waiting; the watch calling out the hour. One by one, the gas lamps are lit and night falls.

"I would like to see your brother. I know what it is to accompany a search party. I know how monstrous a river can appear. How monstrous it is. My father, as you must be aware, also disappeared in a similar fashion. A year ago last January."

Dumont doesn't reply. Regarding him in the artificial light, Martha surmises that he's about to protest the proposal, so she continues with a calm:

"Will you take me there, Mr. Dumont? At once? Tonight will be the worst of many he will face."

"You're very kind, Miss Beale, but with your own loss so analogous, perhaps it's unwise for you to—"

"My father lived a full life, Mr. Dumont. He had more years to enjoy, but that was not his destiny. A spouse is different than a parent, I believe, because a wife or husband must be the soul-mate of the other—the other half. For me, losing the better part of myself would be intolerable. Now, shall we go?"

AS CAN BE EXPECTED, the house kept by Cornelius and his wife is a dreary spectacle. Servants come and go, flitting about on tiptoe so as not to intrude but also plainly curious about the unfolding events—and more than a little nervous, too. For although no one saw her leave, their mistress was inadvertently allowed her freedom. Blame is sure to surface, or perhaps worse than mere reproach.

Martha is asked if she will take tea or a sherry or cake, maybe, or something warm—a spot of soup or roasted meat—or a cold collation if she'd rather, but she declines each suggestion. Her host says nothing throughout. He simply sits beside the withdrawing room fireplace and stares at the logs sparking in the grate. Charles stands next to him, or pokes at the blaze, or paces toward the street-side windows, or else retires to brood over the back of his brother's chair.

"Mr. Dumont," Martha begins after the buzzing of servants has stilled. "I will intrude upon you only for a few moments longer. I came to express my sympathy and to tell you that you're not without friends. Remember that during this time of trial, for friendship is a boon and a blessing. Those whom you value, and who value you, stand ready to help. I would like to count myself one of those companions."

"She can't be truly gone" is the whispered reply to which Charles, now stirring the fire, responds:

"But, brother, unless a miracle—"

"Not truly gone. Not forever. She cannot be dead."

"But, brother, the river...You saw it as well as I—"

"Who dares insist that she threw herself into the Delaware? My Althea doesn't like water, or ferries or boats of any kind. She likes farmland and gardens and the smell of fresh-tilled soil. You invent a calumny because—"

"Cornelius, be reasonable. I would never create a malicious rumor about your wife. It was others in the search party whose opinion—"

"She doesn't like water. You know that."

"Yes. Yes, I do."

"She's not a suicide."

"If you believe so, Cornelius, then so do I." Charles says no more; instead, he crosses the room again. His shoes pad over the carpet in a measured, solemn tread; Martha can almost hear the thoughts accompanying this cautious parade. She yearns to offer words of comfort but knows she should keep silent for the moment and permit Althea's family to adjust to their new situation. "Hard though it is, we need to face the facts presented to us."

"I don't want your facts, Charles."

"I understand that, brother. Nonetheless, the truth—"

"The truth be damned!"

"We have a guest, brother, in case you'd forgotten." The gentle warning, however, falls on deaf ears as Cornelius continue to speak, his voice quivering with anger:

"The truth be damned, I tell you!" To which he adds a quieter but no less adamant "She's always been afraid of you."

"Brother, that's not an accurate statement, as you know."

"She is. Aren't I familiar with my own wife's feelings? You can insist that she suffers maladies of the brain, or any other ailment a physician can invent, but her intuition is acute—"

"No one doubts Althea's sensibilities, or her poetic—"

"You did! You do now! She told me once she thought you were a villain—"

"Oh, my dear brother, I beg of you; tonight isn't the time for—"

" 'A villain hiding in the skin of an innocent man.' Those were her very words."

"If you say so, Cornelius."

"I do. I do."

Another excruciating silence ensues. Martha is aware of both brothers' labored breathing: one full of grief and rage; one full of grief and hurt. Her own chest swells with empathy; she draws her feet under her chair, hoping for a chance to escape from this unforeseen confrontation. There's no consolation she can offer now, and her presence seems not only awkward, but intrusive.

"Cornelius, you know that I've felt only the deepest devotion toward you and your wife. And I've shown my loving kindness, too. Now, let us be at peace with one another. You're distraught, as you have every cause to be, but can we not—?"

"You should have married long ago, Charles. Perhaps you would have learned to revere someone other than yourself."

Either Martha gasps at the cruelty of this statement, or she twists in her chair; whatever the signal, Charles is immediately at her side. In the flickering light, his passionate face has become a mask that she scarcely recognizes. "Miss Beale, our thanks for your sympathy. As you predicted, the night will be difficult. It *is* difficult, as you can attest. I would be happy to accompany you back to your home, but fear I should remain in my brother's house. I'm certain you understand. Let me send a footman with you. And let me extend my sincere apologies for the unnatural acrimony we've forced you to witness. It's not our habitual state." With that, he presents his arm to help her rise. Accepting the gesture, she finds herself all but dragged to her feet.

THE RETURN JOURNEY to Chestnut Street would be passed in silence were it not for Martha's voluble companion. Like the scullery maid, the footman is young and green, and he doesn't fully comprehend the gulf that exists between classes. Or perhaps he's too preoccupied with his own worries to care.

"I never saw Mrs. Dumont, not once," he says. "Not in the nine months I been serving in the house. The lady's maid, she left. I heard tell because she feared for her life—the missus was that dangerous. But I can't say more, because that would be gossip, and the master doesn't permit it."

Martha doesn't answer. She recognizes the extenuating circumstances that have caused the boy to break all rules of domestic employment; besides, his nervous habit of jerking his shoulders up and down as if expecting a whip's lash engenders her pity. She tries not to listen, but curiosity gets the better of her.

"And now the master's in such a lather and telling us we'll be dismissed without references. And all because the missus took it into her head to go for a walk. It's not anyone's fault she crept off like that, is it? I've got the knives to sharpen, the lamps to trim, and the stove to black every morning before the master sends down for his breakfast. The upstairs and downstairs maids and the cook and everyone, why, they're hard at it, too. Why should he care what she wore when she went missing? One of the girls told me the missus's chambers were a shambles, cloaks and other garments all tossed about. But that's what happens when there's no lady's maid, isn't it, miss? Maybe the missus did wear her finery when she lit out; maybe she didn't. It doesn't matter now. If she comes back like

the master keeps muttering, then he can buy her a new gown—
or many. And if she don't...Well, he won't be needing those fine
dresses anyway."

Chapter 21
Darkest Night

EMOTIONALLY DRAINED by her condolence call upon the Dumonts, Martha reenters her house. The hour is far too late for a traditional suppertime, but her servants have faithfully kept watch for her return, and the rooms glow as though it were still mid-evening. She regards the light, the smiling faces, and willing hands waiting to do her bidding and feels such leaden exhaustion that she fears she cannot take another step. The meal so carefully prepared must remain uneaten. Not even the lighter fare proffered—warm chocolate or beef tea or milk toast—holds appeal.

Shedding her outer garments and depositing them with a footman, she prepares to climb the stairs to her chambers when a salver on the secretary in the foyer catches her eye. On it are arranged *cartes de visite* and letters delivered in her absence—one of the latter in Thomas Kelman's hand. Knowing that the missive has been waiting here while she was elsewhere makes her heart twist; it feels as though she'd purposely ignored him, as if dutiful visits with near strangers were of greater importance. She takes up the salt-stained and sea-spattered envelope; as she does so, all sound seems to leave the place. There are no men and women attending her and her home, no dousing of lamps or fires, no bolting of doors and windows; there is only a ringing in her ears and an ache in her chest that causes her breathing to slow and her sight to blur. A message from the departed! What evil necromancer could have conceived such a hideous trick? Her arms begin to quiver in

jittering spasms, and within view of everyone, she rips open the
missive.

My dear Martha,
I pen this in haste, as our good ship Red Cloud *has happily met with*
a northerly-bound vessel—one traveling directly to Philadelphia—with
whom our captain is exchanging news and information. I trust this will
reach you in a timely fashion, and long before I can describe in person the
places and people I've seen during the hours we were moored at various
city docks: Savannah being the most recent.
'Before I can describe in person. . .' Merely writing those words causes my
hand to slip upon the page, for I have determined to disembark and obtain
passage home at the next port of call. My reasons are many; a sense of
cowardice at quitting the city because of unresolved business is one; self-
anger and condemnation is another; but chiefly, the reason is you. I will
say no more of those emotions at present. You know them as well as I.
The difference in our social classes and spheres is very great, as we both
recognize. Sadly, it's probably insurmountable, but I would count myself
worthless if I couldn't continue a supportive friend to you throughout
your life, as well as a friend to your family—a future husband perhaps
and children, too. For now, permit me to remain your
Thomas Kelman

Determined to leave the ship, Martha thinks. *Returning home. . .Is it*
possible Thomas quit the Red Cloud *before the disaster Charles Dumont alluded*
to, or was the letter offloaded but not the passenger? She examines the envelope again; specks of water have made blurry images of her name
and street. She imagines the droplets still in their liquid state, and
the ship rising and falling as Thomas completed the message and
delivered it to the other vessel. *No, the letter was written before,* she
tells herself, *before Thomas. . .*The thought is left unfinished as she
clutches his words to her breast. Everything around her fades from
conscious thought: footmen, maids, her home, the night blanket-

ing the city, the Dumont brothers and their anguish, Althea, the Delaware's killing tides. *Before my Thomas drowned...Unless...But no, there's no point in clinging to false hopes.*

How does she continue upstairs, or undress or slip into bed after this? She doesn't know. Her feet plod forward; her arms move; her dress, underskirts, corset, pantalettes, shoes, stockings: all are removed, and her braids unplaited and the ringlets brushed out by her maid who then tidies the room and replaces specific articles in the wardrobe and carries others elsewhere for a thorough cleaning and brushing. Martha doesn't speak throughout the familiar routine; it's doubtful she recognizes what occurs. Her eyes stare, seeing nothing but the past: Thomas entering her father's house the day they met; Thomas sharing that first intimate luncheon with her, the shy manner in which their two conversations halted or lurched forward; or, later, his selfless and soothing presence while they discussed, oh, anything and everything; and finally, that late night when, against his wishes, she dared enter his private chambers. A year filled with the large and small events of a companionship that burgeoned into something richer and finer than anything she could have imagined or hoped for. When she blinks, she fears he and each precious memory of him will vanish.

But he's already gone, she reminds herself as her head finally rests upon the pillow, her gaze fixed on the draperies that cover the bed's canopy. *Charles Dumont told me. The ship,* Red Cloud, *was lost. A storm, or perhaps an accident....*

Staring upward, her mind's eye can't help but conjure up images of the city's rivers: both in flood, both scouring their banks and burying islands and shoreline trees. The waves hiss with violence, but the palisades on either side are visible and dry, a safe haven for people and cattle.

The ocean is a different creature, and she envisions this deadly picture too: nothing but sea and sky and her Thomas struggling to stay afloat while miles and miles and miles of seawater roll forward. She sees him as though it were her head bobbing beside his, watching for rescue that will never appear. And then he sinks from view.

ᏻᎧ

WHILE MARTHA sleeps and dreams and gasps out her misery, her adoptive daughter lies fully awake and pondering several problems. One is the letter from Thomas Kelman that she espied on the foyer secretary; another is Findal Stokes, his dire words of warning and then his equally worrisome disappearance; the third is that afternoon's conversation with *Mademoiselle* Hédé. All are bundled together in her mind as if the separate dilemmas were related, although Ella's not sure how they could be.

In the semi-darkness, her eyes glitter and her jaw is set in the fixed and stubborn line that mirrors Martha's, making them look like blood relations, which, of course, they're not. Ella listens to the sounds of deep night—the distant barking of a dog, a single cart or wagon dragging slowly over the cobbles in a neighboring street, the watch calling the hour—and considers how pleasant it is to be safely abed in a big and well-guarded house, how nice it is to have clean sheets and a fluffy eiderdown and a gown especially for sleeping in, and feet that are washed and hair that smells of rosewater, and food in her belly and more for breakfast.

Those grateful thoughts, however, carry her back to Thomas Kelman who promised to find her birth mother and then left Philadelphia without saying goodbye. If Ella were truthful, she might also identify the betrayal she feels as the loss of a potentially loving father—which she's certain she'd have if Mr. Kelman wed

Martha Beale. She doesn't admit to this hope, though, at least not tonight.

What she does focus on is who will locate Findal and the criminal Munder and protect her adoptive mother now that Mr. Kelman is gone. With the perfect reason of a child born and raised on the streets, she decides it must be herself. There's no one else capable of the task: Findal's unreliable; Martha Beale's too delicate and well-bred. She never sees trouble coming; she trusts everyone; she's as naïve as a baby who's just been fed. Which is precisely the reason she went gallivanting off to that count's house—*chateau, Mademoiselle* Hédé calls it—and became involved in a murder, a *decapitation* according to Cook.

And then there's Mr. Dumont, whom Ella suspects of having amorous designs on Martha. He'd make a terrible parent! She'd never believe a word he said, and he'd dislike her because of her history, although he'd pretend otherwise. And Mother would listen to him—at least, she would for a while.

"Oof," Ella mutters aloud, then tosses aside the bedclothes, rises, tests the coldness of the floor with her toes, and flops back onto the warm mattress again, drawing the eiderdown around her shoulders while she glares reproach at the room. *What makes everyone think the dead lady is the mill hand's wife?* her brain demands. *People who labor in the Northern Liberties don't take pleasure jaunts into the countryside. They have to walk everywhere, because they don't own fine carriages or have money to use public omnibuses or stagecoaches. Walking to* Point Breeze *would take a day or more.*

The girl's scowl has become so fierce and her eyes so hard and bright that it seems as though she could send sparks shooting along the carpets, like the weird balls of fire that sometimes skittle over the floor during summer storms.

Besides, Mademoiselle *Hédé doesn't believe the murdered lady is Agnes Munder, either. And she would know, wouldn't she? Because her parents worked for the* Compte, *and she grew up in the house, and labored in the scullery when she was my age. She met the* Compte, *too, before he went back to France, and she knows his grandson and the lady who wasn't the* Compte's *wife.* Mademoiselle *said everything is different in France; no one minds cutting off the heads of royal people there or throwing rivals in prison or forcing them to leave their homes and all their handsome possessions. Not that anyone will listen to* Mademoiselle; *she's only a servant, and she can't express her ideas unless Mother or someone in authority asks her to speak.*

The unfairness of this decree refocuses Ella's deliberations. Inequality as a fact of life will never cease to rankle. She kicks at the bed linens and huffs her outrage, but the display of temper brings no solace. Instead, her mind returns to her conundrums, and she imagines the party picnicking on the belvedere (*Mademoiselle* Hédé has described the place in full). Everyone is eating and drinking as much as they wish—sugared fruits, current cordial, macaroons, nutmeg-scented negus, and cakes iced in almond paste—until Mother's friend Mrs. Taitt goes for a stroll and trips over the dead woman. Ella sees a custard-filled fanchonnette tartlet slipping out of the onetime actress's horrified fingers as she shrieks and then collapses in a dramatic faint. But this is pure invention.

In that moment, Ella concludes that Mrs. Taitt's involvement with the crime isn't as innocent as it seems. In her reinvention of the scene, Mrs. Taitt looks like a marionette opening a puppeteer's box and pretending to be shocked at what lurks inside. Ella pictures wooden hands attached to strings and a red-rimmed mouth that opens very wide, a bloodied cape stretched out upon the stage floor, and the puppeteer's big fingers moving above.

A second later, the fanciful notion evaporates, leaving Ella again fretting over how to guard the woman who rescued her. Who saved her life.

UNAWARE OF being the subject of Ella's unflattering scrutiny, Becky Gray also lies sleepless. In the chambers adjoining hers, she hears her husband return from yet another late night of carousing. The sounds of objects falling, of flesh colliding with furniture or walls, and of curses hurled at his valet indicate that Taitt is inebriated yet again. She stretches herself into a taut line on her bed and prays that his intoxicated state will overwhelm him with lassitude and confine him to his own room, but her prayer is not to be answered.

Her door opens and there he is, weaving in the fickle glow of a candle the valet has lit for him and which now leans at a perilous angle allowing molten wax to drip upon the carpet and the flame to flare and sizzle. "Damnation." With a yelp of pain, he drops both candle and holder, and then kicks a shod foot at the burning mess. "Damnation! Damn man…" The odors of singed wool and leather fill the room as he stamps through the fire's remnants while the syllables of his speech slur together in an inarticulate blur. "Damn man…gimme fire…"

Becky considers rising and leaving the space, but where is she to go at this hour? Certainly not Baby's or Nurse's chambers, nor the withdrawing room or Taitt's library—especially not there— and venturing outside into the street is out of the question. So she steels herself and anticipates the inevitable while her husband blunders around the room, muttering something beneath his breath. When he reaches the bed, he crashes down upon it, his collapsing body producing such a fog of fortified spirits that Becky's throat burns from breathing it in.

"How now, wife," he mumbles. "Not sleeping yet? Waiting for…waiting for…?" His fingers grasp at the sheets until they find her neck and face. Becky can't help but recoil. Although she can't see his skin in the dark, she knows from its coarse, clammy touch that it's soiled and streaked. The reek of another woman or women assails her.

"William, I cannot accept you in this state," she tells him, although the defiant words require effort. She raises herself to a sitting position, but here too, the choice is safety rather than assertiveness.

"Cannot…" Taitt's tone is sleepy and distant; his thumbs continue to knead her jaw line and cheeks.

"Take your hands off me, if you please."

"If I…"

"The hour is late. And you are…not yourself."

"Not…"

"Let me go, William." She attempts to pull out of his grasp, but he's more agile than she anticipated.

"My wife's grown cold." His speech is suddenly clear—and hostile. "The pretty wife won't do her duty. My pretty pauper Mistress Grey."

"In the morning, William. When you are refreshed."

"When I'm refreshed." His hands drop to her neck and shoulders, squeezing and pinching her skin as he lumbers closer, his hip now pinning her thigh. "Who are you to tell me what I may or may not do?"

The stench of his breath is terrible; Becky tries to turn her head, but his foul-smelling fingers seize her mouth and hold her in place. "My poor Becky. My starveling. Don't I know why you married me?"

"Have done," she manages to whisper.

"And why I married you?"

"Tomorrow. We'll discuss this——"

"A whore who——"

"Enough, husband. Please."

"Who spreads her legs for any man. Especially when he's as pretty as Charles Dumont——"

"William. Stop. What you infer isn't true. You know I would never——"

"Not true that you don't like spreading your legs——?"

"Husband——"

"You could learn a trick or two from your younger, professional sisters. Or haven't you guessed I've been a-whoring tonight?"

"Take your hands away." The words issue forth between clenched teeth, a nearly inaudible threat. Then, with a grunt of exertion, she jerks free of Taitt's grasp and hurls herself toward the far side of the bed. But her husband is faster. He grabs her again as if she were the slowest of flies and he the quickest of cats.

"One beauty in particular——"

"Let me go, William."

"A really lovely specimen. And docile——"

"Release me, husband. You're hurting my arms——"

"Don't you want to know the lady's name, Mistress Grey? Or how I found her? Or where I've been keeping her? A compliant, black-haired witch living in a sorcerer's hole."

"You can go to the devil, sir. Now, take your hands away before I raise the household." With her back to her husband, Becky doesn't see the blow coming. Even if she were able to watch it aiming toward her head, what could she do? Jump out of harm's way, raise her arms to deflect his fist? Flail at him in return? Because of her stagecraft, she may have more physical strength than most women, but she's no match for a man. So the hand that slams into her fells her in an instant, leaving a handprint on her cheek that will turn livid within the hour, and an ache from the top of her skull to her jaw that will make Becky wonder whether the bone has been shattered.

Chapter 22

William Taitt and the Devil

"I ONLY ASK that you keep me a little while. A few weeks at most. Please, Martha, please. Then I'll return to England, or make some other arrangement, because it's obvious I can't stay in that house—"

"What about Baby?"

Still standing near the entry to Martha's private sitting room and still clothed in the outer garments she wore to traverse the early-morning streets, Becky's body grows rigid while her battered face grimaces as though bracing against a sudden squall. She turns away from Martha; it seems as if she intends to drag herself back down the stairs and out the front door. "William will never allow me to take him. A girl, perhaps, but not his heir—"

"You're the child's mother!"

"Yes. I am. Although I'm certain William can and will declare me unfit as a parent, and that will be the end of what rights I may possess." The fortitude that carried Becky out of her house and into Martha's deserts her. Her shoulders sink; her knees buckle; she tips forward as if on the verge of collapse. Martha, who has stood close by ever since her friend's precipitous arrival, reaches out to steady her while simultaneously pulling off Becky's mantle and bonnet and leading her to a chaise.

"Oh, Martha, what am I to do?"

"Remain here, of course. And as long as you wish. Three weeks, three months…it's for you to decide. Lie down now, and let me put some pillows under your feet. Or does your head hurt too much in this position?"

"I don't know. I'm hardly aware of physical sensation." Despite this declaration, her voice is now marred by pain. Becky touches her jaw with a tentative hand. "I was afraid I'd sustained greater injury. In truth, I don't know how I found the stamina to come here. Now it's deserted me altogether. I feel so dizzy and unwell, and my vision is…oh, everything's become blurry. I should feel fortunate to have escaped worse damage, and yet…" The words trail off.

"Good fortune counts but little if not sustained by human decency. Your husband's hand is imprinted on a large bruise upon your face. If you'd fallen at a different angle or hit your head against a sharp object…" The implication is plain. Martha says no more.

"He doesn't know his own strength" is Becky's response, which plea her hostess disregards by continuing with an assertive:

"Will you take some beef tea? Or perhaps rice milk or barley gruel? You must nourish yourself, no matter the hurt you experience."

"I'd rather sleep, Martha. Here, where it's so lovely and warm."

"So you shall. After you have some food and the surgeon examines you—"

"I don't want an examination! William will—"

"William isn't here. Nor will I permit him entry into this house. Besides, I had my footman send for the surgeon the moment you appeared on my doorstep. You may have imagined your veil and cloak concealed your injuries, but they were plain for all the world to see." Martha pauses. Still bending at Becky's side, she touches her forehead and is dismayed to find it becoming hot and feverish. "Your husband has harmed you before, hasn't he?"

"Yes...although he wasn't so...so unpredictable in the past. Now I think sometimes he wants to kill me."

"And when you fell after he hit you, what happened next?"

"I don't remember. I slept, I suppose, for I awoke on the floor and he was gone and daylight had arrived. Then I dressed, such as it is—I didn't want to summon my maid—and found a hansom cab that conveyed me to your door."

Martha says nothing; instead, she covers Becky's prone body with a lap rug, then crosses the room, rings for her lady's maid, and orders various foods for the invalid and a room prepared to receive her guest and a bedgown and dressing gown readied. "Have the footman bring the surgeon up the moment he arrives," she concludes in a near whisper, "I fear Mrs. Taitt may have suffered a type of concussion of the brain. She showed extraordinary resolve in making her way here, but her body is already feverish. Time is of the essence."

A concussion is a dangerous diagnosis as everyone knows, because it can lead to the dire condition of brain stunning or inflammation. The lady's maid's response to the verdict is a practiced: "Shall I prepare a lotion of sal-ammoniac and vinegar, madam?"

"No, let us wait for the surgeon's recommendation. If he deems the case serious enough, he may wish to apply leeches first. But have the other ready. And a poultice and black draught to lower the fever." Then Martha returns to the patient; she's dismayed to find her asleep. Her skin is hotter than before.

"Becky, dear, you must keep awake a while longer."

The former actress opens eyes that have grown clouded and unfocused. When she speaks, her voice is faint, the words like those mumbled in a dream. 'A black-haired witch, he said, in a sorcerer's cell."

"Who said that, Becky?" Martha pulls a chair close to the chaise and begins lightly stroking her friend's face.

"William. He keeps a girl...a witch..."

"Ah..." Fury almost gets the better of Martha, but she masters her sense of outrage and maintains a soothing tone. "Let's not fret about witches or strange girls now."

"Was gone when..." The speech fades into silence, and Martha, not because she wants to discuss William Taitt and whether he's keeping a mistress, but because she needs to keep Becky fully conscious, asks a quiet:

"When was he gone, dear?"

"*Point Breeze*...before...days...came home...didn't know where gone..."

Martha thinks back. It requires no effort to connect Becky's "accidental fall" prior to the excursion to her husband's brutality. "So he arrived from this unexplained absence when you were preparing for our picnic?"

"Gone..." is all Becky answers. "Didn't know where...black hair..."

"Don't fret about that now. I'll help you handle your wayward husband when you're fully recovered—"

"Girl...kill...me..." is the disjointed reply before Becky falls insensible.

ꙮ

WHEN THE SURGEON arrives, he finds Martha kneeling beside her friend's makeshift bed, trying in vain to rouse her. The lady's maid is again summoned, and the surgeon and she shave Becky's head, the long locks falling in untidy clumps on the floor. There's no time for tidiness or decorum; the curls are trampled underfoot, and some of Becky's fine lace bodice must be cut in order not to disturb her while her stays are unloosened and her body freed from its fashionable constraints. Leeches are applied, but the surgeon's expression remains very grim as if he didn't expect this most reliable of remedies to achieve the desired results. "I fear she may be suffering from a violent inflammation of the brain," he finally concludes. "It's obvious she struck her head on this side when she fell, but the bruise on the other half of her face indicates that the blow she received was severe enough to cause equal damage."

"She won't die, will she?" Martha asks in the barest of whispers, to which the surgeon replies with an oblique:

"Have you sent for the lady's husband? He should be apprised of the calamity."

"He was the person who hurt her." Martha stands as she makes this pronouncement; her eyes and cheeks blaze.

"For his sake, let us hope the damage isn't as great as it seems. Choleric men can be intemperate, but in my opinion, they usually repent of their—"

"For *her* sake, you mean, sir," Martha interrupts. "The devil can take William Taitt."

UNAWARE THAT his wife has quit his home, unaware, even, of what transpired during the night, Taitt awakens in his own bed. His head pains him considerably, and he wonders momentarily whether he incurred some injury: a tumble down slippery stairs, perhaps, or a collision with too low a ceiling beam. Then his stomach churns and he retches, vomiting up an alcoholic bile into the chamber pot he grabs from beneath the bed. Finished, he stares at the floor while self-pity and sickness overwhelm him. He drops back into his sweat-soaked pillows trying to recall the events of the previous evening, but finds he can't remember anything: where he went, what he did, how he returned home. All he knows is that he feels a bitter mortification and an abiding sense of dread. He stares at his hands as if they hold a clue to his unease, but they reveal nothing except an unpleasant uncleanliness. Wherever he was—or with whomever—fastidiousness was of little consequence.

Rising, he must steady himself by grasping the bedpost, a chair back, the chest of drawers, but the simple act of bathing his face in the washbowl is impossible. The water, which is cold, swirls around and around, and the soap that slithers through his fingers makes the surface as greasy and repellant as cooling mutton gravy.

He rings for his valet then submits to the man's ministrations as if he had no more flexibility than a dressmaker's manikin. Several times Taitt must vomit again, but there's nothing left to regurgitate. The valet offers to bring egg wine or calf-foot broth, but the suggestions are rebuffed with a brusque wave or angry purse of the lips. Taitt saves his speech in order to swallow back the rising gorge.

Attired at last, his face slick and greenish, his brain still pounding, he leaves his house. But where to go? Not his club. Not a bawdy house, nor oyster cellar—definitely not there with the odor of rotting fish and rancid seaweed rising from the straw-strewn floor. Nor one of the new hotels constructed on lower Chestnut Street that boast *tables d'hotes* for the discerning traveler. Simply imagining those places makes Taitt's head swim; he grimaces in disgust as if he could smell the mingled scents of cookery, savory pastries, tobacco, and fortified wine.

He presses on and finds himself approaching the Delaware River. The breeze whipping off the still-churning waves begins to revive him, and he determines to walk among the commercial quays, or if they're too crowded, seek out a path along the river's banks. A sense of purpose enlivens his step, and he pictures himself entering the wharves in order to seek news regarding a ship or ship's cargo in which he has a monetary stake. The jangling of halyards and masts, the smells of tar and sun-bleached wood will prove a restorative, especially with the riverine waves whipped into such a frenzy.

Crossing Front Street, he spots a man walking in his direction. He's a shabby creature, a manual laborer of some type, but dirtier than most, with his hat pulled low as though ashamed to show his face. *And well he should be,* Taitt decides, *a youngish fellow like that with big, sturdy hands sneaking around is if he feared his employer would catch him shirking his work. Probably a seaman off one of the ships or a dock hand; either way, he should be gainfully employed not wandering about.*

Unbeknownst to William Taitt, the man about to pass him is Oscar Munder who has spent much of the previous day in the anonymous employ of the Dumont brothers. A coin is a coin, after all, and the mule spinner is well acquainted with hunting for a vanished wife.

The Delaware's lethal currents have afflicted his psyche, however; unlike the other searchers who abandoned the endeavor and journeyed homeward once daylight faded, he has remained at the site like a ghost haunting its banks and moorings. All night and now into the morning, he has roved back and forth unable to stand in one spot for more than a few minutes, or spend his payment on food, or even rest and watch the detritus-filled tide tumble past. Does he imagine his Agnes will rise up wraith-like from its depths and call to him? He doesn't know, although his judgments, grown confused from lack of sleep and sustenance, have begun to confound his lost wife with Dumont's until he has a vision of his own dear Agnes drowning while he, her husband who should have protected her no matter the cost to life and limb, was nowhere near.

Cursing himself, Munder shambles past Taitt. He never looks up; it's as if this gentleman, as well as every other person in his path, was invisible.

Taitt sees him, however. The man reeks of unwashed flesh and fouled linens, and Taitt turns his head away to breathe purer air. As he does, he sees a vision of such malignancy that he stops in wonderment that those nearby don't remark upon it: a black creature, besmeared head to toe as if with soot. It glides over the ground on two feet that do not touch the soil. Both are pointed; both are furred, as is the body, which is almost—but not quite— a man's shape. The head is preternaturally large, the shoulders hunched and narrow, the legs bend like a goat's standing upon its rear hooves, the fingers are talons. "Follow me," the being sings. "I am your comrade, your boon companion; my desires are your desires, your thirsts and hungers alike to mine. Together we shall find pleasure."

Taitt opens his mouth to answer, but his tongue and throat are too dry to speak. He stares and stares; the creature merely drifts along. Were it not for the blackness of its face, Taitt would imagine a smile on its lips. He turns back toward the laborer whose path he crossed, wondering if the weird spectacle is the man's evil spirit, a phantom trailing behind him like his smell and mumbled imprecations. The man has vanished; the demon remains.

"I am your comrade. Come with me. Together we do wonders."

"Who are you?" Taitt demands aloud, oblivious to the stares he now receives from those closest to him.

"You remember, Mr. Taitt. Surely you remember."

"MOTHER, I MUST speak with you." Ella has entered Martha's sitting room. The surgeon has long-since left, and the insensate Becky Grey has been removed to a darkened bedroom where Martha's lady's maid attends her, but the mistress of the house remains in doleful ruminations. Still seated near the chaise where her friend lay, Martha regards the empty cushions, the fire burning merrily in the grate, the windows which now reveal the brightness of a perfect morning. Except, of course, that nothing is merry or perfect or bright.

"Don't you have school today, dear?" is the abstracted reply. Martha's voice echoes as if she were far away.

"I didn't go. *Mademoiselle* Hédé gave me permission to remain at home. So that I could talk to you."

"Ah." It's obvious to Ella that her adoptive mother scarcely hears her.

"*Mademoiselle* wishes to speak with you also."

"About your lessons?" Although Martha looks at the child, her focus is elsewhere. *Will Becky survive this calamity? Will Taitt try to force his way into the house? Will he lie about being the cause of her brain inflammation?* The latter two concerns pale in comparison to the first, which Martha returns to, then immediately queries the efficacy of the fever draught and when the leeches should be removed. She must send for the surgeon again, she decides. Or, no, he should be persuaded to remain until Becky revives. With a commensurate fee increase, naturally.

"No. About what Mrs. Taitt—and you—discovered at *Point Breeze*."

"Ah, yes...*Point Breeze*. The dead woman."

"That's right." Ella is still standing in the center of the room; her natural impatience is getting the better of her, and she shifts from foot to foot.

"That's not a proper subject for a child" is all Martha says. "*Mademoiselle* Hédé should know better."

"But—"

"I will advise her so immediately. Discussing gory scenes produces nightmares. You haven't allowed Cai to hear you, have you? His falling sickness is nowhere near healed."

"No, Mother, I wouldn't—"

"Good. Now, run along, dear. You must do your lessons at home with *Mademoiselle* if you've missed a day at school."

"But, Mother—"

"What is it, Ella? Say what you wish, but be brief. I must order the footman to fetch the surgeon again."

Part of the rehearsed speech comes tumbling out—although not in the precise manner Ella practiced. "A mill laborer and his wife wouldn't have gone to *Point Breeze*. It's too far, don't you see? Poor people walk everywhere. They can't afford omnibuses or stagecoaches. I should know, shouldn't I?" In her frustration at this jumbled narrative as well as her adoptive parent's disinterest, Ella twists her pinafore in her hands while her face takes on an expression both irate and desperate. "Shouldn't I, Mother? I was one of them. Poor, I mean. And *Mademoiselle* says that the *Compte's* grandson—"

"Child! Stop! My friend Mrs. Taitt is very ill. Very ill, indeed. While I applaud your inventiveness, this is no time to discuss the matter. The culprit was arrested; he will be caught again and brought to trial. Justice will be served, and undoubtedly, he will pay for his cruel actions with his life."

"But—"

"The crime has nothing to do with us. Now, go attend to your lessons."

"But don't you see, Mother, no mill hand could travel as far as—"

"Ella. Desist. There are wiser people than we investigating the situation."

"They don't know how poor people think, though, or what they do. When you've got plenty of food in your belly, you can't imagine being hungry."

Martha has had enough of forbearance. "Our conversation is concluded until you can learn to speak politely about your elders. Find *Mademoiselle* Hédé and tell her I wish to see her at once. You should not have been permitted to avoid school."

"I wish Mr. Kelman was still here," Ella lashes back. "He'd listen to me!"

"Enough, Ella—"

"He would! He knows how poor laborers survive—"

"Ella. Stop this nonsense immediately."

"You shouldn't have sent him away! I liked him and so did Cai. And now Mr. Dumont will marry you, and Cai and I will be sent somewhere terrible, or he'll make us go back to living on the streets—"

"Mr.—?" Astonishment fills Martha's face. "Mr...will what...?"

"I don't like him," Ella declares, mindless of the cost. "I think he's mean, even though he pretends to be kind. And he won't be a good father."

"No one said anything about Mr. Dumont acceding to that role. Or anyone else, for that matter. Now, fetch *Mademoiselle*—"

"But you told Mr. Kelman to go away, and I never got a chance to say goodbye to him. What if his ship sinks and he drowns? We learned all about that in school. Ships sinking in terrible storms, or pirates attacking them for the treasure they carry."

The metamorphosis Martha undergoes is extraordinary. She's no longer a person of authority and discipline, but a frail figure that looks to Ella both helpless and very, very old. When she speaks again, her voice cracks. "Mr. Kelman's decision was his own" is all she says. Then she rises and walks to the window, not because she can't face the girl's persistent arguing, but because her emotions threaten to undo her. *Was his own*, she thinks, *was. Not is.*

"But what if he never comes back, Mother? What if that happens?"

"That's enough. There are circumstances you're too young to understand. Or question. Now, go before I lose my temper. You have no idea what you're talking about."

Chapter 23
Said and Left Unsaid

MARTHA HAS NO SOONER concluded the quarrelsome interview than the footman knocks on the door announcing that Charles Dumont has called and is waiting below. Ella, who has only just left the second-floor sitting room, can't help but overhear, and she determines to find a means of eavesdropping (a terrible crime, as she well knows). In her opinion, however, the visit is further proof of the gentleman's amorous intentions; the fact that her adoptive mother receives him when she's so clearly preoccupied and distraught only bolsters the notion.

Nothing could be farther from the truth, at least, where Martha is concerned, but the child has no means of knowing this. Besides, she has already made up her mind; and it will take a good deal of contrary evidence to prove her wrong. Ella isn't a person given to halfway measures. Unnoticed by Martha, or anyone else, she takes up a sentinel position in the foyer the moment the footman slides shut the double withdrawing room doors. She can hear the heavy velvet draping the portal swish with movement and fall back into stately place. When the standing clock near the foot of the front stairs booms out the hour she jumps with fright, but a rapid glance at her surroundings assures her that she's alone in her clandestine mission.

"Mr. Dumont." With her ear pressed to the crack, Ella detects warmth and encouragement in the greeting, although Martha is experiencing the reverse. She does everything in her power to maintain a polite and empathetic pose and remind herself of the brothers' suffering. Were the child to witness the forced smile that accompanies the words, she'd understand how wrong her conclusions are, but of course, she does not. Nor does Dumont recognize how stilted the expression is.

"Miss Beale, I simply had to call upon you and apologize for the miserable exhibition my brother and I forced upon you last night. Cornelius also sends his deepest regrets. We're accustomed to be more honest—and, yes, sometimes more combative—with one another than our acquaintances are comfortable with. Perhaps it's because we're twins: half one person, half another. And then, we know each other so very well. Too well, maybe. I'm truly sorry if we offended you. Or appeared ungrateful for your kindly concern."

"I was never blessed with a sister or brother, Mr. Dumont, so I have little ken of such an intimate companionship. However, I recognize that your family has been faced with extraordinary hardships and that times of trial can induce ire in the mildest person. Your apologies are unnecessary, but I will accept them if it eases your conscience."

"Oh, Miss Beale, you are goodness itself!"

The hidden Ella stifles a disgusted groan while Martha also bristles inwardly. Despite her denial of the child's claim, she knows precisely what Dumont's intentions are and is beginning to wish he'd be less obvious. Maintaining a friendship with someone who has been rejected as a suitor is difficult when the goal has been overtly expressed. She changes the conversation's focus to *Point Breeze*, since the topic seems more prudent. She's unaware that Ella suggested the queries as well as the suspicions they've inspired.

"How is your friend, the grandson of the *Compte* de Survillier? I imagine the shocking events that occurred on the estate must have been enormously disturbing to him. No doubt he and his staff were intensively questioned."

"Oh yes. That brute of a constable prowled around the place for an entire day. From what I understand, the man displayed as little expertise as he did when interrogating our party. Fortunately, business affairs have allowed my friend to leave the area, and he no longer needs to deal with prying eyes. The servants have been instructed to permit no one entry to the park or buildings."

"Ah." Martha can't fully comprehend why she finds the grandson's defection disturbing, but she does. "Will he be gone long?"

"I'm afraid I don't know."

"And the...lady acquaintance?" Purposely referring to the woman in the most ambiguous fashion, Martha's cheeks redden nonetheless.

"She has also decamped from her nearby residence. Her life, as well as those of her children, was made quite miserable. She has relatives in another state—either west or south. I'm not certain which."

"I see..." is the even response. "So there's no one remaining to bear witness to what transpired."

"The *majordomo* and other servants, of course."

"But no one in a more elevated position?"

"You and I, Miss Beale. And, of course, Mrs. Taitt."

"Yes..." Thinking of Becky lying comatose upstairs, Martha's face creases with worry—which expression Dumont misinterprets.

"But let us not stir up painful memories, Miss Beale. Our party's discovery and the subsequent investigation have produced too many ugly associations for all concerned. In fact, my friend intends to close the main residence for a while. As the future ten-

ancy of the estate is unresolved, he believes it's advisable to keep
his distance and thus maintain an appearance of disinterest. For
my part, I'm glad he's free from an odious situation and can recom-
mence his legal suit when the murder trial reaches its resolution.
Now, shall we examine happier thoughts: the current offerings at
the Musical Fund Hall or the new production at the Walnut Street
Theatre. Our city boasts a plethora of entertainments; there's no
need to dwell on misery."

Martha nods. Her thoughts, however, refuse to leave *Point
Breeze*. "I've been told that Mr. Booth is excellent in the role of
King John," she offers before continuing with a seemingly offhand
"Did anyone learn who created such havoc in the *Compte's* library?"
A further query concerning the secret bed chamber is on the tip of
her tongue, but she doesn't mention it.

"Not that I know."

"Curious. It seemed so important at the time—"

"I suppose because our nerves were frayed—"

"Yes, that must have been it. Still, it was disconcerting to
find the room—the two rooms—in such disarray."

The words have no sooner left her mouth than a commotion
erupts in the foyer. Before a footman or the house's *majordomo* can
quell the interruption, or stifle the oaths that slice through the
closed doors, or persuade the interloper to depart, he throws open
the portals himself. How he missed the lurking Ella is a wonder,
but perhaps his eyes only see what they wish, and the hiding girl is
all but invisible to his outraged eyes.

"Mr. Taitt." There's anger as well as apprehension in Martha's voice, but she holds her own, squaring her shoulders as if
intent upon physically preventing him access to Becky.

"Where's my wife?"

"Safe, I'm glad to say. At least, as safe as possible given her injuries."

"Here, do you mean?"

Before Martha can respond, Dumont throws himself into the fray. "Mr. Taitt, what's the meaning of this uncouth behavior? Miss Beale and I heard shouting—"

"Come to woo the heiress, are you? Well, take care of what she may or may not promise you. My wife told me her heart was pledged elsewhere."

"Those are most unpleasant accusations, sir. As well as being obvious calumnies. Were it not for my admiration for my hostess—and your hostess, too—I would challenge you."

"To a duel, do you mean?"

"That is precisely my meaning."

"Well let's have at it, Dumont! By all means, let us have at it." Taitt stumbles as he speaks, revealing how unwell he is: a man who has slept poorly, dressed badly, and who gives off the acid odor of stale spirits and undigested food. "I'll send for my man and my pistols, and you can send for your brother—unless he's cowering inside, grieving for his lunatic wife."

"Mr. Taitt! That's quite enough." Martha's voice cuts across the room. "I order you to leave my house at once. Otherwise I'll be forced to summon the constabulary."

"And charge me with what, madam? Of desiring to see my lawful spouse? You're the one who should be queried by the authorities. You're the one who's holding a lady hostage—"

"How dare you, sir!" Dumont is truly angry now. His hands clench; his pinched lips go white. "How dare you insult Miss Beale." He strides toward Taitt who manages to elude him with the slippery grace of a man still partially drunk.

"You didn't know my wife was hidden here, did you, Dumont? While you engage in a private tete-a-tete, my wife is sequestered somewhere in this house, allowing her purported friend's twisted views on marriage to manipulate her. Well, let me tell you, madam, that as long as Becky remains under your roof, I will number the days against her. She has fled her conjugal duties and her child. I needn't explain to you what becomes of wives who deserts their homes and families, do I?"

"Your wife," Martha interrupts in a tone so full of fury that it seethes, "may not live to see your threats executed. The damage you caused by your heartless blows has produced severe inflammation of the brain. And you are aware of what becomes of husbands who murder their wives."

"My Becky?" At once, all bravery and bravado desert the man; he rocks backward on his heels while every spot of color drains from his face. "My Becky?" He stares at his hands as if they'd betrayed him. "This can't be true."

"The surgeon left not an hour ago. I've had need to send for him again."

"I must go to her—"

"Your wife is insensible, sir. Even if she weren't, I swore to her that I wouldn't allow you to come near."

William Taitt, so proud, so filled with his own superiority and invulnerability, merely gazes at his alien hands. The demon he envisioned while walking the waterfront seems to have invaded each finger, and he pictures black fur growing there instead of smooth white flesh. "She won't...She won't die, will she?"

"The surgeon could give no assurances as to her recovery." Martha maintains her rigorous pose. Although it's obvious to her how upset Taitt is, she remains implacable. "Will you leave of your own accord? Or must I have you bodily removed?"

Both Dumont and Taitt regard her with astonishment: Becky's husband because he has momentarily forgotten where he is; Dumont because he's startled at finding this seemingly gentle soul grown so merciless.

"She should be home with me," Taitt begins to mutter. "She must have had a bad fall, for I would never harm her. Upon my life, I wouldn't…An accidental stumble…Yes…Yes, that's what must have occurred." He frowns then ducks his head as if suddenly recalling the scene. "No gentleman would—"

"I must attend to my friend. The footman will see you both out." Martha walks to the open doors, but before departing she turns back. "Mr. Taitt, do not attempt to visit again. You're not welcome in this house. Good day to you, Mr. Dumont."

REMOVED FROM THE woes of Becky Grey Taitt, or Oscar Munder, or the Dumont brothers, and as far from the cosmopolitan confines of Philadelphia as imagination can fly, the public stagecoach with its uncommunicative female passenger journeys on. The night spent at a wayside inn has produced an artificial but lively camaraderie among the male voyagers, and they chat animatedly with one another as the carriage body buckets back and forth, causing them to bump into one another and then brush against their still-silent companion. Despite the lurching motion, the men's over-loud voices, the smells of hastily consumed breakfasts, and the sweaty odor of begrimed travel clothes, and of horse, she continues to gaze at the passing scene. Her attention is so rapt that she gives the impression of having never ridden in a vehicle before, which can't be true, of course. Or so the gentlemen assure themselves.

By means of coded phrases and knowing glances, they maintain a dialogue questioning and discussing her parentage, her motives, and her ultimate destination. The dry goods merchant who has been assiduously studying her attire is now convinced the woman is of lesser birth, a household servant who stole her mistress's clothes, perhaps; but the schoolmaster disagrees. He sees tragedy stamped in the dreamy face and decrees her the runaway wife of a wealthy manufacturer who abused and perhaps even imprisoned her. The tannery owner agrees with the first part of the verdict, but believes she was cast out of her husband's home due to an indiscretion. Thus, the haphazard quality of her dress, as he points out to his fellows. Clearly, she grabbed whatever came to hand and escaped before her husband's righteous indignation could become physical. The preacher deems her none of the former; it's obvious to him that she's mentally unstable, a person with unhealthy humors nesting in her brain. How she came to ride in the stagecoach, he doesn't know.

Only the ironmonger is unconvinced by the varying theories. But then, he's younger than the other men, and the game with which they idle away the time begins to feel repugnant to him. She's a person, after all, and a defenseless one, at that. While the men bunked together the prior night, she remained in the inn's one-room reception and dining hall, sitting on a bench with her back pressed against a wall.

He sneaks glances at her mouth, at her yearning eyes, at the dark curls that creep out from beneath her bonnet and experiences such sadness and loss that he can't help but speak.

"Where are you from?" he asks, by which he means, *Who are you, and how did you find yourself in these circumstances?*

The answer is straightforward. If she's surprised to be addressed, she doesn't show it. "From Philadelphia."

"And why are you traveling?"

"I'm going to Williamsport. And then further west, I think. The stagecoach is bound there, isn't it? Toward Williamsport?" A smile accompanies the response, a dazzling one, full of white teeth, pink lips, and promise.

"Yes," the ironmonger says. He leans close as if by doing so he could protect her from the innuendoes that have circled throughout the confined space.

"From your questions, I was afraid I was wrong. This is my first time in a public conveyance." She returns her gaze to the passing scenery, although the effect of her declarations has generated a change in the carriage that's impossible to ignore; and the others simply can't permit her to retreat into herself again.

"Have you family in the western part of the state?" the dry goods merchant asks, which elicits a cheerful laugh, but nothing more.

"Surely your loved ones must be concerned for your well-being: a lady journeying alone. Unless, of course, they're unaware of your travels." This is the school master speaking; his probing receives a polite but elliptical:

"Is the trip very long? Will we be forced to stop at other inns?"

"I don't have the answers, I'm afraid," the ironmonger tells her. "Perhaps these other gentlemen have more experience with—"

"Oh, no matter. What will be, will be." She smiles again then turns her back upon the group, sighing as she watches the road course past until silence envelopes her again.

Her rejection of their advances proves more nettlesome to the lady's companions than her prior abstraction. Their jovial mood is broken; save for the ironmonger, they feel as if a surly foreigner had been thrust amongst them. They raise their voices in gruff dispute and begin to talk of serious affairs: politics, Andrew Jackson's disastrous war upon the central bank, the labor riots that often hold Philadelphia in their thrall, and, of course, the sensational murder at the Bonaparte estate.

"I've heard rumors that it might not be the fellow's wife, after all. Some say it's the Frenchman's mistress," the tannery owner begins.

"Then who killed her?" the preacher asks.

"The grandson. On account of the estate's ownership being in limbo. She's the mother of the count's bastards, so they have legal claim to the property."

Only the ironmonger considers the rude language inappropriate in mixed company, but he's too young to reprimand his elders.

"Who else but the grandson has ready access to the place? That's what I'd like to know. Not a simple laborer. At least, not any I've employed. Besides, I've also heard that the grandson has hightailed it. And the woman in question hasn't been seen either. So there you have it. She could be dead. And he could have flown the coup."

"The devil, however, remains very much alive," the preacher declares.

"Amen to that, sir. It would take a fiend to saw off a person's head."

"They did that in France, though, didn't they? Lopped off the royal pates," the dry goods merchant observes.

"That was a kind of war, though" is the tanner's reply before he falls to musing about the gory scene and how he believes it must have affected those who discovered it. Because his trade deals in carcasses and blood, he spends some considerable moments verbally recreating the imagined details until he's satisfied that he has given the slaying sufficient ferocity. The name Beale rattles around the cabin, then Becky Grey Taitt, then Dumont.

The female passenger leaves her steady perusal of the scenery and turns to her fellow travelers. Disgust and dismay cause her to frown and bite at her lips. "What slaying is that?"

"Why, the one up at *Point Breeze*," the schoolmaster announces. "On the Bonaparte estate."

"Bonaparte...*Point Breeze?*" she echoes as her frown deepens. "A dead woman was found there?"

The tanner laughs. As he does, the odors of his trade escape his clothes and fill the coach with the stinging reek of lime and sulphur. "You must be the only resident of Philadelphia unfamiliar with the tale."

"But I heard you mention other names...not Bonaparte."

"The toffs who discovered the corpse," the ironmonger tells her. "And welcome to it, I say. Those types can use a bit of heartache and mayhem now and again. Make them understand how the rest of the world lives." His egalitarian approach fails to win her over; instead of another glowing smile, he's awarded an almost reproachful stare. "Trying to pin the blame on a simple man whose wife—"

"Remember, he did escape custody," the tanner interjects. "Honest fellows don't flee the constabulary, so he must have a nasty secret or two, even if he's innocent of slaughtering his wife."

"You're correct there" is the preacher's resonant addition to the discussion. "Honest men have no need to hide their faces when justice draws nigh."

"Tell me how he took himself out to that grand house if you're convinced he's evil," the ironmonger persists. "Him and his missus? Did they journey by private charabanc? Hire a public carriage? No, I'm thinking something is woefully amiss in this investigation—"

"The lady's head, for one thing," the schoolmaster quips at which the ironmonger rounds on him.

"This is all a jest to you educated gents, isn't it?" he demands. "A poor laborer whose wife was none too faithful. What does it matter if he killed her if it makes a spicy tale to enliven the evening? Those impoverished types are no better than alley dogs going at it; that's what you think, isn't it? Breed, whelp, eat their young and each other. Those are your grandiose opinions of men like me who work to keep you in your fine houses, aren't they? Well, I say Munder's been wrongly accused—"

"Munder?" the woman asks. Her voice is no more than a whisper.

"That's right. Oscar Munder. A mule spinner. It was his wife's body that was found at *Point Breeze*—"

"I need to leave the coach," she tells him in rising agitation. "I need to leave the coach. *Now.* Take me back to Philadelphia."

Chapter 24

Resurrected

CORNELIUS DUMONT'S HOME is draped in mourning black, the curtains drawn according to custom, the doors affixed with swags and wreaths indicating that a death has occurred. In the withdrawing room, the pier glasses are covered and funeral cloths darken what light and joy remains. The business of grieving is an exacting and expensive one, especially for persons of means and social stature. Cornelius loathes every convention: the luster-less leather gloves he must wear when outdoors, the long widower's weed affixed to his hat, the dyed crape and serge, the servants attired in black livery, the interior of his carriage transformed into sepulchral gloom.

"Why must we do this when Althea might be living, brother?" he demands.

"Because she's not, Cornelius. As you well know."

The unwilling widower turns his back on his twin, wandering toward the fireplace, then stopping when he spots an arrangement of inky feathers and purplish, preserved flowers spreading across the mantelpiece. He views the display with disgust, wrinkling his aristocratic nose as if the thing gave off a rank odor. He doesn't speak, so Charles continues:

"We must discuss the funeral. Until a fitting memorial service is arranged—"

"A church service for a suicide? Additional sacrilege? Is that what you're suggesting? I suppose you believe you can manipulate the priest as easily as you do me."

The response is icy self-control. "I'm suggesting the appropriate manner of grieving a beloved wife and sister-in-law whose sensibilities were too impaired to sufficiently protect herself from the elements."

"Charles of the silver tongue and the serpent's wiles. A perfectly fashioned speech, as always." Cornelius raises his hand as though intending to sweep the ghoulish floral display into the fire, but sudden languor overwhelms him and the gesture falters. "I should never have listened to you. Never. And now I'm damned. Both of us. Damned for all eternity."

In two rapid strides, Charles is at his brother's side. "Keep silent, man. You know what I told you." He grabs his twin's shoulder, but Cornelius shakes off the restraining grasp.

"I know what you told me. What you continue to tell me."

"Then be quiet!"

"Are you worried that God can hear us? You should be."

"The household is full of servants, in case you'd forgotten."

"But God doesn't need to listen to our conversations, does He? He knows what's in our sinful hearts. Even before the deed was done, He knew what you were conniving and what I was permitting myself to—"

"Stop this at once, Cornelius—"

"And I obeyed you! I obeyed you. Better the river than..."

Charles raises his fist and strikes his twin, slapping his cheek with enough force to startle him into silence, but not enough to inspire retaliation. The two countenances are so similar that Charles has an eerie sense of hitting himself, and his corresponding features also glow red.

"It was the Delaware that took your Althea's life. Remember what I've said."

Cornelius regards his sibling. His tortured expression rearranges itself until a kind of sickly belief in the impossible glimmers in his eyes. "Yes, the river..."

"Your dearest Althea who suffered so long from melancholia and other mental disorders...Repeat the words. Just as we rehearsed them."

"My dearest Althea who suffered so long..."

"And whose death often leaves you at a loss for rational speech."

"...for rational speech." The effort ends in a grunt of anguish. "She never trusted you. Never. She believed that you'd cast a sorcerer's spell on me. For my entire existence, she said. As if you were the sole child of our parents and I was nothing but an invented shadow."

The voice that responds is deceptively soothing and sweet. "A spell, Cornelius? And you a ghost rather than a man? Poor, poor Althea to have imagined such malevolence. And you, for having to withstand her eccentric accusations. Those unhealthy notions were due to her tendencies to mania. Come now, repeat after me: Her tragic tendencies to—"

"Mania..."

"That's correct. As well as other brain fevers and often sordid apparitions."

"Sordid..."

"And although you're presently overcome with sorrow—"

"Overcome..."

"You recognize that your dear...your darling Althea is resting in the bosom of the Lord."

At this reference to heaven, however, Charles's honeyed approach fails and Cornelius's wrath resurfaces, although now it's tinged with terror. "We'll be hanged for what we did, Charles. Hanged! The both of us."

"Silence, I tell you—"

"How did you imagine this lunatic plan would work? A sweet and gentle soul hacked apart, so that you and your frivolous party could *discover* a corpse conveniently left upon a hillside—"

"Cornelius, I warn you—"

"What if the other woman turns against you or refuses to keep away from the city? What if the payment wasn't sufficient—?" The questions disappear beneath another blow. Cornelius wilts under the attack, then gazes his twin with helpless yearning. "You promised the plan was foolproof, Charles. That's what you said. And the Beale woman would—"

"I'm afraid you're turning as lunatic as your late wife, brother. Perhaps laudanum should be prescribed in your case, too."

"Better that than become a replica of you." With that, Cornelius begins to weep; the tears course down his face, and he does nothing to brush them away. The noise of his sobs increase, filling the room and doubtlessly traveling through the shut door into the foyer beyond. Charles raises his own voice as if consoling the bereaved husband.

"Let me call your valet and order a calming potion. Your distress is too terrible to bear. Indeed, it seems to have induced a nightmare-like state, and I'm having trouble discerning the truth in what you tell me from the fantastical. I deeply regret that Althea escaped from the house; we all regret the tragic occurrence: every maid, every footman, the cook, your valet, everyone! However, we must face reality. Now, let us continue planning an appropriate testimony to your dear Althea's life—"

"You can't blame the murder on someone else," Cornelius hisses.

"I can and I will," Charles fights back in a tone both whisper quiet and hard as steel. "If the mill hand Oscar Munder proves too elusive a suspect, there's always Bonaparte's grandson and the *Compte's* mistress—who has conveniently vanished. Trust me in this, brother. I promised to make you a free man, and I intend to keep my word."

"This is the fire of Hell you're playing with—"

"When have I ever failed you, Cornelius? Tell me that. And now I have Lemuel Beale's daughter to aid me."

IT'S NOT UNTIL late the following day that Agnes returns. Exhausted from the hasty retracing of her route west, she creeps through the dark city, avoiding the busier thoroughfares and cleaving to the empty alleys. When she encounters another person, which she seldom does for the hour is approaching midnight, she ducks her head and hides her face. But who would recognize her? Or imagine the fine garb belonged to a onetime mill hand? Or that Oscar Munder's slaughtered wife had been miraculously resurrected? Perhaps her neighbors might be startled to find her among the living, but she purposely avoids the building where she once dwelt until she can be certain of entering it unseen. What she expects to accomplish by communicating with her husband, she doesn't know. But then, Agnes has never been one to ponder her actions.

The chamber she once shared with her Oscar is black as pitch when she silently pushes open the door and latches it behind her. And cold, too, she notes with dismay. No supper was prepared there that evening. From the dank and musty smell, she wonders how long it's been since any form of cookery has been attempted in the place. Thinking of her husband hungry and alone, her heart swells with pity. She tiptoes across the floor, which crackles with dirt—another sign of neglect. Imagining scuttling creatures darting over the boards or climbing the whitewashed walls, she doesn't dare strike a match, but blunders forward, bumping against a chair that previously stood elsewhere.

"Oscar? Are you awake?"

Two eyes regard her awkward approach, but they don't belong to Munder, and Agnes doesn't see them.

"It's your own girl, my dear. Come home at last."

There's no answer, and so she pauses, listening for a breath, a snore, a growl of resentment—or of welcome. "I didn't mean to stay away so long." This is a lie, however; Agnes never intended to return. At least, that was the pact she made. Gold coins for silence, for a new identity in another town, for dreams with which to build a different future. "Please tell me you forgive your little Agnes."

Again, there's no reply, although she begins to detect someone's presence. Shallow breaths, at first, and then a shape emerges upon the floor when her eyes become accustomed to the gloom. "Who's here?" Fear freezes her. *I wasn't supposed to reveal my true name to anyone! Not to anyone ever again! Oh, what have I done?* The fact that she's also broken her promise to keep distant from Philadelphia is momentarily forgotten. "It's not Agnes, I'm afraid, Oscar, but her...her sister...come to pay her respects to...to you...the widower. Please, if you're not the mule spinner, tell me where I might find him."

"Agnes Munder has no sister," the huddled mass on the floor announces. If she were less frightened, she'd realize the voice belongs to a child, and one who's as confused and startled as she, but she's too self-involved to notice.

"Who told you that?"

"Mr. Munder."

The age of her unknown interlocutor becomes apparent, although worries for her personal safety now take precedence; she edges back toward the door all the while wishing that she hadn't locked it after she entered. "You're a thief, aren't you? Come to steal a poor man's meager belongings while he's absent from his home. An evil little sneak, waiting to pounce."

"Better that than a runaway wife."

"I'm no such thing. I'm a relation from—"

"Didn't you just declare your name was Agnes?"

"I did not. You misunderstood. Besides, who are you to question me? A trespasser hiding in an honest man's room." She tries to take the high road, but she's growing more agitated by the moment. The impulse that propelled her out of the anonymous safety of the stagecoach seems horribly misguided, and she yearns to transport herself back again, like a winged angel or a fairy creature. "Speak, boy!"

"I'm Findal Stokes, Mr. Munder's piecer, and I'm paying him for the privilege of sleeping here." The tone is confrontational. Findal rises from his makeshift bed and lights a candle. In the cold air, the tallow-soaked wick sizzles before accepting the flame, then the light flares up spreading a garish white across the boy's face before subsiding to a muzzy glow that turns his skin yellow. Agnes notes the child's peculiar ears, his bedraggled clothes, and finally the jumbled state of the place that was once her home.

"Where's Oscar?" she asks.

"What does it matter to you where he's gone? He could be dead for all you care. And he will be, too. He'll be hanged if they catch him. On account of killing a female who didn't happen to die." Findal also inspects Agnes: the fine if mismatched attire, the muddy hems, boots begrimed, more dirt streaking her cloak. "Where did you go?" he demands. "How did you get that fancy gown?"

"Never you mind about that. I need to find Oscar. He can't be at the mill, can he?"

"He hasn't been at Quaker City for days and days. Kicked out, he was. Me and him both, but I connived my way back in after he was arrested for killing you. Which he clearly didn't..."

"So it's true, what those gentlemen told me." Agnes sinks into the chair. The dust from all the roads she's crossed rises from her clothes in a cloud. "A corpse without a head, they said, and Munder found guilty of the crime—"

"That's what I've been trying to explain, isn't it? They'll hang him on account of the mistake, and it's all your fault."

"Oh, but they can't...They can't. Oscar wouldn't harm a fly. Not even a bluebottle fly about to sully his porridge."

"Then you need to admit to the constable what tricks you've been playing so he can start a proper investigation."

Weary and heartsick though she is, Agnes leaps up at this suggestion. The chair clatters to the floor. "No. I cannot do that. I can't."

"*Won't* is more like it, missus." Findal is about to use a derogatory epithet but recognizes the woman's irrational faith in her own superiority and decides against language that could give her the upper hand. "You're selfish, you are; and Mr. Munder will die because you won't explain the mistake that's been made."

Poor, lost Agnes begins to weep. "Oh, what am I to do? I gave my word...And I don't want to lose everything I've won—not this nice dress and my pretty locket. Oh, how did this awful thing happen...?" The words trail away in hiccoughing tears.

Findal regards her with contempt. "Some rich gent handed you those things, didn't he? That's where you was on the nights when Mr. Munder and me were a-hunting you. Holed up with some snooty old fellow—"

"Not old. No indeed." The words are out before Agnes can stop them. She claps her hand over her mouth.

"You make me sick, missus. You do. Poor Mr. Munder, he was worried near to death about what had become of you. And then, when they found that body, and he went out to Bordentown." The narrative ceases while Agnes hangs her head and sniffles in despair. Every gilded dream she's ever clung to starts to evaporate like shiny soap bubbles popping in the wind.

At length, her tears dry and her spine straightens. She didn't begin transforming her life to be confounded by a boy. "Tell my Oscar I was here. But you mustn't blab to anyone else. Just him. Tell him I'll finagle some plan to save him. I will. I promise I will." The pledge made, she edges closer to the door. "I have some money now, and I. . .I can help him. But I must go now, for it isn't wise for me to linger."

"Not so fast, missus. You're not leaving until you reassure him yourself. He won't believe me—"

"No. You must tell him." Agnes smiles her lovely smile. "Please, Master Stokes. For me."

Findal is not to be won over by these wiles, however, and he lunges at the door just seconds before Agnes can reach it. "You'll not hurt him again. Coming around and pretending you want to make amends—"

"Why, Master Stokes, haven't I promised to help—?"

"The only aid you can give Mr. Munder is to confess the truth."

"I can't do that, don't you see? At least not at present, I can't."

"Then when?"

By now, the two are wrestling for control of the latch, and although Agnes is taller than the boy, he has justice on his side—

and loyalty, too. The battle turns one-sided; Findal takes the advantage.

"Please...let me leave, Findal dear. Haven't I said I'd aid poor Oscar?" She attempts another winning smile. "I could give *you* the money, if you'd like...to show my good faith."

The idea that his devotion can be bought so disgusts Findal that he drops his hand, which permits Agnes to make her escape. He hears her tearing down the stairs, and it takes him a long minute to comprehend her treachery. Then he takes to the stairs himself, softening his footfall when he realizes it might be more advantageous to slip after her unnoticed.

THROUGH THE STREETS the pair rush: Agnes heedless of everything except her flight; Findal keeping easy pace. He decides she looks like a madwoman as he watches her pelt along, for her bonnet has fallen from her head to jounce upon her shoulders, and her hair, loosed from its pins, flies wild and free. He's relieved there's no member of the night watch to apprehend her. Then he wishes there were and considers hallooing in her wake, only to decide against it. He'll discover more about her and her destination through craftiness and guile. Wherever she's going, he means to nab her there. This time he won't be tricked into releasing her.

At last they reach Callowhill Street and an expensive though inconspicuous residence that Agnes obviously recognizes. There she pauses to catch her breath, fidgeting back and forth from one foot to the other while she regards the house and mutters under her breath. Findal can see how torn she is about whether to remain or leave; several times she glances backward over her shoulder or gazes up the road and into the distance. At last, she appears to make a decision; she dashes up the front steps where she commences banging on the door while the boy sequesters himself nearby. "Please!

You must help me. I. . .My carriage was set upon by highwaymen after leaving here. . .awful ruffians who robbed me of nearly everything." No one responds; not a light stirs within.

Not a private bawdy house, Findal thinks, or the madam or one of her minions would have grabbed the weeping woman before she'd uttered three words.

"I only need a place to rest, and then I'll leave as I was instructed. I swear I will. I wouldn't be here at all if it weren't for a cruel trick of fate. Besides, he wouldn't want me to be forced to sleep out in the elements. Not after the many kindnesses he showed me."

A lamp glimmers inside. The door is opened. Findal spots a slatternly female blocking the entrance. She looks very severe, and her dressing gown has been hastily tied—proof to anyone who spots her that she considers the hour too late for hysterical visitors. She doesn't speak, nor does she permit Agnes to slip inside. In fact, she looks as if she'd like to knock the offensive woman down the steps and into the street.

Agnes, however, isn't deterred. "Just for this one night," Findal hears her cooing. "He doesn't need to know. . .I can make it worth your while. . .I have coins on me despite the attack, real silver and gold, not paper. . .He needn't learn where you got them. And you were good to me when I was residing here. Don't think I've forgotten."

But the guardian of the house remains obdurate. She listens to the beseeching speech in a manner that suggests she's deriving a good deal of pleasure from her position of power. Then, without ever uttering a single grunt of warning, she slams the door. The sound echoes as loud as a gun report in the still street, and Agnes all but tumbles backwards.

"That witch must be in on the plot, too," she grumbles. "Yes...of course...And she'll warn him that I've returned to the city, and then he'll..." Her hands reach upward to stroke her throat. "Oh, oh..."

She clambers to her feet, her eyes staring in all directions as if wondering where next to flee. Before she can take a step, however, the door behind her flies open, and the servant bounds down the stairs, grabbing Agnes and dragging her inside.

Chapter 25
Emil Rosenau's Verdict

NOT TWELVE HOURS after Agnes's reappearance and subsequent flight, Martha is seated in her dining room eating her midday meal. Or, rather, she's merely moving the food across the various plates the footman proffers. She can hear faint whispers emanating from the butler's pantry; without distinguishing individual words, she knows they relate to her lack of appetite. The vermicelli soup has been exchanged for baked mullets that in turn have been replaced by a roast loin of veal surrounded by mashed turnips and a garnishing of Brussels sprouts. The scents of nutmeg, rosemary, and thyme add perfume to the air, but Martha can only think of Becky lying upstairs in her darkened chamber unable to eat. She puts down a silver dinner fork, takes up a vegetable spoon, and then replaces it, sighing as yet another dish is removed uneaten.

Although there have been slight signs of recovery, she reminds herself; one set of leeches has been replaced by another, and Becky's fever appears to be diminishing. The problem continues to worry the surgeon, and his visits, as Martha has noticed, follow a foreboding routine: a minimum of words accompanied by numerous stern expressions and dour nods of his head. He strokes his beard and clears his throat as if in consultation with himself, then walks back down the stairs without offering a definitive prognosis, and so patient, sick nurse, and all within the household wait.

When the rhubarb tart (a favorite delicacy) appears, Martha can no longer keep up the pretense of dining. She lays aside her napkin and rises while the footman immediately pulls out her

chair. "I will attend to Mrs. Taitt," she tells him, "before I return
to the brokerage house."

Climbing the stairs, however, she hears a visitor being ad-
mitted; she turns, worried that Becky's husband is attempting to
gain access to his wife again. Looking down, however, she sees
Emil Rosenau. His expression appears as grim as the surgeon's.

"I'm glad to find you at home, Miss Beale. The gentlemen
in charge of the *Point Breeze* murder investigation seem determined
to thwart me at every turn. I must appeal to you again." Rosenau's
habitually restrained speech reveals a depth of exasperation that
Martha didn't believe he possessed. The word "gentlemen" is akin
to a sneer while the subtler "appeal" has a painful ring. This is a
man unaccustomed to requesting favors or having his authority
challenged.

"I'm sorry to hear of your travails, sir," she tells him as she
descends.

"Incompetents, the lot of them. The group in Bordentown,
as well as here in the city. Do you know, they informed me that
dissecting the subject was unnecessary? Despite the letter you'd
written as well as my obvious credentials. Laziness, I call it. Or in-
eptitude. Or both. If they had their wishes, we'd all turn blind eyes
to illegitimate activities, and then our metropolis would sink into
deeper sloughs of lawlessness and venality. Not one of the supposedly *honest* citizens would be safe while the dishonest ones would
slaughter each other—and anyone else—with impunity."

Martha doesn't argue with the physician's opinions. She's
well aware of the frustrations Thomas experienced when faced
with similar dilemmas.

"Sometimes I wonder if criminals aren't more evolved mentally than the men who hunt them. I don't mean in a scholarly
sense, but in an innate aptitude for cunning and perspicacity. Per-

haps I should begin examining the crania of policemen and comparing them to those of their prey. I might make startling discoveries about brain capacity."

Martha can't help but be amused at Rosenau's pique. The meditative gentleman she first encountered seems nowhere in evidence. She masks her feelings, however, and responds with a pensive nod.

"I won't burden you with the details of my work, Miss Beale. The language isn't appropriate to the feminine ear. I made a thorough investigation of the body in question and committed my findings to paper. Perhaps you—with your influence—can affect a judicious deliberation on my conclusions." So saying, he places a leather-clad notebook on the foyer table; the gesture is final, as if he wishes no further attachment to the work. Martha observes that he's still wearing his outer coat, though not his hat. "In brief, however, I'm certain the body is not Agnes Munder's. You suggested as much; your intuition proved correct."

Martha is almost too astonished to speak. "Dr. Rosenau... please...will you take some refreshment and explain what you mean?" She indicates that he should follow her into the withdrawing room, which he does, although with obvious unwillingness. His heavy coat remains fastened; the notebook is left on the table.

"I'm afraid I can't say more, Miss Beale, as the details aren't suited to a lady's sensibilities. I previously explained that dissecting the human body is deemed a mysterious—some might even say 'unholy'—business by those unfamiliar with the medical arts. For a thorough study of anatomy, however, the process of dissection is necessary. The cadavers of women are rarely examined. I once thought the anomaly was because there were fewer female subjects, slain criminals and the like, but I've come to realize it's simply a habit among doctors of medicine. On those relatively rare occasions when a woman is examined, the audience is exclusively male—due, naturally, to delicacies of language and so forth."

"What do you mean 'delicacies of language?' "

"Anatomical references...to a lady's body."

"But shouldn't any female be aware of those parts of the anatomy? Our anatomies, I should say."

"I assume so, Miss Beale, but the terms should never be discussed in mixed company."

Martha's frustration at this antique credo is beginning to show. "Then how on earth can the conclusions you've just delivered alter public opinion? If Munder is suspected of killing his wife, which he is, and the victim is another person entirely, your examination must be fully explained. And in the most concrete terms. Originally, you told me that without defining characteristics, you had no means of identifying the woman."

"Nor do I. I'm simply saying that the cadaver doesn't belong to Agnes Munder."

"But—"

"Let someone of the stature of Judge Craig read my notes, Miss Beale, and a barrister, as well. Their corroboration of my verdict is all that's required."

This time Martha doesn't suppress an irked sigh. "What if the case comes to trail?"

"It won't, if my assertions are accepted. Which any learned man would do."

"But public opinion—"

"Public opinion is easily swayed. Now, I will bid you good day. I don't regret the information I gained, but additional use of my time would prove a psychic hardship. Some men may forgive the dull-witted and inefficient; I am not one of them."

"Please tell me how can you be certain the dead woman isn't Munder's wife?" Martha persists.

Rosenau hesitates for a moment before speaking; he's obviously annoyed by his hostess's continued queries. "You indicated that the couple was childless, did you not?" He has no time to finish this discourse, because the footman enters to announce another visitor. Following immediately on the servant's heels is Charles Dumont, who strides into the room exuding health and bonhomie as if it were freshly applied cologne.

"Another intrusion, Miss Beale. Forgive me. Forgive me. I'll never learn manners, I'm afraid."

Martha turns to him; exasperation flits across her face, as it does Rosenau's. However, he doesn't disguise his feelings; a cold stare is leveled at the young dandy while Dumont apprises the older man with curious antipathy.

"You're the famed Emil Rosenau." The statement is devoid of awe; in fact, it borders on mockery.

"At your service, sir."

Surprised by this impolite exchange, Martha intervenes. "May I present Charles Dumont, Dr. Rosenau? And Mr. Dumont, let me be the first to apprise you of Dr. Rosenau's astonishing verdict. He recently finished an examination of the murdered woman we found at *Point Breeze*."

The two men shake hands, Rosenau's pale and papery fingers vanishing in Dumont's hearty grasp.

"What verdict is that, doctor?"

"My report is intended for use in a criminal investigation; it has no bearing here."

Watching the two men, Martha frowns; it seems to her that they might as well be arming themselves.

"Ah, then I shall wait until the mill hand's trial" is Dumont's offhand reply.

"Which will never happen, sir, because the deceased is not his wife."

"Of course she is," Dumont laughs.

"Then you must possess information I do not, sir."

"But he confessed as much."

"Did he? I seem to recall a more complex conclusion to that affair."

"I happened to learn that Agnes Munder was childless," Martha interjects, "when I visited the couple's home. Dr. Rosenau had just begun to explain that the body we—"

"Miss Beale, I did no such thing," he corrects with the same authoritarian tone he employed with Dumont. "There are matters I neither can nor will discuss with a lady. If you choose to read the report I left in the foyer, I can't prevent you. However—"

"Are you insinuating that the deceased woman you examined gave birth at some point? Is that it, sir? Is that the basis of this capricious theory?"

Rosenau's long nostrils flutter in disgust. "I bid you both good day."

"You can't possibly corroborate your hypothesis," Dumont insists. "A dead woman left out in the elements."

"There are means, sir, for medical professionals. If Miss Beale were not present, I might consider explaining them to you—"

"Come, man, Miss Beale's not made of wax. She won't melt, nor dissolve under the onslaught of medical terminology. I want to know how you came to this fantastic conclusion."

"There is nothing fantastic—or capricious—about it." Rosenau's voice is ice.

"Oh, you 'bone collectors' and your games," Dumont sneers. "Resurrectionist men, all of you. Hiding behind a Hippocratic Oath. Hypocrisy, I call it."

"I take that amiss, sir!"

"Mr. Dumont, please...I asked Dr. Rosenau for his expertise in this matter—"

"You asked him?" A surprising amount of vehemence reverberates through the words. "Whatever for?"

"Miss Beale wished to see justice carried out," the doctor declares, and Martha again finds herself reduced to spectator in the peculiar battle.

"For a homicidal mill hand?"

"For a laborer wrongly accused of a crime."

Dumont sneers. "What nonsense! Of course the woman was the fellow's wife. Who else could it be? A female well known for her infidelities, I needn't remind you. A vile situation, all around, but one this city should forget as quickly as possible. And you, sir, with claims of motherhood you won't or can't confirm..." He shakes his head. "Don't think I don't know how you fellows work. Cutting off the legs—and other appendages—of your victims. Or your penchants for male and female body parts to add to your repulsive collections—"

"Please, Mr. Dumont," Martha interrupts, but he's only just started his attack.

"Did you take the bladder and reproductive organs, too? Marred, though they must have been if this mysterious lady produced a brood of offspring as you insist—"

"Mr. Dumont, please—"

"I had a friend whose sensibilities were warped when studying under anatomical professors like you, Rosenau. He told me the fellows made a regular party when a female cadaver—"

"Listen to your hostess, sir, and cease your odious comments at once," the physician orders. Then he bows to Martha. His polite expression is the thinnest veneer, as if Dumont's his boorish interrogation was her fault. "Good day, Miss Beale."

The moment Rosenau departs, Dumont again addresses Martha. His manner has lost none of its belligerence, although now it's taken on a protective quality. "I hope you didn't pay an exorbitant sum for that quack's supposed expertise," he says, but she's too angry to reply.

"I see I've put my foot in it again, haven't I? I seem to spend an inordinate amount of time apologizing to you, Miss Beale. I do so now and ask you to forgive my ill-mannered outburst. It was inexcusable to attack one of your guests. Unfortunately, I have personal experience with those damnable dissection practices. The friend I mentioned quit his studies altogether rather than perform the ghoulish work…I know you meant well. How could you not have? But, you see, it's barbarous what those fellows do in the name of science. 'Anatomical specimens,' they call those poor, dead souls. A person isn't a specimen, Miss Beale. We're not insects or examples of fungi affixed to a scientific display. We're God's creatures."

"So are insects, Mr. Dumont" is Martha's weary reply. She can't bring herself to be more cordial or to berate him. "I ask that you leave me now. I have pressing business."

"Of course. Of course." He opens his arms in a sign of penance allowing Martha to notice a rust-colored streak on his right cuff. Seeing her eyes on the stain, he lowers his hands. "My normally meticulous valet cut me while shaving me this morning. It was partly my fault, I'm afraid, for moving into my brother's house and causing additional burdens upon the servants. Thus, the gory result of a home in turmoil!" He shakes his head at his own folly.

"Fool that I am, I tried to stem the blood with my shirt and then refused to change it. So not only am I wearing dirty linen, but I've also besmirched your noble intentions. I bow my head in sorrow, Miss Beale. If the constabulary ever apprehends Oscar Munder, let me promise you that I'll make certain he knows who his guardian angel has been."

With that he departs, and Martha waits in the withdrawing room until she's certain the house is empty of visitors. Then she again prepares to visit Becky. Walking past the foyer table, she notices Rosenau's notebook is missing. Her lips purse with disapproval. *All that palaver and sword-rattling for nothing,* she thinks. *Why did he bring the thing here if he didn't desire my involvement? Didn't he request my help? And Dumont, what a bother he is with his high-handed mistrust of the medical profession. Oh, these men!*

Chapter 26

Fate

BECKY SUFFERS. Of course she suffers, battered as her body has been. But her husband also labors under sensations of grief and pain. And rage, too, although his anger is focused inward and has tunneled so deep into his soul and psyche that it has created holes and hollowed-out courses like ant passageways carved in dirt.

He hates himself, berates himself, then mourns that he could be so misunderstood. Hasn't he provided the best for his wife and child? Isn't he admired within the community? Doesn't he always execute his duties well? Manage his church's financial affairs, serve as a pillar of respectability, dispense prudence and wisdom? Aren't there scores of laborers at his southern plantation who depend upon his rigorous leadership, as well as neighbors there who applaud him for his firmness? And doesn't he possess wealth and the ability to increase it daily? Shouldn't he be acknowledged as an exceptional human being?

The numerous testimonials weave through riddled emotional soil, however. When William Taitt walks or sits, climbs into his bed, or even turns his head to survey a different landscape, all manner of inward implosions are liable to occur, altering his opinions and his behavior in a moment.

And so he drinks to avoid the noise of his inner ravings and the echoes of his inner fears. Wines and fortified spirits conjure up for him genies as beneficent and forgiving as gods or perfect mothers. When those illusory spirits evaporate and reality opens black and cavern-like below him, he must seek out the bottle again. Despair sits and sips beside him.

Leaving his gentleman's club late in the evening two days after being expelled from Martha Beale's house, good humor blessedly reigns. He decides the night is far from spent and embarks upon a stroll to the Northern Liberties in order to sample the feminine wares in a fancy house there that recently opened its doors for business.

The air is dulcet; the scent of spring is upon the breeze, and the city streets all but shout out rebirth and joy. Or so it seems to Taitt. He's none too clear-headed, however; he hums to himself with delight, and his gait begins to match the tune: a private dance enacted in his mind.

He walks northward, leaving behind the familiar bawdy houses on Lombard and Locust Streets that he's been accustomed to frequent. They seem sordid to him now, their over-perfumed receiving rooms unhealthy and vaguely sinister. A new place and new female companions is precisely what he needs. A Miss Sarah Zeisse owns such a shop on Wood Street near Seventh; her establishment's entry in *The Guide to the Stranger*, the well-thumbed publication left in all the city hotels, lists the place as boasting a "fine address," where "a genteel gathering of lovely and accomplished ladies play musical instruments, lift their lilting voices in song and otherwise entertain their gentlemen patrons while more discreet negotiations are arranged." Taitt thinks the manse sounds like heaven itself.

He crosses Mulberry Street, passing the Friends' Meeting house sitting stolidly within its own park, a testament to Owen Biddle and the other English Quakers who produced structures that gave shape to the city. At other times, Taitt might be remind-

ed of his own ancestors and feel the weight of their reproach as if
their scowls had been transmuted into the building's staid walls.
Tonight, he saunters by; he whistles, too, and smiles at this imper-
tinence.

Then on toward Sassafras Street where equestrian competi-
tions are held—"Race Street," as it's dubbed by the wags. Taitt
murmurs the name several times; he likes its hiss and its hint of
decadence. Wagering isn't for respectable citizens. With a smug,
self-congratulatory nod, he also notices that the architecture is becoming more garish as he journeys further from his normal haunts.
Gone are the dental moldings and Greek-inspired columns; in their
place, wood tracery clings to cornices and eaves like lacework cut
from paper. Pausing, he considers how odd it is that the pragmatic,
German burghers—for these are the owners—would build homes
that resemble images in a child's illustrated book. Then he decides that it must be the wives who dictate the outlandish designs.
He pictures well-dimpled *fraus* bestowing bumptious gratitude for
their new stained-glass windows, the peaked lintels, the roof-lines
that jut upward at angles as steep as mountains; he wishes his own
marriage consisted of cooing adulation and pretty handfuls of
warm flesh. The thought fades with his next step, however. Late
nights for William Taitt aren't conducive to lengthy meditations.

By this time, he has reached Wood Street where he begins
ambling west to the desired address. Finding it, he's perturbed to
see a crowd of young rakes gathered outside the door. They're so
colorfully attired and wear so many of the latest styles in gentlemen's attire that they look like actors hired to promote a tailor's
new designs. Although Taitt prides himself on his choice of garments, he feels old and outmoded in comparison. He crosses the
street in order to avoid the throng and decides to return when the
group has dispersed. The noisy level of the men's inebriated laugh-

ter indicates their evening's amusements are drawing to a close, but Taitt has no wish to mingle with them, not even for the time it would take to enter the house. If the watch is summoned to disperse the rowdies, he doesn't want to jeopardize his good name.

But where to venture in the meantime? Not south again, certainly. Nor west, nor east. He has no desire to prowl back and forth along Wood Street until the Zeisse establishment is clear.

So fate takes William Taitt to Callowhill Street, where by remarkable coincidence he spots a man toward whom he bears a special grudge. His sunny mood melts like ice on a hot day, leaving a black stain in place of what was once sparkle and glitter. "You! Dumont!" he yells out. "A word, sir!" He doesn't stop to consider the lateness of the hour, or whether his angry shouts will rouse the neighbors, or even why Charles Dumont is on Callowhill Street. "Sir! Halt, I say!"

Whether or not Dumont hears Taitt calling to him is uncertain. He ducks his head and enters a house on the northern side of the street while Taitt strides across the cobbles, convinced that the man is avoiding him.

"Hiding from me, are you?" he bellows. "As well you should after the misery you've caused my wife. And me. My fine name connected to a heinous crime. Come out, man, and face me: gentleman to gentleman." He tries the door, but finds it's locked. "Dumont! Show yourself at once!"

The house remains shuttered; not a lamp is lit; not a soul stirs within. Another person might wonder if a mistake had been made, but not Taitt. Righteousness is on his side. He pounds upon the wood and screams out oaths and threats. The peace he recently experienced has become a rage he's incapable of stanching. Charles Dumont is to blame for all his woes: his loss of reason, his wife's

injury, this late-night escapade, his drunkenness. "Coward," he
roars. "Coward."

The noise eventually alerts a member of the night watch
who approaches the irate but obviously well-dressed gentleman
with trepidation. "A bit late for visiting, isn't it, sir?" He keeps
his distance, for Taitt looks capable of physical as well as verbal
assaults.

"I tried to murder my wife because of this knavish rascal."

The watch frowns. Despite the slurred speech, the word
"murder" leaps out. "That's a powerful accusation, sir," he says.

Taitt, however, has already forgotten the interruption. He
commences kicking the door. "Dumont, face me at once!"

"I'm afraid you have the wrong residence, sir," the watch in-
forms him. "No one of that name here. So, seeing how you made
an honest mistake, perhaps you'd like to permit the owner to have
his rest—"

"I saw him entering. Not ten minutes ago. Charles Dumont
who caused me to—"

"I don't know who that would be, sir, but it's not the inhab-
itant—"

"It is, I tell you!" Taitt rounds on the watch who steps backward several paces, trying to decide whether to run for assistance
or remain with a person who's clearly laboring under dangerous
delusions. The only thing that keeps him in place is the word murder. Perhaps, he thinks, here's a clue to that peculiar slaying on the
royal gentleman's estate. Maybe the laborer who was nabbed and
then escaped is innocent as he claimed. Maybe there's a reward.

"But you didn't kill your wife, did you, sir?"

"I don't know," Taitt howls. He turns his back on the watchman, gesticulating wildly. "I don't know. These hands which you
see...these hands..."

The watch's eyes grow very wide. He's not a youth, nor is he new to his position, but his brain is slow to process information, and so he appears less experienced and more naïve than he is. "It is *Point Breeze* you're referring to, isn't it, sir?"

"Of course" is the surly reply. "She was there, wasn't she?"

"You would know that, sir. I wouldn't."

Taitt glares at the man. "Imbecile," he snarls. He begins to stalk away, but the watch, naturally, can't permit this challenge to his authority.

"I must ask you to come with me, sir."

"Whatever for?"

"I think you know, sir."

"I most certainly do not." By now, Taitt has all but forgotten what brought him to Callowhill Street; what he does recognize, though, is insubordination. He squares his shoulders, staring down at the watch who continues to stand in the street's gutter. "And you can go to the devil if you believe that I'll obey the likes of you. I'm William Taitt, you fool." He begins marching away, forcing the watch to scamper after him. Not for anything will this nervous guardian of the peace physically accost the larger man, but he knows he mustn't let him escape.

"You, sir. Hold, I say. I speak for the law."

Taitt's pace increases, so does the watchman's.

"Stop, sir. In the name of the law."

The strides stretch out; the watchman scurries behind. "Mr. William Taitt. Halt, I tell you."

Who can say what causes Taitt's reaction to the orders: bewilderment at finding himself in an unknown corner of the city, incredulity that his good name is being sullied, or simple panic? Whatever the impetus, he begins to run in earnest, pelting along with a scared, jerky motion that makes him look guilty of any number of crimes.

The watch runs, too, calling to his fellow guards for support and yelling Taitt's name over and over.

Dawn is nearing, however. Many members of the night watch have crept home early. Their daytime colleagues aren't yet arisen, nor are the drovers and farmers who populate the city's morning hours yet in evidence, for they would certainly join the chase.

Pursued and pursuer fly along until the watchman, because of his smaller stature, must stop to catch his breath. Taitt disappears before his eyes.

BY MIDDAY, the rumor mills have already produced "reliable" witnesses who claim they saw the watchman's attempt to do his duty; added to those questionable accounts is the fact that Taitt fled when queried about *Point Breeze*.

The penny press accepts the hearsay as gospel. "Patrician Butcher: Noblesse or Bleed" is one of the headlines.

Chapter 27

Bone to Bone

NATURALLY, OSCAR MUNDER soon learns the peculiar story about William Taitt. Still dodging from hiding place to hiding place, too fearful to attempt returning home, he can't help but hear newsboys hawking broadsheets and issues of the penny presses, or the excited commotion the sordid tale generates. It seems that Agnes's name and that of the diabolical aristocrat are on everyone's tongue; he can't round a corner or sidle through a back alley without overhearing theories about the attempted arrest on Callowhill Street.

As speculation regarding Taitt's motives and methods builds, the theories grow more and more lascivious. Too weary and malnourished from his vagabond life to question whether the reports are correct (the penny presses are notorious for their errors), he latches onto what facts he gleans and finds they replicate others he already knows. He recollects a woman named Taitt being a member of the elegant party who discovered the headless corpse; Dumont and Beale were there, too.

By now, the former mule spinner can't remember that he'd claimed the body wasn't his dearest wife's; he only recalls clutching the mantle and dress and sobbing into the blood-streaked fabric. Thus, William Taitt becomes the ogre who slaughtered—no, *butchered*—his Agnes. What other unspeakable acts the villain may also have committed, Munder cannot, will not, consider.

The fact that his wife is alive is information he doesn't possess.

MARTHA IS EQUALLY UNAWARE of this fundamental shift in circumstances. Although Rosenau insisted the dead woman wasn't Munder's wife, like Oscar, she has no means of knowing that Agnes returned to Philadelphia or that someone close to her household actually met her. And chased after her, too, hoping she'd explain her heartless disappearance.

As to William Taitt, the reason for the attempted arrest as well as his subsequent flight becomes immaterial to her, because the hue and cry raised over his reputed depravity makes her examine her own memories of him.

Weren't there early hints indicating his potential for brutality? Didn't Becky show obvious signs of unhappiness in her marriage? Didn't she suggest that her husband was in the habit of leaving their home for extended periods? Martha thinks back. *When did I learn that piece of information? Was it the result of one conversation or several? And what precisely did Becky say—or infer?* The more Martha recalls, the more apparent her friend's distress becomes. *The supposed fall that resulted in those livid bruises the day of the ill-fated picnic, her terrified dreams later that night, and finally the beating that forced her to flee her home.*

Pondering, Martha berates her lack of perception. Blame settles in her chest, and she prays more fervently that Becky's brain fever will abate. Martha believes she has much to regret and countless apologies to make.

In the meantime, she recognizes that she has work to do. Everyone in her household must be warned that Taitt and his fugitive status must not be discussed in the patient's presence. Insensible though she appears, Becky could improve at any moment. Besides, Martha has peculiar notions concerning dreamlike states. Perhaps her theories are the result of experiences with mesmerism and somnambulism, or maybe they're produced by a mind accustomed to solitary meditations; whatever the cause, she's convinced that sleep or other trancelike conditions leaves the psyche vulnerable to suggestion. How else does a tightly-wrapped sheet turn into a shroud or the pressure of a pillow become choking fingers grasping your throat? How to explain intuition or seemingly irrational fears? How is it possible to fly when no human is thus equipped? Men and women aren't angels, after all.

Her second task is to convince Emil Rosenau that he must swallow his pride and deliver the results of his dissection procedure himself.

"I CANNOT DO THAT, Miss Beale."

Martha stands at the foot of the stairs leading into Rosenau's exhibition gallery and consulting chambers. The physician has arisen in order to receive this unexpected guest, although his posture indicates that he's not pleased with the interruption or likely to permit the visitor to linger. He doesn't offer Martha a chair. Nor does he instruct the footman who conducted her downstairs to light extra lamps. The rooms lie tomb-like in their shadows. The ghostly skeletal figures gathered in every corner do nothing to dispel the gloom; in fact, they increase the lugubrious effect.

"Why not, doctor?"

"I believe I explained that continuing with this unpleasant business would prove too taxing to my mental condition."

"You did, sir, but unless you reveal your—"

"That's precisely what I indicated you should do on my behalf." Obduracy hovers around the man; he seems as hardened and inflexible as the bones around him.

"I can't be as persuasive as you, sir. And now, with William Taitt—"

"If he's innocent of a crime, he has nothing to fear."

"In theory, I agree with you, sir, but the truth—"

"What is deemed 'true' can be elusive, Miss Beale. You requested my aid. I provided it. Willingly, I might add. For my labors, I was insulted when at your home; my years of scientific experimentation were derided. That is my understanding of the 'truth.' If you can walk down those stairs without apologizing for Charles Dumont's egregious behavior, it seems to me that you possess a different attitude toward reality."

Justified though Martha realizes Rosenau's pique is, her temper rises. "Mr. Dumont is the merest of acquaintances, sir. I'm neither responsible for his actions, nor in a position to atone for them. I cannot unmake a nettlesome situation."

"Then I can only repeat my injunction that you inform a judge and barrister of my verdict yourself."

Martha looks around the room: the anatomical models fixed in their sentinel positions, the rows of crania staring sightlessly forward. She has an image of the dead waiting for life to be restored to them, like the dried bones left in the valley in the prophet Ezekial's vision. "Sir, when last we met, you expressed a desire to see justice triumph—"

"That was your wish I was interpreting, Miss Beale, not mine. I'm a scholar of science. I cleave to the objective opinion rather than the subjective. The 'vaguaries of the soul' as you put it—"

"But don't these…people speak to you, sir? Don't you feel their histories? Yes, I recall you explaining many here committed crimes, but what of their unknown victims?"

"These are not living humans, madam, waiting for sinew and flesh to reattach itself; instead, they're a collection of carpus and jawbone, ischium and tibia, and so forth. As to 'victims,' let us not commence upon that subject. What causes a man or woman to murder? Is it destiny? Is it the Devil's work? I believe not. Cruelty is a taught condition, just as goodness and mercy are also. These long-dead villains gathered here most certainly suffered at the hands of someone else—and when they were too young to recognize or escape the aberrant behavior."

"I didn't come here to quibble with you, Dr. Rosenau—"

"Then pray, do not."

Martha ceases speaking. It seems to her that the deceased in the chamber are urging her toward action. She turns her head, wondering if she'll catch some ghostly movement, but, of course, she does not. "You refuse to reveal what you know." The words form a statement; the tone is level.

"No. I readily submit my verdict. Although not in person— as I stated."

Martha releases a sigh that signals both exasperation and defeat. "Very well. If you supply me with your notebook, I'll endeavor to make certain the proper people examine it."

"I left it in your house, Miss Beale, on the table in your foyer. Now, I must wish you good day. You interrupted my studies."

RETURNED TO THE STREET, Martha's brain whirls. Rosenau's notebook was not on the foyer table after she'd bid Dumont and the doctor adieu. If she's to believe him, which she does, that can only mean that Charles Dumont took it. But why? Everything he said indicated that he found the physician's theories and practices odious in the extreme. To delve into the records of a so-called "bone collector" would be an abomination to him.

The fact remains, however, the report detailing of the corpse's examination is gone.

A verse from *The Book of Ezekial* enters her mind: *And the breath came into them, and they lived, and stood up upon their feet.*

What does this mean? she asks herself. *How can the words of a He-brew prophet have bearing on this situation?* Frustration quickens her foot-steps; she frowns. *If Thomas were here, he'd understand*—The thought isn't even completed before loss overtakes her, and the brisk stride ceases. *When good comes from thinking about him now? Or wondering what conclusions he'd draw regarding Rosenau or Charles Dumont's private motives. Thomas will never be able to counsel me again. Or love me, either.*

Eyes blurring as she gazes at the brick walk below her, she eventually moves forward, stepping down into the street proper. A fully-laden omnibus is speeding toward her although she's un-aware of its proximity just as she's unaware of all other surround-ings. The horse is pulled up short; the coachman swears; several female passengers scream out in alarm; their gentlemen attendants shout imprecations upon the oblivious Martha who passes safely to the opposite pavement, her head bowed, her mantle clutched close to her body.

Or love me, either... her heart repeats while her reasonable brain interjects a disillusioned: *If Charles Dumont took the notebook, what dif-ference does it make to me? I have no business associating myself with this problem. Why should I fret about William Taitt, or the dead woman's identity, or whether some unfortunate mill hand receives fair treatment? Aren't there predicaments clos-er to hand that demand attention? I should concentrate my energies on ensuring Becky's recovery.*

Martha continues on her way, resolving not to set foot in the Dumonts' household again, or demand an explanation for Rosenau's missing work, or further engage herself with the two brothers. Instead, she'll sit at Becky's side and nurse her. *My one remaining friend*, she thinks. Self-pity wells up inside her like a surg-ing tide. *My one friend.*

☙❧

ELLA HAS BEEN waiting for Martha's return. Anxiety has propelled her upstairs and down: down into the kitchen and pantries where she got in the servants' way and was ordered to leave or up to the day nursery where *Mademoiselle* Hédé admonished her for fidgeting and told her to depart if she couldn't attend to her lessons or permit Cai to study his schoolwork in peace. "The blood of springtime is in your veins," *Mademoiselle* cautioned. "If you cannot keep your mind from wandering, then find a different part of the house for your daydreams."

It's not daydreams or the blood of springtime, Ella wanted to respond. *It's real blood. From a real person.* But she didn't; she simply left, roving around and around while she pondered what she'd just discovered.

How to explain her latest secret encounter with Findal Stokes? How to justify the meeting or describe her sly and wrongful behavior? If she doesn't, will anyone believe this strange new tale? She mutters and mumbles, the sounds full up with frustration and woe. *The lady Agnes was alive when she was supposed to be dead, but now she's really been murdered—at least, that's what Findal said. And he thinks the Dumonts are responsible. No, he's certain they are. And he should know; he followed Oscar Munder's wife to a house and saw one of the brothers enter it.*

This, however, isn't the proper approach. Ella knows her adoptive mother will immediately admonish her for consorting with wicked characters and that the information will remain unspoken while a lecture on proper conduct is delivered. Isn't that what happened before? It did no good to argue that Findal wanted to warn them about the mule spinner, that he feared for their safety.

Her mouth pinched with worry, Ella huffs through the house: her footfall dragging up the servants' rear steps or hurrying down the main staircase when she imagines hearing the entry door open. The maids she passes murmur a pleasant "Miss Ella," to which she answers a distracted "Good morning." At other times, she'd stop to talk or maybe help clean the gilt picture frames with an onionskin broth or polish the fire irons with a paste of emery-powder and turpentine. She likes those homely tasks, loves the now-familiar aromas, and talking with the maids; above all, she enjoys the sense of belonging.

Which draws her back to Findal and his odd notions of home and kinship. Although she hasn't criticized his devotion to the mill hand, she does question it. His loyalty makes her envious, too. She wishes someone would defend her to the death.

Her brooding ceases as the front door opens in earnest; Ella hears Martha's voice. Finding herself on the second-floor landing, she flies down the stairs, gripping the banister so she can leap the steps two at a time.

"Mother! Findal said—" The words are out before she can stop them. It does no good to clamp her lips shut because her adoptive mother is already scowling and yanking hard on the ribbons that tie her bonnet.

"Didn't I forbid you to talk to that boy?"

"You did, but—"

"Rules are rules. They're not made to be treated cavalierly."

"I understand that, Mother—"

"They're also for your own good," Martha continues as if Ella hadn't interrupted. She hands her mantle to the footman; her shoulders are rigid and lordly. Knowing for certain that the dreaded lecture is on the way, Ella stifles a sigh.

"I know, but—"

"Do you remember last autumn when a young lady vanished from her home? Do you remember all the talk about kidnapping and ransom monies?"

"Yes."

"Good. Now, I don't want to frighten you, but you must be cautious."

"I am."

"Not if you hold conversations with a street urchin."

"But he said—"

"I don't care what he may or may not have told you, Ella. I mistrust the boy's motives. I know I sound harsh; I intend to be harsh. If any hurt befell you, I would never forgive myself."

This time Ella does sigh. How on earth is she to divulge Findal's theory if she can't mention his name? "Mother, you know the dead lady you and Mrs. Taitt and Mr. Dumont found at *Point Breeze*—"

Martha has ceased listening, however. Instead, she's holding aloft an envelope containing a letter from Charles Dumont. Opening it, she scans the message. "More apologies," she mutters. "The man dresses himself in 'sorry' as if it were worsted wool. Now he wants to return the pilfered notebook. Where is his common sense?" She crumples up the missive, then turns to the footman, inquires after Mrs. Taitt, and begins climbing the staircase. Halfway to the landing, she looks back at Ella who tries again to explain what Findal told her.

"It's about Mr. Dumont—" she begins, but Martha wants no further references to the brothers.

"You must guard against excessive noise, Ella. We have an ill guest in our home. I know you have an exuberant nature, but you should curtail running up and down the stairs for the time being. Spring isn't an easy season in which to be demure and docile, but you can do anything you set your mind to."

"But, Mother—"

"I'm sure what you wish to say can wait. I plan to spend the afternoon with our patient, and I'm sure you've got schoolwork to finish. When you take your evening tea, we can talk.

◕◕

THE PROMISE IS FORGOTTEN, however. On entering Becky's chamber, Martha is immediately aware of a change in her breathing. Beneath her closed lids, Becky's eyes flutter, and the tips of her fingers quiver; her skin feels cooler, but damp. The nurse considers the situation perilous. The surgeon is summoned, but before he can arrive, a miracle occurs. Becky opens her eyes. She looks at Martha, surprise at first flits across her countenance; a labored comprehension replaces the initial reaction.

"Ah," she murmurs before her eyelids again close. As they do, the body beneath the sheet and counterpane relaxes. The rigid outline of fear and fight gives way to peaceable sleep.

"Becky dear," Martha says as she draws a chair near the bed and takes the limp fingers in her own. "You're safe and well—and welcome—in my home. My house is yours as long as you wish it."

The response is a sigh. Martha knows her message has been understood. She lightly strokes her friend's hand. "Doze as long as you wish, and awake hungry and order a feast prepared. I'm very glad you're here."

◕◕

THE REMAINDER OF THE DAY sees the Beale household reenergized. A calf's-foot broth is set simmering; rice-milk with finely minced suet is boiled; an invalid's lemonade is produced; barley gruel and beef tea are commenced. Becky will want for nothing. Each time she wakes, the delicacies are urged upon her; the merest sips, at first, that grow into teaspoonfuls. A pillow is propped behind her back, raising her body slightly. She nibbles the rice-milk, drinks the barley gruel, and drifts again into a wholesome slumber. Martha never leaves her friend's bedside. Naturally, there's no mention of Taitt, and when Becky suddenly asks about Baby, she's informed that her son is well and thriving. Martha even assures her that she's seen the child herself, although this is a lie.

Dozing atop a chaise while the patient also sleeps, Martha experiences an odd semi-dream. It's so real, however, that she becomes convinced the vision is true: Two spiders cling to an upper corner of the chamber; they're preternaturally large and they hang from their webs in a sinister fashion. Martha and the nurse both take up brooms in order to dislodge them, but before the women can commence their attack, they notice the webs are empty.

"We'll have to move Mrs. Taitt," the dreaming Martha commands.

No sooner have the words been uttered than a spider jumps down from the door jam, flying straight at her. It's now grown as large as a rat. Grabbing a blanket, she captures the horrid thing whereupon it commences to squeal and hiss and produce a noxious stench. She stabs it repeatedly through the covering, which makes the hisses increase in intensity and volume. A leg emerges, then another. Lashing Martha's flesh, they emit venom so painful she drops the evil bundle.

"We must move Mrs. Taitt," the sleeping Martha cries out. "She's in danger." Leaping to her feet, and simultaneously waking, she finds the nurse standing in front of her.

"If you wish, madam, although she's resting so serenely now, I'm not certain it would be advisable to disturb her."

Caught between the dual worlds of illusion and reality, Martha can't relinquish her horrifying image. "But the spiders—"

"Oh, madam, your staff is extremely conscientious; I can't imagine finding any vermin here."

"Two of them," Martha persists. "And both poisonous."

"If you permit me, madam, you must have been dreaming. You've had an arduous day, and that chaise can't be comfortable. Why don't you retire to your own chamber? I'm accustomed to these unusual hours, you are not."

"No, I will make my makeshift bed here" is the quiet reply, which Martha does, although she watches every shadow flitting over the floor until she truly sleeps.

Chapter 28
Another Sunday

AS IS HER CUSTOM, Sunday morning brings Martha to services at St. Peter's. The first of April seems especially beneficent, for not only has the weather turned unseasonably mild but because of Becky's continuing recovery. Walking south and east into Washington Square with Ella and Cai, Martha experiences a kind of grace as if the sun had decided to bless her and the children with its rays. Patches of daffodils that yesterday appeared stunted and drab now display gold petals while new leaves unfurl, greening the air surrounding each tree. Warmth, like a human embrace, spreads along Martha's shoulders and back. She takes the children's hands and swings them back and forth. Were it not a Sunday, and were there not somber figures nearby, the three might laugh aloud.

The mood vanishes the moment they pass through St. Peter's doors. Martha's accustomed to stares, and whispers, too. Adopting children of questionable lineage and histories has garnered her much disapproval, especially when one child is mulatto and another rescued from a bawdy house. "Iconoclastic" is the kindest critique; if Martha weren't a Beale, the denunciations would be severe. Today, however, it's not a basilisk frown or two that mars the pleasant moment, but Ella's reaction as she spots Charles and Cornelius Dumont beckoning to them to join their pew.

"I don't want to sit with him," she says in a frightened whisper. "Neither one of them." She drags at Martha's hand as if she intends to back straight out of the church.

"Ella!" is the swift reprimand. "I will not permit you to be rude. You must apologize at once."

The girl doesn't reply, nor does she yield; and murmurs of censure abound. "In my day…" several voices begin. The conclusions to the litanies are lost, but Martha can imagine what they contain.

"You will sit where I choose," she orders, although she has no desire to join the Dumonts, especially as her customary place is vacant.

Despite every lesson Ella has been taught about childhood etiquette, she glares at the twins. "I can't. He's mean. He'll hurt me and Cai."

"For goodness sake, what nonsense—"

By now, however, the girl's anxiety and palpable fright have begun to affect Martha's adoptive son. He commences whimpering in a sing-song fashion, something he hasn't done in several months.

"Oh, look, you've upset Cai." Martha bends down to the boy. Afflicted with the falling sickness, his health can be precarious. "Come now, little man, Ella didn't mean to worry you."

Cai closes his mouth, although silent sobs begin to wrack his body. If Martha doesn't act quickly, a fit will overwhelm him. She touches his cheek, keeping his gaze focused on her own eyes. The condemnation of nearby congregants increases, and Martha must shift positions to permit passing parishioners to take their seats. "Would you like to go back outside, little man, and watch the squirrels?"

The boy shakes his head no, but there's so much despair in his features that Martha gathers him into her arms.

At that moment, Charles Dumont walks to her side, his expression one of kindly concern. "May I assist you, Miss Beale?

Your boy looks too big a lad for you to easily carry. Let me take him to our pew."

"No!" Ella yelps while Cai tightens his grip on Martha's neck, hiding his face while refusing to accept Dumont's outstretched arms. Martha feels an anxious tremor shoot through the boy's body.

Furious that her adoptive daughter should engender such turmoil, she spins on the girl, but the clinging Cai demands full attention. During the year he's lived in her house he's grown a good deal heavier and taller, and his gangly length nearly causes Martha to trip on her long skirts.

Then the organ commences the prelude to the hymn, the choir masses in the center aisle preparing to process, and she feels she has no choice but to allow Dumont to lead them toward a box pew on the nave's north side. *If it weren't for Ella's outrageous behavior, we wouldn't be in this awkward position. Well, let this be a lesson for her. She must learn to temper her emotions and abide by her elders' decisions,* she thinks as her face assumes an expression of unchristian ire, and the Processional begins:

"A mighty fortress is our God,

"A bulwark never failing..."

Singing in a showy tenor voice, Charles Dumont proffers a hymnal, holding it aloft for Martha to read. She accepts with a grateful nod although she's aware that the origin of her gesture is spite.

"...And though this world, with devils filled..." At the word "devils" Martha catches Ella's eye, fixing her with a look of imperious disdain.

As the service continues, however, Martha grows to regret her decision to join the brothers. Despite the invitation, it's obvious that neither relishes the presence of children; the rapport

Thomas always enjoyed with Ella and Cai is nowhere in evidence. Cai remains mute rather than displaying the enthusiasm he does with Kelman; Ella's face is a blank, her body motionless as if she'd turned into one of the church's wooden columns.

Then, too, Charles must keep whispering to her during each pause between lessons and psalm and prayers. At first, the comments and questions are of an innocuous nature, centering on her and her family's well-being. Soon, however, an underlying motive emerges.

"I was beginning to worry you weren't coming today, Miss Beale," he whispers. "You see, I brought Dr. Rosenau's notebook in hopes that I could return it."

"You brought it here? To church?" Martha isn't certain why she finds the fact so distasteful, but she does.

"Guilt wouldn't permit me to keep it in my possession an hour longer. I hope you will permit me to walk you home and discuss this remarkable work. I was mistaken about the man. Woefully so. I must admit I couldn't quite understand his conclusions, but no matter. I'm sure the scientific terms are there, and I'm merely unaware what to look for."

"What you did was wrong, Mr. Dumont" is all she answers.

He continues undismayed. "*Mea culpa*, Miss Beale. And the very reason, I brought it with me." He taps the pew cushion. Nearly hidden beneath his hat and gloves is Rosenau's notebook.

Another hymn commences; the congregation again rises. Instead of taking up a hymnal for Martha, however, Dumont tries to press the book upon her.

She shakes her head, drawing her finger to her lips in hopes that he'll cease his continuous talk. She wishes she could escape the claustrophobic box, escape Charles's persistence and Cornelius's dreamy indifference, which she suspects may be the result of an over-dosage of laudanum.   Before the Gospel reading can commence, she seizes her chance, grabbing each child's hand and hurrying outside before her hosts can protest. She's aware that her rapid exit is causing another uproar.

Freedom isn't so easily gained, however. Charles Dumont appears in the churchyard moments later. In his grasp is the note-book. He waves it at her as he approaches, his countenance still wreathed in a seraphic smile as if he's unaware of her snub.

"Didn't Dr. Rosenau ask you to provide his verdict to members of the legal profession?" he calls out.

Martha can't help but express her exasperation. "I'm no longer willing to perform that role, sir. I suggest you return the book to its rightful owner."

"Oh, but you should—"

"Please take the work to Dr. Rosenau. It has nothing to do with me."

"But you were the one who—"

"I no longer wish to participate in this affair, sir. I leave it to others to sort out the truth."

Crestfallen, Dumont regards her. "Miss Beale, I sincerely hope I'm not the cause of your decision. I'll never be able to forgive myself."

"Forgive me if I bid you good day" is the curt reply. "As you see, my children require my attention."

"Let me call upon you this afternoon, Miss Beale. We can discuss my lapse
        then—"

"The remainder of my day is occupied, sir. Now, please, al-low me to go." Pulling Cai forward as well as the still-icy Ella, Martha walks to the churchyard's Fourth Street entrance. Her father's grave marker lies close to the path, but she neither slows nor looks at it. Her heart is racing as if it were peril rather than tedium she'd just escaped.

AT HOME, CAI is delivered to *Mademoiselle* Hédé while Ella is consigned to her chamber for the remainder of the day. Martha is still angry with the girl, and the exchanges with Charles Dumont have only exacerbated her ill humor. "He's like a spider waiting to pounce," she mutters to herself before marching upstairs to inquire how Becky fares. There, she's astonished to find the patient up and dressed.

"I couldn't bear it any longer—wrapped up in a cocoon. You and everyone here have been kindness itself, but I'm well enough to go home now."

"No, you're not." The tone is sterner than Martha would like, which causes Becky to laugh. A purplish bruise still covers half her face,

"You've become quite the tyrant, Martha Beale. There'll be no questioning your decrees now."

"I didn't intend to be harsh, but don't you think it's advisable to wait until the surgeon declares you're completely healed?"

"I'd hoped to see Baby..."

"We'll bring him here, then. With his nursemaid. There's ample room. *Mademoiselle* Hédé can go there at once and assist in the move."

"And William..." Becky adds, although the tone is cautious.

Rather than respond, Martha weighs her choices. *How to explain Taitt's bizarre flight, or tell Becky that her husband hasn't been found, or that her son has been parentless for the past two days?* The dilemma is postponed because of what her friend says next. In place of her former eloquence, Becky's voice is halting. She sits on a settee as she speaks, curving her neck downward as if her thoughts were too odious to bear.

"Martha, I believe William may have killed that woman… the one we found at *Point Breeze*…Agnes Munder—"

"He couldn't have" is all Martha has time to reply, because Becky's words rush forward.

"Do you remember when I came to see you…it seems a hundred years ago…before the picnic. You intuited that I had a problem I wasn't divulging. You were correct; I did. My husband had disappeared. Given his predilections and the timing—"

"You're wrong," Martha argues, but Becky won't permit any interruption.

With her head still bowed and her gaze affixed to the carpet, her words spill out. "And what he tried to do to me…what he *did* do…He has hurt women before…at his plantation…slaves, so he's never been held responsible—"

"Listen to me." Martha sits beside her friend, taking her shoulders and turning her until they're finally face to face. Becky's expression is one of utter desolation.

"I didn't understand why he was so furious that we'd gone to *Point Breeze*, or why he kept alluding to the fact that our names were associated with a murder, but it has suddenly become clear…Don't you see? If we hadn't visited when we did, the crime wouldn't have been discovered. I know, I know, it's awful to think of that poor, dead body lying there exposed to the elements, and…and the—"

"Listen, please. You're—"

"But what if he didn't intend to kill her?" Becky continues as if Martha hasn't spoken. "He didn't mean to hurt me, after all. Not the way he did. When he's been drinking, he has no comprehension of his strength. And he's always so full of repentance afterward. What if this was another horrible mistake, like hitting me so hard I fell...? Then he became terrified, which he would... I know he would...And then...and then he cut off the woman's head so no one could identify—"

Martha squeezes Becky's shoulders hard; if she weren't afraid of inflicting damage, she'd shake her. "Listen to me. Whatever apologies you feel you need to make for your husband aren't important now. The dead woman isn't Agnes Munder."

Becky's face creases in confusion. "Isn't—?"

"The mule spinner's wife, Agnes Munder."

Within her friend's tight grasp, Becky's frown deepens. All her arguments have become meaningless. "Who is she, then?"

"That hasn't been determined. It may never be. Another impoverished and forgotten creature in a city teeming with similar people. If no one comes forward with information about a missing family member, her identity will remain a mystery and she'll be buried anonymously in a pauper's grave."

"Oh..." is all Becky can manage to reply. Her body loses its nervous energy; Martha's grip slackens and both women sit for several minutes, thinking back to the scene at the Bonaparte estate: the coarse cloak, the dress's cheap fabric, the undertaker's men hefting the body as if it were of no more value than a sack of flour. Becky opens her hand as if the crimson ribbon were still there, then gazes at her empty palm.

At length, Martha leans back against the cushions; her corset stays pinch, her several crinolines are twisted beneath her, but her physical discomfort is nothing compared to her mental unease.

"That Sunday, two weeks ago, after you and I were accosted by the mule spinner, and your qualms about the situation were so apparent, I made a private decision to help you. I approached Emil Rosenau and asked him to examine Oscar Munder. My reasons were simple—at least they seemed so then. Rosenau would determine whether or not Munder was capable of a crime of that magnitude; either verdict, whether no or yes, would eliminate the rumors distressing your husband, because your name would no longer be—"

"The famous craniologist Emil Rosenau?" Becky asks. It's obvious that she's only grasping fragments of the conversation.

"*Difficult* might be a better term for the man. But no matter. Obviously, the plan miscarried. An escaped prisoner can't be scrutinized. Instead, Rosenau performed a dissection on the victim and determined that she'd borne a child. Agnes Munder is childless. The doctor recorded his conclusions. If the matter comes to trial, at least the world will know who the victim was *not*." Martha leans forward; her expression has assumed an appearance of cheerful competence although it's the opposite of what she feels. "So, you see, Mistress Grey, your worries are for naught."

"And where is she now, this Agnes?"

"Missing. Apparently, she isn't the most faithful of spouses." Martha shakes her head; the self-confident mask dissolves into one of regret. "I blame myself for much of this tragedy. My good intentions have produced nothing but misery. If I hadn't interfered and sent Munder to Bordentown to view the corpse—" She doesn't finish the thought. "I wish the silly woman had just come home."

"Has my husband been told?"

"Why on earth would he have been, Becky? The case has nothing to do with him. Nor with you, either—or me. Now, let's dispense with it, and pray that the woman returns, and that she and her fugitive husband are reunited. As for Quaker City Mill... well, I'll say no more. Now, let me ring for *Mademoiselle* Hédé so you can have Baby delivered to his loving mama."

There's no reply to the suggestion. Instead, Becky murmurs a nearly inaudible "There were things William said...the night he hit me...I think he's been keeping a mistress...and he may fear that—"

"That what?"

When Becky looks away without answering, Martha loses her patience.

"You don't propose that your husband is afraid he slaughtered this purported mistress and sliced off her head, do you? Oh come, Becky! William behaved brutally to you and may do so again. That's not the issue, however. You must forsake these morbid notions—"

"They're not my notions. Don't you understand that?" She rises suddenly. "I must go to William. He needs me."

"You'll do nothing of the kind—"

"What if this Agnes is my husband's mistress? Or was, perhaps."

"Philadelphia is a large city. Many women of questionable morals dwell within it—"

"But don't you see? If she was William's...lover...and then we found that awful butchered corpse, and the mule spinner became convinced the body belonged to his wife...Oh, can't you realize what demons William must be facing?"

As Becky speaks, Martha's mind fills with disconcerting memories: Taitt disappearing following an altercation on Callowhill Street; the fine carriage she saw near the same address during the return from Quaker City Mill, and how she thought about the mule spinner as she watched it pass. None of the recollections does she voice; instead, she answers with a brisk "And you will face a veritable demon in me if you don't remain a docile patient.

Come, madam, promise you'll remain within these chambers until the surgeon again examines you. I'll order you a warmed egg wine, or would you prefer sherry-lemonade?"

Becky regards her friend; the robust coloring has now deserted her. "I'll do as you suggest, if *you* promise to send one of the footman for William. I must speak to him."

Martha doesn't answer. What can she say? That Taitt is also being hunted as a criminal? The news would only confirm Becky's hypothesis, and she's not recovered enough to face those burdens.

Seeing her hostess's hesitation, Becky misinterprets its source. "You're correct in stating that my husband can—and does—behave cruelly, but I won't desert him in an hour of need. Send for him Martha, please. I'll write the missive at once."

And so Martha unwillingly agrees to carry out her friend's wish. She quits the house, waving enthusiastically toward the upper windows to signify that her mission has begun, but out of sight, her progress halts. *How can I find William Taitt if he's managed to elude the constabulary? And when I return home without him and tell Becky the truth, won't her worst fears be justified?* Pondering these insurmountable dilemmas, she grimaces. *If only I hadn't accepted the Dumonts' invitation to* Point Breeze…Without completing the thought, she hails a passing hansom carriage and directs the driver to Callowhill and Seventh Streets where Taitt was seen last. Before the horse is set in motion, however, she changes her mind, raps on the carriage door, and alights.

I'll elicit Charles Dumont's aid in this matter. Unwelcome though his company is becoming, I dare not attempt to track down William Taitt alone. Dumont will be circumspect—and strong, if need be.

The decision made, Martha turns her path toward the home the Dumont brothers now share. Not three hurried steps have been taken when she again questions the strategy. *If Charles Dumont doesn't prove discreet, Becky will be compromised. No, I must delve into William Taitt's affairs alone.*

Another hansom cab approaches, but before it can stop, she reverses this latest decision. It would be absurd to embark upon her task without a gentleman's protection. Unreliable as Charles Dumont may be in regards to keeping confidences, she must go to him and request his help.

Chapter 29
Hellfire

"THINK NOTHING OF IT, Miss Beale," Dumont tells her as they journey to Callowhill Street. "You know how happy I am to be in your company, and how quickly I would—and always will—come to your aid. I also promise that I'll be the soul of discretion, although I sincerely hope that Mrs. Taitt is mistaken in her suspicions."

The hansom cab jostles their bodies closer together as it speeds northward. Dumont deemed it more expedient to travel by hired coach rather than order his own carriage equipped for usage, and Martha readily agreed. However, the wisdom of the undertaking—if not the cramped quarters—is becoming increasingly debatable as the streets roll by.

"My gratitude, sir" is all she replies. She clings to a leather strap, pulls her skirt from beneath Dumont's leg, and sighs over her impetuosity. *What do I expect we'll find? A hidden and villainous William Taitt? The faithless Agnes Munder? An unsuspecting householder who's unfamiliar with either name and irked at being disturbed by two strangers? And if we do discover something amiss, what can we accomplish? We have no authority, no constable at our side, no one to lend credence to our tale.*

In exasperation at her own rashness, she expresses these many misgivings to her companion, but he soothes her qualms, adding a calm:

"Callowhill near Seventh Street, that is the address we're seeking, isn't it?"

"It was where a watchman attempted to apprehend William Taitt, yes."

"I pray your friend can put her mind at ease when we're finished with this exercise, Miss Beale."

"As do I."

♋

FINDING A HOUSE that appears similar to one of the newspapers' descriptions, Martha again experiences uncertainty. Although obviously new, it has an air of desolation: no draperies swag the lower windows; no furnishings appear visible in the room facing the street. Were it not for curtains drawn across the third story panes, the building would look as though it had been uninhabited for some time. "This cannot be the place," she murmurs. "Clearly, no one lives here."

"An unpromising prospect, I agree. But come, let us complete the task we've begun."

Accepting his arm and lifting her skirts in order to protect them from the worst of the roadway's mire, she crosses the cobbles at his side and then waits on the brick pavement while Charles Dumont climbs the front steps and raps upon the door.

Several long moments of waiting extend into minutes. He knocks again and, again, is rewarded by silence. After additional time has lapsed, he looks to Martha for guidance.

"Use my name. If I'm wrong, the Taitts' reputation will be unsullied," she urges in a whisper, which he does, declaring it in a tone loud enough to be heard throughout the house. "I represent Miss Martha Beale. If you would be so kind, she and I desire a moment of conversation."

At that, the door opens several inches. Still standing upon the pavement, Martha sees a drudge of a woman who looks as though she's come face to face with a ghost. The pinafore indicating she's a maid-of-all-work is stained and graying, but her skin compensates for the drab hue by being very white. Fear makes her brow waxier still, and she clings to the portal as if guarding it against strangers is a matter of life and death.

"Is Mr. Taitt available, by any chance?" Dumont asks. Mindful of potential passersby, his voice is now lowered.

Chewing on her lower lip while staring down at Martha, the woman gives her head a vehement shake.

"Mrs. Munder, perhaps?" Martha adds in an equally confidential vein. "Agnes Munder?"

The same unspoken but rigorous denial greets the request, although Martha recognizes that the name is a familiar one. "Oh, Mr. Dumont, I fear my friend's suspicions may be correct."

An expression of disgust crosses his face. "Miss Beale, let me accompany you back to the safety of your home. This…place is not for you." He turns in order to descend the steps, but she hurries up them before the maid can shut the door.

"Agnes Munder, is she here?"

In response, the maid tries to slam the door, but Martha is quicker; her tall frame outmatches the squat body pressing against the wood. It occurs to her that anyone seeing the struggle would find it peculiar: a well-dressed woman intent upon forcibly entering a shabby house. "Mr. Dumont, if you please, sir."

At that moment, the door flies open, and Martha with Dumont on her heels all but tumbles inside while the maid slinks into the shadows of the cold and unlit foyer, staring in dread at the intruders before scuttling forward to again bar the entrance. Finished, she holds a ring of keys aloft as if uncertain what to do next, and Dumont seizes it from her. "Wretched woman! Lock us in this mausoleum, will you?"

"Oh, don't strike her. She's obviously a mute and may be mentally impaired. She's merely following whatever orders she was given."

Despite this reasonable appeal, he glowers at the servant before returning his attention to Martha. "Miss Beale, let me take you home and then return with members of the constabulary." While he speaks, the maid slinks toward the rear of the house. Before reaching a door that undoubtedly leads to a larder or pantry, she looks back. The clandestine glance conveys a combination of horror and warning. She shakes her head from side to side, opening and closing her mouth in an attempt at speech, but the only sound produced is a bearish whimper.

Hearing her, Dumont spins around and the woman flinches, tripping over her own feet as she seeks the safety of the door that then bangs behind her. The hurried clatter of her shoes echoes in her wake, as do several animal grunts as she descends into a basement kitchen.

"I implore you, Miss Beale. Who knows what dangers may lurk here. Although the construction is obviously not old, neglect or shoddy building practices may have rendered the flooring unsafe."

But Martha is already proceeding toward the staircase. Cobwebs drape the ceiling, and the chill within the abandoned structure seems greater than in the street. Here is no cheery manse, no well-scrubbed hearth spreading heat and joy. Dumont was correct; the building has the feel of a tomb. "No, I believe the servant witnessed something vile and that she's too frightened and dull-witted to express herself in a coherent fashion."

"In that case, at least let me precede you. If a floorboard gives way, my attire will permit greater freedom of movement."

Martha permits herself a wry smile. "But I am the lighter in weight."

"Then you and your long skirts shall rescue me."

Up they climb and then walk through three empty rooms on the second floor. Dirt and neglect are everywhere in evidence, and it's obvious that mice and other vermin have claimed the chambers as their own.

"I can detect no sign of human tenancy, Miss Beale."

"Let us proceed upstairs. I saw curtains upon those windows."

"Perhaps I should force that idiot maid to accompany us, lest she do some mischief behind our backs."

"She's too cowed to act in a sinister fashion, Mr. Dumont. And if she were with us, who knows what she might attempt to hide?"

The third story lies in darkness. The draperies blotting out the sky are of a heavy woolen fabric. Opening them, Martha finds two large rooms that comprise a pleasant suite: a bed, pier glass, and chest of drawers in one; a table, several chairs, and a settee in the other. There's also a smaller chamber fitted out with a hipbath and armoire. Like the remainder of the house, the area is cold, but the mice and spiders haven't invaded.

"Curious" is Dumont's sole comment while Martha wanders back and forth. She notes that the bed has been stripped of its hangings and that the water jug used to fill the bath is missing. In every other respect, the rooms appear serviceable and comfortable. She walks to the window in order to appraise the view; other rooftops are visible, and in the distance, the spire of Christ Church. Startled by some unseen disturbance, a volley of pigeons wheels past, their flapping shadows darkening other panes of glass in other buildings, and she wonders whether the drawn draperies were intended to shut out light or prying eyes.

"At least your suspicions haven't been realized, Miss Beale. Whoever dwelled here is clearly gone. And for some days, I imagine."

"Yes, so it seems. . ." As she speaks, she spots a rumpled, blue ribbon lying nearly hidden beneath the bed's footboard. Bending down, she finds a necklace similarly discarded. An inexpensive and garish piece of paste, it's something that might tempt a woman unaccustomed to more costly finery. The clasp has been torn loose and a number of the counterfeit stones are missing. Its forlorn state fills Martha with pity for the unknown owner. Without hesitation, she reaches for both ornaments.

"What's that you've discovered?"

An instinct that she'll never be able to explain prompts her to conceal them in her long sleeve then compound one deception with another. "Dust and more dust, I'm afraid. You're correct; my worries are unfounded. Shall we quit these dank premises before we take a chill?"

"I saw you take something from the floor."

She rises and smiles, tightening her grip on the objects. If she were to question her own behavior, she might answer that she didn't want Dumont to scoff at the shabby fripperies or the woman who once cherished them, but the real motive is less innocent. And so Martha concocts another lie. "Despite the protection of my gloves, I wouldn't retrieve anything from a place as soiled as this. Now, shall we leave? You've been kindness itself, and I thank you—as well as apologize for my invented phantasms. Mrs. Taitt, however, will be greatly relieved, so I extend her gratitude in absentia."

"If you found an object that might aid the constabulary, you should leave it where it is," he insists. "I promised you I'd return with members of the day watch, and so I shall. If you're correct about the servant keeping a secret, then we must be diligent whether or not you believe our work here is finished."

An additional falsehood is on her lips when the sound of male footsteps in the foyer below arrests them both. Another person has entered the premises. As there's been no knocking or stumbling footsteps from the maid, it must be the building's owner.

She watches Dumont turn and listen. Alarm darkens his features; his fists clench. He walks to the landing door, passes outside, and latches it firmly behind him while Martha scarcely dares draw a breath. She looks around, uncertain whether to attempt to hide or join Dumont and hope for the best.

Feet begin climbing the stairs. On the uncarpeted wood, they reverberate, thud upon thud drawing slowly upward. Out of the corner of her eye, she sees pigeons again circling though the sky as though the loud and measured footsteps had disturbed their uneasy peace.

"Charles?" she hears a muzzy voice shout. "Charles? Are you up there?"

And then the relieved reply: "Cornelius! Miss Beale and I have been playing amateur secret service investigator. I'm glad the footman told you where I'd gone, but you mustn't trouble to ascend when we were just on our way down. We had some uneasiness regarding a dear friend of Miss Beale's, but I'm happy to report that all is well." Without waiting for his sibling's answer, Charles raps lightly upon the door. The signal sounds like an inconsequential reminder, as if Martha were merely attending to last minute preparations before departing, tying her bonnet or affixing a brooch. "Madam, shall we go? Cornelius has discovered us at our games.

Let us leave before that hellish servant summons the constabulary
and accuses us of illegal trespass or another absurd offense."

What does he mean by this, she thinks, *trespassing is the very act we're
engaged in.* "Why did you come here?" she hears Cornelius demand-
ing.

"I just told you, brother. Miss Beale requested my aid. Now,
let us descend to you, and then we'll journey home."

"But you shouldn't be here."

"Yes, brother, I understand." The tone isn't merely irritable;
it's angry. "You needn't tell me what I already know."

In that instant, Martha recognizes the truth. *William Taitt
never entered this house, although the Dumonts are well acquainted with it, and
with the servant.*

Her fingers curl around the paltry treasures in her hand;
she has a sudden vision of their owner that's as real as the image
she received when visiting the Munders' home. *Agnes has lived in these
rooms as one or both of the brothers' mistress—not as Taitt's.* No sooner has
this revelation appeared than Martha understands the meaning
of the necklace. The woman who wore it must be dead. If not, it
wouldn't have been lying hidden beneath the bed. Martha touches
the broken clasp, the ruined settings; violence lives in each shard
of twisted metal.

"Madam," Dumont calls a second time, "shall we relinquish
our explorations and join my brother downstairs? The calmative
potion he's been prescribed can make even a few steps an arduous undertaking." His voice is again full of bonhomie; Martha
can picture his smile as if he were still in the room with her. She
hears Cornelius speak again although only a smattering of words
penetrates the door:

"...The fire of Hell you're playing with...She...you...
afraid..."

All at once, the larger crime reveals itself. *Althea! Althea, who Cornelius insisted wasn't a suicide. . .It was her body we found at* Point Breeze, *not Agnes Munder's. . .Althea, who no one saw vanish from her home.* The discovery explodes in Martha's mind. *Althea, who hated the water. . .*

Martha's thoughts fly back to her condolence visit after the futile search for the missing woman: the husband full of reproach and sorrow, his brother's fierce resolve, the ugly confrontation. *Why didn't I recognize the root of their battle? "A villain hiding in the skin of an innocent man,"* that was the phrase Cornelius used. *And equally bitter ones, too. He said his wife was afraid of his brother.*

The scenes rush forward in her mind, each as carefully constructed as a lantern show: *Charles's original appeal to aid his melancholic sister-in-law; the picnic at Point Breeze; the library in disarray; the hidden bedchamber; the gossip about Bonaparte's mistress; the missing grandson. . .everything designed to mislead. . .And the corpse of a wealthy lady clothed in the garb of a mill hand. Even the crimson ribbon must have been artfully placed: a clue to be discovered as if by chance, so the ruse could succeed.*

Except this house. I was the one who insisted on visiting it.

Martha's skin grows icy. *No wonder Rosenau's verdict was discredited and the notebook stolen. Althea produced a child—*

Her deliberations cease as Cornelius reaches the third-floor landing. She can hear murmured conversation: one twin's breathy but vehement entreaties; the bitter rebuffs. She transfers the two ornaments to a pocket and shakes her lace cuffs free as though nothing more than a little dirt were troubling her. Then she walks to the door, a sham expression of polite anticipation fixed upon her face. If the Dumonts can be adept at guile, then so can she.

The scene that confronts her, however, isn't one she can bluff her way past.

Charles, ever superior, has his back against the wall. Facing him and leaning upon the banister for support, Cornelius is attempting to level a derringer pistol at his brother's head, although the exertion of his climb causes his hand to tremble. "And you'd kill her, too, wouldn't you?" he says.

Martha freezes where she stands.

"You would, wouldn't you? Just as you robbed me of my Althea."

Charles doesn't look at Martha, but she knows his smooth reply is crafted for her ears. For her *gullible* ears, she'd add if she weren't so frightened. "Dear brother, I'm afraid the laudanum is producing hallucinations. I have neither robbed you nor killed anything larger than a gaming bird. I'm your devoted sibling. Step closer to me now, and let me take that fearsome weapon before you do some damage to the woodwork. Don't you see how much you're upsetting Miss Beale?"

The response is a snarl. The derringer weaves back and forth through the air.

"Cornelius. Do as I say. Please."

"Never...never...never again. All my life—"

"Enough theatrics, brother. Come now, let me—"

"All my life, all of it...You..."

"I have what? Harmed you? Hurt you? Certainly not, dear brother. My efforts have always been for your betterment, as Miss Beale can attest. These past days have been a trial, I know, but put that monstrous thing away. Your mind is inventing—"

"No!" Cornelius's voice is a howl, his face contorted in a rictus of grief. "No—"

A noise below disturbs him: the timid footfall of the maid creeping slowly upstairs. As he turns to peer over the balustrade, Charles lunges for the pistol.

Inching back toward the doorway, Martha watches the two struggle; their countenances and physiques appear so identical, it almost appears as if one man were wrestling with himself. When their faces pull close together, they meld into a single unit like lovers locked in an embrace.

Finally, Cornelius breaks free, waving the weapon and forcing his sibling to retreat. It's obvious, though, that his victory has exhausted him. He bares his teeth; his breathing is labored. "No more" is all he says. He gazes at his twin who stares coldly back.

"Allow Miss Beale to leave us, at least, Cornelius. Surely you don't wish to see her come to unintentional harm while you play out whatever unhappy fantasy your brain has concocted."

"My Althea—"

"Is gone, I know, brother—"

"You...You—"

"Miss Beale," Charles interrupts, "walk past my poor twin and proceed down the stairs. I promise you won't come to harm. Cornelius isn't well; you must forgive him. He hasn't been well for some time. I should have sought help for his condition earlier." His attention fixed on his brother, he reaches for Martha while he speaks, but she flinches away from his touch.

Charles spins toward her; fury galvanizes his body. "You do believe me, don't you?" The outrage in his voice is plain. *No*, she's about to say, *no*, but Cornelius speaks the word for her.

Then he fires. Blood, flesh, and flecks of skull bone explode, spattering the wall and Martha's face. In the instant between life and death, Charles stares into Martha's eyes. Not even surprise softens his wrath.

Watching the body slide downward, Cornelius whimpers. Hefting the pistol again, he presses it against his own temple as he gazes at the pool of black-red blood leaching over the floor beneath what remains of his brother's head. The pool grows; seconds pass; Martha doesn't move. She waits for the second shot.

It never comes; instead, Cornelius sinks against the railing, his lips open in a soundless shriek.

Chapter 30
"It Must Be"

MAY, IN ALL ITS refulgent glory, has arrived. The city bursts with blossoms; the air is sweet as if farmland and field have been transported into dingy alleyways and byways. If only for the space of time, the tanneries and factories and those employed within them are transformed. Faces beam; hope is aloft.

Boarding the paddle steamer *Robert Morris* for a sojourn in the seaside resort of Cape Island in New Jersey, Martha smells the fresh breeze and smiles. Near her on the crowded deck, the children and Becky Grey ramble. And *Mademoiselle* Hédé, of course, as well as two lady's maids and numerous trunks and valises. Travel among the well-to-do isn't a simple task; half a floor of one of Cape Island's hotels must be requisitioned for the party. Naturally, Baby is too young to join the adventure and has been left behind with his nurse, as has Becky's husband, but Martha doesn't want to consider that complicated matrimony at the moment. She wants only pleasure and laughter, strolls on the beach, health, sunshine, and a dearth of introspection.

She grasps the ship's rail; beneath her gloves, the wood is warm, almost hot. Her fingers curve around it as if taking solace from its solid presence. At two-hundred-seventy-nine tons, the steamer is as sturdy as a house: two giant wheels on either side that might be garden pathways if the thing were on land; a smokestack replacing a chimney; the deck, a what...? Martha cannot find an analogy. A piazza, perhaps? An upstairs gallery? Picturing this odd invention, she smiles. Although, the happy expression falters momentarily as she remembers Charles Dumont's ferocious glare fixed upon her; she shivers as if she were still pressed against a clammy wall watching one brother murder another. *No more*, she tells herself, *no more*.

Within her view, gulls drift back and forth, crisscrossing the lines of masts and spars—a full complement of vessels amidst the busy wharves. If she were to close her eyes, she might question in which nation the steamer was berthed because so many foreign tongues can be heard. Instead, she watches it all, even the plodding arrival of a ship that's seen more wear than is wise. It's an insignificant craft, nosing its way in among the greater merchantmen, a coastal trading vessel, probably, designed to sail brief distances only.

Ella appears at her side, and Martha wraps the child's shoulders with her arm, bundling her inside the fabric of her mantle as though within a giant, human wing. Neither speaks for several peaceable minutes until Ella stiffens. As she does, Martha's own body involuntarily follows suit. *No more anxieties over what's past*, she silently begs, *no more questions, no more demands*.

"Look!" Ella shouts, pointing. "Over there! It's Mr. Kelman! Mr. Kelman, come home."

Martha follows Ella's finger but sees only the same battered boat she noticed before. She turns away, her eyes grown suddenly blurry. *It cannot be*, she tells herself, *it cannot*. "Someone who looks like him perhaps, dear. Don't you remember? I told you Mr. Kelman—"

"No! He's right there! That tall man standing near the back of the ship that's docking near us."

"Ella, I know you don't mean to hurt me, but—"

"Look! Look!" the girl orders. Reaching up, she grabs Martha's face, twisting it until she focuses on the neighboring wharf. "Don't you see?"

Bowlines are attached; stern lines made fast. Ella's fingers continue to hold Martha's head in place. "It is," she insists, "it is, Mother."

"Dear, you cause me pain if you—"

"It is. It is!" Releasing her grasp, Ella begins to wave, both arms flashing wildly through the air. "Mr. Kelman! Look up here!"

Martha stares and stares although her sight is still clouded and her mind fixed on impossibilities.

"Here!" Ella continues to shout. "Here! Up here! Mother, look! Isn't he calling to us?"

Taking her hands away from the rail, Martha lifts her skirts and pushes through the throng of embarking passengers, hurrying down the gangway and onto the pier where she begins to run in earnest. *It is Thomas. It must be. Please, dear God. Oh, please.*

Finis

Withdrawn

**Indianapolis
Marion County
Public Library**

**Renew by Phone
269-5222**

**Renew on the Web
www.imcpl.org**

For General Library Information
please call 269-1700

DEMCO